Wild *and* Distant Seas

Wild *and* Distant Seas

A Novel

TARA KARR ROBERTS

WEST BRIDGEWATER
PUBLIC LIBRARY

W. W. NORTON & COMPANY
Independent Publishers Since 1923

This is a work of historical fiction. Apart from the well-known actual people, events, and locales that figure in the narrative, all names, characters, places, and incidents (other than the obvious, from Herman Melville's *Moby-Dick*) are the products of the author's imagination or are used fictitiously. Any resemblance to current events or locales, or to living persons, is entirely coincidental.

For information about permission to reproduce selections from this book, write to Permissions, W. W. Norton & Company, Inc., 500 Fifth Avenue, New York, NY 10110

For information about special discounts for bulk purchases, please contact W. W. Norton Special Sales at specialsales@wwnorton.com or 800-233-4830

Manufacturing by Lake Book Manufacturing
Book design by Patrice Sheridan
Production manager: Julia Druskin

ISBN 978-1-324-06488-6

W. W. Norton & Company, Inc., 500 Fifth Avenue, New York, N.Y. 10110
www.wwnorton.com

W. W. Norton & Company Ltd., 15 Carlisle Street, London W1D 3BS

1 2 3 4 5 6 7 8 9 0

For my mother, aunts, and grandmothers

Chief among these motives was the overwhelming idea of the great whale himself. Such a portentous and mysterious monster roused all my curiosity. Then the wild and distant seas where he rolled his island bulk; the undeliverable, nameless perils of the whale; these, with all the attending marvels of a thousand Patagonian sights and sounds, helped sway me to my wish. With other men, perhaps, such things would not have been inducements; but as for me, I am tormented with an everlasting itch for things remote.

—Herman Melville, *Moby-Dick*

Part One

EVANGELINE

Nantucket, 1849

I was called from these reflections by the sight of a freckled woman with yellow hair and a yellow gown, standing in the porch of the inn, under a dull red lamp swinging there, that looked much like an injured eye, and carrying on a brisk scolding with a man in a purple woollen shirt. [. . .]

"Come on, Queequeg," said I, "all right. There's Mrs. Hussey."

And so it turned out; Mr. Hosea Hussey being from home, but leaving Mrs. Hussey entirely competent to attend to all his affairs.

—*Moby-Dick*, "Chowder"

Chapter 1

IT TOOK ME some time to appreciate the smell of dead fish. When I
arrived on Nantucket I was nineteen, claiming myself to be the niece
of a businessman who was due to visit the island in search of a ship
to sponsor. I took a room at the Try Pots inn, and there I met its proprietor, Hosea Hussey. Over a bowl of thin and gritty clam chowder,
I told him I could make better. Perhaps this was overconfident, as I
had never so much as touched a sea creature, but he said he would be
pleased to see me try. When I told him the uncle and the ship were
lies, Hosea laughed. We were married six days later on the deck of
the whaler *Deborah* by a half-drunk minister who had stumbled over
from the mainland some days earlier. Hosea wore an ill-fitting suit left
to him, alongside the inn, by his late father; I, my yellow gown. As its
skirts brushed the polished planks, they released the stench of whale
oil, and I wondered if I should ever again smell the sea air without the
smell of its inhabitants, deceased.

I spent the early days of our marriage learning to gut cod, to slice
off their heads with a steady hand, to pry open the tiniest clams with
the twist of a knife tip. It turned out I was good with chowder—and
the previous cook had been bad with it, too generous with the water
and moldering biscuits. I fried salt pork, softened the onions in its

drippings, doubled the clams, skinned the cod, finished each batch with cream and butter. Soon we had to keep the pots on to cook day and night.

The cloud of chowder air released from the Try Pots' kitchen filled the halls and rooms, leaked from the doors, hovered above the roof. Our room smelled of clam and cod—hearth and chair and headboard and sheets—and Hosea wore a sheen of scent in the pockets behind his ears, in the coarse, fair curls on his chest, in the soft skin on the insides of his thighs. Before long the smell worked its way into my own palms and knuckles. Some nights I would lift my hands to my face as I slept and wake at the shock, and once I wept over my pots as I wondered if I would ever again smell the sweetness of woodsmoke without the body of a fish above it. But time and love wear down sensitivities, and chowder is delicious.

We had two good years. Early one September morning when the inn was silent, Hosea woke me with a promise to return with something new. I kissed him goodbye, thinking only of our guests, who would soon begin streaming in for breakfast. As I milked the cow and put on the first pots of the day, I rearranged recipes in my head. Lobster might go well with basil, scallops a splash of white wine. What if it were mackerel, or some unknown fish? I planned to test Hosea's gift in my midday chowders, yet he had not returned as I filled the bowls of the morning stragglers. Concern crept in, and I assured myself I had no need to worry. I could ease my own fear.

I was born with the strange power to peer into the minds of those near me and see their recent moments, memories fresh and soft as paint on a canvas not yet dried. I had rarely used this skill on Hosea, rarely needed to, so open was he to me. I searched for him that morning, expecting to arrive at an image of him lost in thought as he fished, letting his boat drift through the mist, a bit too far from shore. What I found was the echo of him clutching his chest and stumbling, his hand twisting in a rope as he fell, the sea filling his boat and lungs.

Back in my kitchen, I stopped looking toward the door.

I knew what the neighbors would whisper when they realized my husband was gone. I knew they would scoff if I insisted he had fallen ill on his boat and drowned. More likely, they would say, it was his marriage to an outsider, the ceaseless chowder, the inn without the thumping feet of children that drove him away. Perhaps he had snuck to the mainland, boarded a ship to Boston, hopped a whaler to Tahiti. They would not help me find him, though I would know the location of his bones.

That night, after the last weary, beer-logged lodger departed to his room, I chopped potatoes for the next morning's chowder, rinsed the starch from my hands, and retrieved the skeleton of the day's largest cod. Already I had picked the bones clean, and a dip in boiling water stripped the last bits away. As my thumbs pried apart the translucent vertebrae, I let my mind wander over the possibilities of life without Hosea. Nantucket was full of women widowed by the sea, left to keep shop with their mothers and sisters-in-law and cherub-cheeked children, but I could claim no kin on the island, and I would not claim the kin I had left. Hosea's parents were long dead, and though his relations doted upon him, I knew they saw me as a trifle of his fancy at best, a trespasser at worst, either way easily swept aside. I had nothing of my own. I could drift elsewhere as I had drifted to Nantucket, call myself by a new name, craft myself a new story, find a new husband, a new kitchen, new pots. But I saw the silver scales embedded beneath my nails despite my scrubbing, the round white scar at the base of my finger from a slip as I split clams, the callus where the thin silver ring Hosea had given me rubbed against my skin as I milked the cow each morning and evening. I closed my eyes, and the ever-present briny steam of the kitchen filled my mouth, my throat. The smell of him. The smell of home.

It would not be long, I knew, before the whispers and suspicions became questions. A preacher would arrive, solemn-browed and white-knuckled, to wonder if I might need prayer. One of Hosea's fleet of cousins would stop in for a chat, rejecting the chowder I set before him as he folded his hands and inquired about my obvious need for assistance. A creditor would come, asking for the man of the house though he knew he would never be home. The questions would not stop until they became actions, and I would lose all I had left.

As I slid the vertebrae onto a length of string and tied the cool bones around my throat, I formed my plan. Some years before, I had discovered how malleable memory could be. How, with sufficient will and enormous effort, I could suggest to someone that a recent moment was not quite as they remembered it. And I wondered whether, if I smudged the paint enough, I might be able to create a new picture.

The next morning, when the first lodger arrived in the public room, I looked into his mind and saw him dropping into Hosea's office, expecting to find the proprietor. I greeted him with the reminder that Mr. Hussey had gone away on business and would return soon. When one of Hosea's old friends visited at midday, reporting that Hosea had invited him, I reshaped our conversation so that he remembered asking when my husband would return, to which I replied that Hosea was expected any day. The next week, Hosea's cousin Peter Coffin arrived from New Bedford for a visit—and four bowls of cod, all in a row—and I explained Hosea's business trip once more. Peter's memory of walking in, assured he would find his cousin, became a memory of knowing, bitterly, he would find only me.

Again and again, through days and months, I nudged more memories with the same tale. Those I told it to spread it to others, until enough people believed the lie was the truth and the whispers ebbed. It did not feel so much like a lie, at times. I still wore Hosea's ring, left his books open on his desk, awoke at night sure I had heard him breathing. Sometimes I, too, almost thought he would walk back through the door someday. I wanted to believe I had changed the story, that the painting of my life on Nantucket now hung on my wall in unchangeable form: I at the inn, Hosea forever on the edge of returning. Yet I came to see I had wrought something far more fragile, an illusion etched on a pane of glass.

A CRACK APPEARED on the day the young sailors arrived, two years after Hosea's death. Mr. Davidson, a regular for ale and chowder most evenings at the Try Pots, tugged me to him by the sleeve of my gown and whispered with sour breath that if Mr. Hussey was so lax as to leave his nice things lying about in the open, he might take one for himself. I yanked the mug from Mr. Davidson's hand and hauled him out the front door by his sleeve. It struck me as my fingers twisted into the fabric that it was not Mr. Davidson's usual checked work shirt, streaked with fish blood, but his Sunday woollen, rich purple. For all his brutish indelicacy, I feared he had higher intentions. Perhaps he was beginning to see through my illusion, to guess Hosea was never coming back—and so I had to ensure his thoughts on the subject ended that evening.

I meant to march him out into the street, but two figures stood in the moonlight just outside the door. A pale young man, nearly a boy, gaped at the massive pots Hosea had hung to signal the inn's name. His tall, dark companion tipped his hat my way before turning his face to the dim street, as if to avoid interrupting either my business or his friend's reverie. I kept Mr. Davidson to the porch, where in the dampened red glow of the lantern I hissed between my teeth that he had no claim on me or anything else in Mr. Hussey's house.

Soused and sheepish, he folded into himself. "I was just trying to say to you . . ." he mumbled.

"You have nothing to say to me other than clam or cod, Mr. Davidson," I said. "You'll have nothing else of mine. Now get along with you."

He shuffled his feet and ran a hand through his thinning hair, and I realized he'd left his hat at his table. I was about to insist upon fetching it myself when the young man who'd been entranced by the pots suddenly strode toward us, the clamshell pavement crackling beneath his boots. He cleared his throat and said, "I see we have found the Try Pots, then."

He stepped into the lantern light as Mr. Davidson slunk out of it.
A skiff of beard shaded his round cheeks, but deep furrows crossed
his forehead and gathered in the corners of his amber eyes, which
darted about, examining everything around him as he talked. He
wore the outfit of a sailor, yet when he clasped my hand in his, I felt
the soft, unmarred skin of a boy from the city. He had perhaps never
sailed, other than across the Nantucket Sound, though surely he had
spent many hours reading and thinking about it. He said I should call
him Ishmael. His friend stood patiently as Ishmael chattered about
lodging and supper and "the best-kept hotel in all Nantucket," and
I beckoned them to follow me into the public room. The sooner the
young men sat down, the sooner I could return to making certain Mr.
Davidson was firmly under my illusion.

I paused to retrieve Davidson's hat at the table I had forced him
to abandon. Ishmael took my action to be an invitation and sat down,
staring for a moment at the dregs at the bottom of Mr. Davidson's
bowl and the damp spot on the table from the ale I'd caused him to
spill. Ishmael's companion, whom he introduced as Queequeg, took
the opposite seat, and I saw him clearly—the thick, black lines and
crosses that patterned his face, trailed down his neck, disappeared
into his collar, flowed back out across the backs of his large, brown
hands. As I stared, he clicked his teeth, drawing my attention back to
his face. He tilted his chin toward Ishmael, who sat rubbing his hands
together as he glanced about the room. Supper first.

"Well, gentlemen, would you prefer clam chowder, or cod?" I said.

Ishmael continued to study the room with a sweet smile, saying
nothing.

I cleared my throat. "Clam or cod?"

He blinked and shook his head, sending his dark curls waving.
"What's that about cods, ma'am?"

I gathered up Mr. Davidson's dishes. "Would you like clam," I
said, slower, crisper, "or cod?"

Ishmael rambled on about clams, chuckling at his own jokes. I noticed a movement in the doorway and spotted Mr. Davidson, still looking for his hat but apparently now understanding that he ought not step back into the public room that night. My patience with men was spent for the evening.

"Clam for two," I shouted to Betty, the taciturn widow I'd hired to help me serve. I tossed the hat to Mr. Davidson, and stepped into the kitchen to deposit the dishes.

I presented my new guests with two steaming bowls of clam chowder. Ishmael's expression, so full of restlessness and distraction before, shifted to a smile, softening the lines on his face as he closed his eyes and breathed in the salty steam.

"I confess I'd missed your meaning at first, Mrs. Hussey," he said. "Clam or cod chowder, of course! The mystery is solved."

"I suppose so," I said. I turned for the kitchen but felt a tug to linger a moment, uncertain of what I was about to offer, yet unable to stop myself. "Call me Evangeline."

~~~~~~

UPSTAIRS, I FRESHENED the sheets and lit a fire in an empty room. I leaned against the warm stone of the hearth, intending to take a moment to rest before returning to my guests. I let my mind flit to Mr. Davidson and saw him tossing sleeplessly in his bed, so obviously ashamed that I should have felt relieved; he seemed to have put aside whatever idea had driven him to make his proposition. But relief did not come. I rushed a broom across the floor, hoping the movement of my body would quiet my thoughts. I could not escape the feeling of dread, as if a firm hand pressed against my glass picture, testing its thickness, considering the weight it would take for it to shatter.

If Davidson's proposition was not the source, what was? The young sailors on the clamshells—Ishmael and Queequeg must have arrived just as Mr. Davidson grabbed my sleeve, if they were already standing there when I dragged him outside. I found them with my mind, but they were as I had left them at their table, Queequeg's head

tilted toward his friend, Ishmael's flung back in a laugh. I knew so
little of them. What could they have brought that would endanger me?

I could not abide such fragility. The life I had crafted was not
as good or pure as when Hosea was alive, but still it allowed me to
keep the only home I'd ever loved. I thought of the years before Nantucket—my mother dead at my birth, my father gone before I could
speak, my grandmother terrified when I began to speak of more than
a child should know. Her fear made her cruel, and I learned to say
nothing, reveal nothing, if I wanted a roof and food beneath it. And
I made myself want nothing, until the day I listened from my toil in
her kitchen and heard a visiting gentleman speak of beaches dotted
with shells and knolls tangled with wild roses, of noble homes and
busy wharves, of a place where the sun melted into the ocean. By the
time I had gathered the courage to set out on my own, I had no doubt
where I would go.

I was not about to lose what I had found on Nantucket. I had to
stop the cracking. I reminded myself I had overcome such a threat
once, more than a year before.

Hosea had been gone for months, though the townsfolk still cheerfully asked what hour he'd be back. The Try Pots received a visitor
named Zephaniah Stiggs, tall and reedy and so quiet he was almost
silent. Nearly three years on a whaler, with nothing to show for it
but windburned lips and an empty purse, had discouraged him. The
abandonment of his shipmates—whether they returned immediately
to sea or left for warmer climes—bent him lower. What broke him
was the discovery upon his arrival home in New York that his wisp
of a wife and their tiny child had taken ill with scarlet fever and died
when Mr. Stiggs was not more than six months out to sea. He fled the
house in New York and returned to Nantucket without even a stop to
visit their graves.

Mr. Stiggs took up residence in the smallest, darkest room at the
back of my inn. He haunted the hallways, gaunt and unspeaking, pacing but never leaving, rarely pausing to eat more than a biscuit. I left

bowls of chowder on his bedside table each morning and took them back to the kitchen, crusted over, each night.

His presence alone did not usher in the sense that my illusion was cracking. It was two weeks into his stay, late in the evening, when he appeared behind me as I rummaged through a closet.

"They are dead," he said, his voice loud but dry, crumbling.

I stiffened at the sound, and the lamp I'd been searching for slipped through my hands, shattering against the stone floor.

Stiggs did not flinch. "Dead and gone."

"Yes, Mr. Stiggs," I said. "I am so very sorry for your loss."

"But you know," he said. "You know what it is like to be alive and carry the dead with you."

The pressure came swiftly. I realized that in all I had done to stave off the questions and whispers of my neighbors, I had stolen from myself a chance to mourn my husband. I had stifled the need, but it bubbled to the surface, drawn by the phantom of Mr. Stiggs. Shouldn't I weep and moan? Shouldn't I grieve, as he did?

I tried to swallow but my throat was parched. I forced the words from my mouth. "No, Mr. Stiggs, I do not know such things."

He began to sob. I should have comforted him, led him back to his room, whispered to him that he could let them rest. But instead I rushed past him. Abandoned him.

He had been a harpooner on his unfortunate voyage, and that night he guided the barbs into his own side. I found him the next morning spread across his counterpane in a sea of his own blood and water, and though I wailed over his body, I felt the pressure release. I could continue on with my illusion undisturbed. All it took was a death.

Betty called from the base of the stairs, releasing me from the memory of Mr. Stiggs. I laid my broom down and drew three slow breaths. I would find another solution this time. I had to. I smoothed my apron and returned to the public room, where the young sailors had finished their supper.

For all I had seen on Queequeg's face and hands, I had not noticed the harpoon he carried until he drew it from beneath the table as Betty gathered the dishes and I prepared to escort the men to their room. My shoulders seized and I fumbled my lamp. Though I caught it, I could hear in my mind the sound of thin glass striking floorboards. I reached toward him and demanded the weapon. Queequeg made no move to resist me, but Ishmael stepped between us.

"Why not let him keep it?" he said. "Every true whaleman sleeps with his harpoon."

I tasted copper; I remembered the smell of Stiggs's blood. "Because it's dangerous," I said, and spit out a story of the suicide.

I did not have to ask again. Queequeg moved around his friend and handed me the harpoon with a nod of his solemn, patterned head.

"I'll keep this for you until morning," I said, my breath coming back to me in gasps as I stretched my lips into a smile. "But the chowder, clam or cod for breakfast tomorrow, men?"

Tension forgotten, the joy returned to Ishmael's face. A sudden warmth banished for a moment my fearful thoughts.

"Both," he said, clasping his hands. "And let's have a couple of smoked herring by way of variety."

Early the next morning I gathered bay leaf and fennel from the larder, milked the cow, and left Betty instructions for starting the recipe before leaving through the back door of the kitchen. Whether because of my panic or the limits of my power, I could not understand why the young sailors had introduced my sense of doom. If I did not know what was coming, how could I stop it? Would this be the time I shattered? Would the price of relief again be blood and water and wailing?

For all my strange abilities, I was no prophet. But I knew a man who was.

Chapter 2

THE STINK OF Elijah's room bled into the air as I navigated the decaying stairs leading to his door: the beer that dripped through the floor of the tavern above, the rotted boxes stacked in the corners, the moldy straw of the mattress, the permanent layer of fish. I knocked hard despite the early hour and heard the soft stumble of his footsteps.

His ragged voice came through the salt-weathered wood. "Be you angel or be you demon, woman?"

I laughed. "You know the number of my wings."

As the door flung open and the full stench reached me, I pressed my hands to my nose, turning away in shame at my reaction to my friend's home. Elijah patted my shoulder with his good arm and closed the room behind him.

"Do not worry, girl. Prophecy pays poorly, but sea air is free."

We walked along the wharf beside the silent, looming figures of whalers. The spoiled-oil reek of the nearby tryworks tinged the air, but we were both accustomed to it, and dawn bloomed with pink and lavender tendrils of light. I pulled my shawl tight across my shoulders as the winter wind swept across the water. Even in his tattered jacket, Elijah did not seem to notice. Though the old man was beneath the attention of many on Nantucket, even when he was stalking the docks delivering his nebulous prophecies, I had first come to know him on account of his stalwart resistance to weather. Not long after I'd married Hosea, Elijah had wandered into the Try Pots for supper during a terrible storm, shaking the sleet from his beard as if it were a gentle spring shower and requesting a bowl of clam chowder. Wind was nothing to him.

"Do you know why I've come?" I asked him.

"Must be something important, waking me at this hour." He grinned from behind the tangle of his whiskers.

"Two young sailors, guests at the inn. They've . . . unsettled me. Do you know of them?"

His fingers combed through a knot of hair behind his ear. "I have seen them."

"And have you seen why—"

He stopped me, swinging out his stricken arm, palm open in front of my chest.

"They are sailors. They will sail. You're an innkeeper. You'll keep."

I pushed his hand away, marching down the wharf as he lumbered behind. He could not play his games with me. I knew something was happening. Images of the night before flittered across my brain: Davidson's hand on my sleeve, the ink across Queequeg's throat, Ishmael's face in the lamplight. I spun back to Elijah.

"Do not speak to me as you do to your wandering sailors, old friend. The arrival of these men is a harbinger of something. I want to know what."

He breathed out through his pockmarked nose and nodded, a motion that involved his whole body. "Much is coming. I will follow these men and see what part they play."

A large wave rolled in and the ships rose and settled with a ripple of cracks. "I want to know what part *I* play. Follow them, but tell me. Please."

He bobbed himself again. "What's to be, will be, Evangeline. And then again, perhaps it won't be, after all."

WITH ELIJAH'S PROMISE to follow the sailors I had at least some hope of an answer, though no assurance that it would be intelligible, and I was distracted from my fears for a while by the demands of my pots. Betty, who liked the quiet of morning in the inn, had already delivered bowls of cod to the earliest risers, and the smoked herring awaited only my final touches. I plucked a sprig of dried thyme from a bundle that hung from the ceiling and rubbed it between my hands over the pot, releasing the scent of wet, green earth. I imagined Ishmael's smile when he smelled it.

When I emerged from the kitchen, he sat alone at the same table as the night before. His face, when I placed the bowl before him, was exactly as I had pictured, and I stepped back in surprise at how quickly his image had found a place in my mind.

"Don't run off before I can thank you, Mrs. Hussey," he said. "Smoked herring chowder. I hadn't meant for you to actually make it."

"You'd best appreciate it, then."

He tucked in, speaking between bites about his morning plans to find a whaling ship for his companion and him to join as crew.

"Queequeg insists I choose for the both of us," he said, the statement tinged with a mixture of confusion and pride. "He's having some sort of ceremony today."

"Alone?"

He nodded, wiping his mouth with the back of his hand. "Fasting and prayer and whatnot."

While I awaited Elijah's answers, I could seek some of my own. For all his posturing as an experienced sailor, Ishmael seemed an open book, eager and green, focused on simple pleasures and the voyage to come. Yet Queequeg gave off the air of a man who knew more than he let on. If I could get him alone, perhaps I could learn something I was missing about these young sailors. I fetched a second bowl for Ishmael, excused myself citing business to be done, and hastened upstairs. I knocked softly, and Queequeg called for me to enter.

He was kneeling before the fire, eyes locked on the hearth. He was stripped to his waist—and yet not naked, for the tattoos that wound across each inch of his skin. I closed the door and stood waiting, unsure how to proceed, studying the tattoos. They seemed to shift and join, the way the marks on the moon become a face when one stares at them long enough. Queequeg spoke, unturning from his vigil.

"What is your name, woman?" His words came slower and smoother than they had in the public room the night before, his voice high and songlike.

"I'm called Evangeline," I said.

He repeated it, lingering over the vowels in the back of his throat, letting it hang a moment in the air before tapping his fingers against the floor. "That is not your name."

A burning sensation rose in my nose, a sudden fear that he had met me mere hours before yet had guessed something no one on Nantucket had ever known, save Hosea. Perhaps I was becoming more transparent than I had realized. I considered a lie, but I suspected he was beyond the reach of my manipulations.

"My father named me Nell, after my mother. But they are gone. It is no more my name than yours is Queequeg."

He laughed then, his shoulders sending a ripple through the patterns of his back. He held his hands before him and turned them, the tattoos twisting along with the sinews of his arms.

"These are my name," he said. "I tell the sailors I do not know what they mean."

"But do you?"

He shrugged again, letting his hands return to his knees. "Can a man know himself?"

I crossed the floor and knelt before him, my back hot against the fire. He stared past me but did not seem bothered by my presence. I realized I did not know what to ask that might help me understand why he and his companion caused me such alarm. Perhaps it was as simple as getting to know him. "Do they tell a story?"

His unwavering eyes met mine. "They tell the truth."

I hesitated, and he nodded his permission. I let my eyes drift over the markings. I saw squares and spirals, mouths and brows and pupils, shells and suns, woven together in an endless parade as he bared himself to me. As the marks filled my vision, I sensed the smoke of unfamiliar wood, the breeze across warm blue waters, the glint of stars I had never seen. I felt the presence of seafaring men, their wives wailing on soft-sanded beaches until the sails tipped over the horizon; the same women rising, smoothing their skirts, leaving to weave frond baskets to hold the babies that would slip from their bodies into the hands of other women. I saw Queequeg in such a basket, borne by the tattooed arms of his grandmother, carried by her own grandmother, and hers, back and back, endless lines, forming him, pouring themselves into him with each cross and swirl and line. Even here, miles and years away, they were with him.

A realization struck me, wrenching me from the trance. I was alone. I had escaped the tatters of the family I was born to and lost the family I had tried to build for myself. I was alone in an illusion I feared I was not strong enough to hold.

Had Hosea been all that held up the weight of the world for me, that allowed me to pass the days with thought of little more than the warmth of our bed, the rush of the ocean outside our windows, the smell of sage and shellfish on my hands? Perhaps this was what I needed to secure my future, the reason these sailors had captured my attention: if my illusion shattered, I should not be alone.

I crawled from the dark of my mind and saw Queequeg there, strong and present. He did not have Hosea's breadth and softness, but seemed made of wood, each shining limb shaped by the edge of a knife. I drew closer to him, the heat of his body as near as the warmth of the dwindling fire. I lifted my hand to his jaw, ran a finger along the raised edge of the tattooed block spanning his chin. I leaned in to kiss him, but he turned away, his eyes dropping as he placed a hand on my arm. I understood—he was a man of other tastes.

With a snap the last log of the fire broke and crumbled into the coals. I jolted to my feet, intending to run for the door, but he caught my hand. "Evangeline," he said. "It's a good name. You seem to be a good woman. Whatever you are so afraid of, I do not think you should be."

I did not believe him, but I thanked him and apologized for disrupting his ceremony. Queequeg adjusted the cloth on his hips and returned to his vigil before the fire, nodding to me once on my way out before sighing and leaning back, his mouth curving into a smile.

ALONE. I THOUGHT of it through the midday rush of men seeking chowder, as I cleared tables and mopped floors in the public room, as I updated my ledgers in Hosea's office, as I hauled potatoes and leeks from the cellar. As Betty served supper, I stepped out back for a quick breath and found Freddy, the schoolboy I hired for occasional kitchen chores, feeding the cow a pile of apples, though she slid about in the spilled peelings and leavings he was supposed to be delivering to a neighbor's pigs. As I opened my mouth to divert him, I was interrupted by a voice behind me.

"Give the little fellow a break, now, Mrs. Hussey, and come inside. I've wonderful news to report," Ishmael said, his words threaded with glee.

When I turned he winked over my shoulder at Freddy. "I've found us a ship, and I'd like to surprise Queequeg with a celebration."

I bent and scooped the scraps back into their bucket, dropping it into Freddy's hands before turning back to where Ishmael waited, his smile broad and expectant.

"What sort of celebration?" I asked as I pushed past him into the kitchen, my hands held straight in front of me to avoid streaking my dress with fish guts and mud.

"I was thinking I might bake him a cake."

I couldn't contain my laughter, but he seemed not to realize it was directed at him. I laughed as I scrubbed my hands, laughed as I dried them, laughed to see him scanning the shelves as if I might already have a cake waiting.

"Have you baked many cakes in your life, sir?"

"My mother, God rest her soul, always baked them when good things happened," he said. "I was thinking a strawberry cake might be nice."

The man was more naive than I'd realized. "You do know it's winter?"

His cheeks pinkened. "Yes, Mrs. Hussey, it's only that you seem to work magic in your kitchen, and I hoped perhaps you might have some dried in the cellar, or perhaps some preserves. I'll be missing strawberries when we go out to sea, and I'm not sure if Queequeg's ever had a strawberry cake. But never mind, I'll just go on upstairs, and tell him the jolly news. That will be plenty."

I intended to let him go—asking me for such frivolity as a cake!— but before I could stop myself, I reached out to stop him. "I have dry cranberries and butter. Did your mother ever make you a pound cake?"

"Oh yes, ma'am, many times."

"And have you ever made one yourself?"

He blushed again; once more impulse overcame me, and I offered to help him.

He was hesitant in the kitchen but not clumsy, waiting for my direction but measuring flour with a steady hand and cracking eggs in a way that assured me he'd helped his late mother at some point in time. As we worked he rambled on about the ship he had found, praising its venerability, its proud masts, its well-worn decks, its bulwarks bedecked with the teeth of past kills. It sounded like any old whaleship to me, but he refused to name it, insisting he must tell Queequeg first. He had not yet met the captain but assured me he was a man of great reputation, as were the ship's two owners, one solemn, one fierce. He was so taken with excitement, he had signed his papers and promised to return in the morning with his friend.

"Can you believe they seemed to want to convince me not to?" he said. "Warning me of the dangers as if I hadn't thought of them. One of the owners, he asked why I even wished to join his crew. As if it weren't perfectly obvious!"

It was obvious, as he said. He wore his restlessness like a too-large coat, its sleeves and hem knocking into everything around him, tipping objects as he passed. His eagerness was no less clear. He had attached his affections to Queequeg, though he told me they'd only met days before on the mainland. He seemed primed to lavish loyalty upon this new captain he'd never met. And though I'd done nothing other than serve him chowder and provide him with a warm bed, he trusted me.

"I want to see the world, Mrs. Hussey," he said as he took the bowl from my hands and began to stir. "Doesn't everyone?"

I did not answer, crossing the kitchen to stoke the oven. I could barely hold on to the piece of the world I wanted to keep. Such a boy to want it all.

He filled the pan, scraping with his spoon until the mixing bowl was clean, smoothing the top of the unbaked cake three times before he was satisfied.

"Shall I call for Queequeg?" he asked as he slid the pan into the oven.

It was then I saw the last piece of his spirit. What I had viewed as greenness, ignorance, was these things, but also something purer. Innocence. "I suppose your mother always sent you out to play or run errands while her cakes baked?"

"Yes, ma'am."

"It will be an hour, then half an hour to cool enough to eat. You might wait to call your friend, unless you'd like to serve him raw cake."

He nodded, the deep lines in his brow appearing. "Then I shall wait."

He tried to coax me back into conversation, but I did not have the luxury of standing around in the kitchen. Betty was scrubbing pots, and I needed to take inventory before I made my monthly dry-goods order. As I stood among the jars and jugs in the cellar, I heard Ishmael's attempts to start a conversation with Betty and remembered my conclusion that I should not be alone. I pushed the thought away, silencing my mind with work.

Ishmael's cheery shout brought me back. He held out the cake, flipped from its pan onto a plate, its golden-brown scent competing with the chowder smell of the kitchen.

"Queequeg's finished his ceremony by now, surely," Ishmael said. "Come with me, won't you?"

I followed him up the stairs to the closed door of their room. Ishmael balanced the plate on one arm and knocked. No answer. He knocked again, harder, and in the silence that followed he frowned and began to search his pockets for the key.

I recalled Queequeg's contented smile when I'd left his ceremony that morning, and realized I had neither seen nor heard from him in the hours since. He had not appeared for the midday meal. I had not passed him on his way to the washroom or seen him stop into the public room for coffee before supper. It seemed he had stayed in there all day, which he couldn't have. I searched for him with my mind and saw him, still in the room, having just folded his hands around his harpoon and raised it before the fire.

My memory rushed to Mr. Stiggs, his harpoon stabbed into his side. My throat squeezed shut, and I felt as if chill water had poured into my stomach. Could Queequeg, so solid and sure, have taken the path of unfortunate Stiggs, have stopped his heart upon a counterpane? Fear seized my ability to see more.

"Mrs. Hussey?" Ishmael said, muffled and distant.

"His harpoon," I whispered.

"Oh. I— Well, to tell you the truth I was bothered you'd taken it, so I snuck into the closet after you'd gone to bed and brought it back to him."

I tried to respond, but my words came out a thin wail. My knees gave way, Ishmael's helpless hands flailing after me, the cake sliding off the plate that clattered to the floor, splitting in two. I heard Betty scream. The walls went gray and shapeless.

When I opened my eyes, the two young sailors were standing above me, and Betty's trembling hands held my head.

"He's fine, do you see?" Ishmael said. "He was only enjoying the end of his ceremony. Aren't you just fine, Queequeg?"

The other man nodded, his eyes attempting to read mine.

I sat up, shying away from their help.

"I'm sorry about this whole strange affair, Mrs. Hussey," Ishmael said. "You must leave us and rest. Queequeg and I will finish the washing-up."

~~~~~~

I RESTED, AS THEY INSISTED, because my body gave me no choice. But I awoke with a refreshed mind. I could not live with the kind of fear that plagued my thoughts and collapsed me over the image of a missing harpoon. While I had developed a fondness for the young sailors, I could not cling to them as the solution to my troubles. They were the portents of fragility in my world, and for all my efforts, I still had no clarity as to why.

I found them up early, in good spirits. Neither mentioned the distress of the night before, and Queequeg was silent about my visit to his room. They devoured eight bowls of chowder between them, clam and cod and the last of the smoked herring, plus halibut Betty had made while I slept. They praised us as good cooks, and Queequeg patted his belly, the patterns on his skin showing through the faded linen of his shirt. I wondered if he would ever see his family again. He and Ishmael rushed out, giddy as children, to sign their lives away to a whaler.

Betty tiptoed from the kitchen not long after, timidly informing me of her resignation after the previous day's clamor—her nerves were frail and she'd never been one for much commotion. I sent her away with an apology and an extra week's pay, though it meant I would have to work myself even harder as I waited to hire her replacement. As I cleared the dishes alone, my second visitor arrived. Elijah stepped inside, his appearance clearing the last of the men lingering from breakfast. I ladled him a bowl of clam, as his scarred throat never could abide the thin bones of fish, and sat beside him. He knew what I waited for.

He wiped the last bit of cream from his mustache. "Know you the *Pequod*?" I did—one of the ship's owners was fond of my chowders. "And know you Captain Ahab?"

Everyone on Nantucket knew the story of the white whale with the twisted jaw, the captain with the mangled leg, the weeks of fever and delirium that, some said, never quite subsided. I had never met the man but had seen his wife, a delicate petal of a woman, at the market.

"Your young sailors," Elijah said, "have found a ship."

"They're sailing with Ahab?" Ishmael had said the captain was a legend, not a nightmare. Not mad, not cursed.

"Some sailors must go with him, I suppose."

I yanked the napkin from his hand and waved it at him.

"You're no help, old man. I already knew they found a ship—that is no prophecy at all. When those men arrived here, they changed something. I will find out what is coming, whether you jabber on or not."

He looked pained, his milky eyes growing watery. He lifted his stiff arm and reached for me, and I allowed the crumpled fingers to rest against my cheek.

"I'll pursue nothing more for you, Evangeline. You should not concern yourself with these men's souls. Or any man's."

A rage boiled up from my stomach, and I flung myself from his grasp, sending the napkin and my handful of spoons clattering against the wall.

"If my own soul alone were enough, perhaps I wouldn't have to. Have you thought of that?"

He turned his head and left me standing, huffing, waiting for answers I knew he did not have.

"Miss Tistig will be in town on the morrow," he said, finally. "She'll want to see you."

"And I her," I said, keeping my tone harsh. "Perhaps she will have something useful to tell me."

He stood, grasped his empty bowl with his good hand, and passed it to me.

"What's to be, will be."

I yelled after him as he limped away, "You've said that before!"

Chapter 3

MY HANDS FUMBLED to fold sheets as I waited for Tistig the next day, my mind reaching for hers. I rarely had warning of her visits—she was a Wampanoag from Gay Head on the Vineyard, and her trips to Nantucket were at her whim. Her younger brothers were celebrated harpooners on one of the wealthiest whaleships that still sailed from the harbor, and she tended to arrive a few days before their crew returned to port. Other times she came to deliver packages to the Wampanoag elders or her distant cousins on the island, or for no apparent reason at all. I liked to think those times were just to see me.

I used my power to see the moment she stepped onto the wharf, and I watched her path to the Try Pots as I paced the kitchen, ignoring the onions waiting to be chopped. When she arrived at the back door, I flung it open. We embraced, and I pressed my hands into her back, breathing in the comfort of her. New silver strands had entwined themselves in her black hair, but she smelled as she always did, of soft deerskin and green-throated orchids and kelp-strewn beaches. It had been several months since she had last visited the island, yet the gap slipped away as we held each other.

"Look at you! Have you somehow gotten younger in my absence?" she said, flitting a fingertip across my chin.

"Perhaps, madam, you have gotten older," I replied, giving her a mischievous smile. "Shall I get you a chair to rest your weary bones?"

She pulled away from me, grasping my hands to hold the connection. "It's good to see you, Evangeline."

"And you the same," I said, my voice cracking with sudden tears. "I have been . . . lonesome. I felt such relief when Elijah said you would come."

"I see." She paused. "We have much to discuss."

Tistig and I met on the morning of my wedding to Hosea. I had readied myself for the occasion alone in my room at the Try Pots, struggling with my stays and worrying over each strand of hair before giving up and stepping outside to breathe. I was still unfamiliar with Nantucket, and my restless feet carried me away from the wharf where Hosea and his family waited, heading instead down quiet, angled streets toward the edge of town. As I reached a patch of what passed for forest on the nearly treeless island, I heard a woman call out. I did not slow, assuming no one could possibly be speaking to me, until she called again. When I slid to a stop, she met me with a kind smile and a clean handkerchief, for in my haste I had not realized I'd splattered mud from the previous night's rain up the back of my gown. Tistig introduced herself—revealing her full name was Beulah Constance Tistig but insisting I call her by her surname—as I dabbed the stains until they blended well enough with the light diamond pattern of the fabric. When she inquired as to where I might be headed all alone that morning, I blushed and admitted I was due to be married in less than an hour.

She laughed. "And I suppose your bridegroom is waiting up by the pond?"

"He is at the harbor, along with all his aunties and uncles and cousins and friends," I replied.

She must have heard the strain in my voice at the thought of that mob of relations, none of whom were particularly thrilled at becoming related to me, for she placed a gentle hand on my arm.

"If you'd like, I can walk as far as New Guinea with you," she said. "Or perhaps we should head for the hills instead?"

I appreciated a woman who understood the need for a route of escape. But my mind found Hosea, watching the streets for me, and I knew where I wanted to be.

"I suppose I am ready," I said, and she fell into step alongside me.

I had no friends on the island. I had not, in fact, exchanged more than cursory words with anyone other than Hosea before that morning, and so I trusted Tistig without hesitation. As we dodged the puddles in the roads toward town, I shared the truth of my flight to Nantucket and the bleak life I had left behind. She assured me she could keep my secrets, but declined when I invited her to join me as a guest at the wedding.

"You will find this place is like any other in its tendency toward contempt," she said before we parted ways. "And yet you will find kindness here, as well, if you are willing."

I did not understand for many years that her words were, perhaps, a prophecy.

My wedding day was in so many ways Hosea's—the endless aunts kissing his cheeks and friends slapping his back, the ale-laden regulars from his inn, the townsfolk who had known him since he was too small to sit in a boat without trying to toddle out. No one approved of the match, but they could not help but approve of him. As I stared at the sea of Nantucketers when the minister asked us to turn and greet the congregation as man and wife, I imagined Tistig's face among them.

Later, when I told Hosea I had made a friend, he huffed and told me to stay away from such trouble—some of the only unkind words I ever heard him speak. I soon learned the kind of trouble for which Tistig was known on Nantucket: pointedly ignoring the preachers who tried to convert her from her so-called heathen ways, failing to cower when sailors spat at her feet and mocked her to their friends as she passed, using the reputation of her brothers to gain passage to places she would otherwise

have feared to tread. Whispers abounded of her supposed power to fore-
see the future, but she refused to answer questions on the matter in any
public way. When I asked, she sometimes answered, but just as often
laughed. She embraced the air of mystery, taking advantage of it as a way
to live her life as she pleased, as much as she could.

After our initial meeting, she stopped by the Try Pots whenever
she visited the island, and our friendship grew as we shared stories
and sorrows and joys over fresh chowder in my kitchen. It was strange
to see her faded and weary that morning I learned my young sailors
had signed on with the *Pequod*. I saw her tilt toward the wall in the
hallway and caught her elbow.

"Shall we go to my room to talk? Perhaps you can rest."

I expected her to scoff at the suggestion of rest, but she let me
escort her.

As she sank into the pillows of my bed, her dress shifted and I saw
the thinness of her flesh over her shinbone and femur, the knot of knee
that bulged between them. My hand felt her cool skin, my nose found
a sourness I had missed before.

"You're sick."

She did not move to cover herself. "I am dying."

I did not know how to respond; I found myself with nothing
to say, nothing to do other than to crawl into the bed beside her, to
stretch my body against hers, to warm her. I nearly shuddered at her
lightness beside me. We had lain in that bed together many times, on
days she visited while Hosea was away, gossiping until dawn or, in the
days after Hosea died, curling together to cry. She had never seemed
to take up so little space.

She reached to twist a strand of my hair around her finger. "I
won't be coming back to Nantucket. I need to be with my family."

"I'll be your family," I said, flinging my arms around her, forgetting her frailty.

I felt her laughter shake her ribs and the bones of her shoulders. I
feared she would break beneath me, but still I could not let go.

"Evangeline," she whispered in my ear, "I saw this in you, the first time I saw you."

I rested my cheek against hers. "Saw what in me?"

"Loyalty," she said. "You are not one who abandons things easily. But you must be ready to let me leave. My brothers' ship arrives tomorrow."

I could tell she had more to say but leapt at the opportunity to turn the topic away from death and abandonment.

"Yes," I said, nearly shouting. "Yes, a ship—that's why you've come. You've come to tell me more about the young sailors."

Her laugh became a cough. When she regained her breath, her expression remained amused.

"What are you talking about, young sailors?"

I did not explain the fracture in my illusion; I felt she did not require me to. I was filled with certainty that she would tell me what I wanted to hear.

"Two young sailors have been staying here these past few days. They are an omen of something, I can feel it. A disruption of all I've done to protect myself. They are shipping aboard the *Pequod* with that mad Captain Ahab, and Elijah would tell me nothing about the future. But you will, won't you?"

She rolled out of my embrace, facing the beams of the ceiling. Her tongue touched her lips in thought.

"So, my words about Ahab live on," she said. "His mother was a friend of mine, you know. Not so crazy as they say—like many of us. She chose the name in hopes he would be a warrior, a man worthy of a story, a fighter who would die in battle rather than lost at sea like his father."

I had never heard her speak of the old captain before; I knew only the murmurs around town that Tistig had predicted his dreadful encounter with the white whale.

"When I met him I could see the name was well chosen, but I told his mother she was wrong as to why. He's no warrior. He's only another poor man who thinks he can fight death and win."

She turned her face back to me, her cheeks damp with tears. "I did not come to prophesy for you, Evangeline." She sighed and I felt a crackling through her lungs. "Don't think of young sailors and mad captains and whaleships. Tonight, be here with me. Tomorrow will bring what it brings."

～～～～

I LEFT THE stove cold after Tistig departed the next afternoon, my pots empty and filthy, the air of the kitchen taking on the scent of sea and cow dung from outside. I shooed away the customers who had come early for supper, informed my lodgers they would have to visit another establishment for their evening meal. I had never closed the Try Pots' public room; Hosea used to boast how he and his father before him perpetually kept the fires hot and the doors open. Yet I snuffed the lanterns in my room while the sun was still hovering on the horizon and wrapped myself in my counterpane so tightly I could not move my arms. I had to hold myself together, but it felt like I was losing limbs, eyes, organs. How had I fooled myself for so long, believing I could ever stay anything more than alone in the world? My lies to others could not protect me from what I knew to be true. Hosea was dead. Now Tistig would die. Frail, doddering Elijah could only hang on so much longer, and in the meantime I had shoved him aside with my anger. The young sailors were meaningless, their seeming significance nothing but my desperate attempt to solve a problem I'd long known to be true: My illusion was bound to fail. I would lose the inn, and with it the last shreds of connection I had on Nantucket, or anywhere.

My husband is away. His bones strewn across the seafloor, buried in sand, carried away by creatures, partly dissolved.

My husband will be home soon. I wanted to have a headstone carved for him, to place it beside his mother's and father's in the cemetery on the hill. I wanted something of his to bury there, so I could be near him. So he could be home.

I took Queequeg's harpoon from the closet, where he'd quietly returned it. At the beach closest to my destination, I stole a rowboat, dragging it to the surf, the harpoon tucked inside. I was unused to rowing but strong from the work of the inn. The first flecks of rain hit my cheeks as the shore faded into mist and clouds shaded the last of the sun. My lantern did little, but I did not need it; I remembered every detail I had seen on the day he died. I knew the place where his boat sank, where I might find his bony hand still curled around a frayed and decaying rope.

When I reached the water above the wreck, I lay on my stomach, ignoring the splinters that dug into the skin on the underside of my arms as I hung over the side of the boat, lowering the harpoon into the water. If I could catch the rope with the sharp barb, I could bring Hosea home at last. I felt a current resist the harpoon as I reached deeper, where I found nothing solid; the sea and my movements had pushed the boat beyond my target. I rowed back, the strain of my muscles keeping me from shivering in the insistent rain. I leaned out farther, stabbing the harpoon into the dark water, but again felt nothing. I had not understood the depth.

I stood, bracing myself against the shudder of waves by digging the tip of the harpoon into the lip of the boat. It could not be much deeper. I could dive. As I tore at the top button of my dress, someone screamed, the words caught up by the wind. Though I strove to ignore the sound, my fingers began to quake, too numb to undo the next button. I heard the scream again, and a figure splashed through the mist. I was distracted for only a moment, but it was enough for a wave to buck beneath the boat. I struck out with the harpoon as I lost my footing, keeping myself out of the water but driving the shaft into my ribs, pushing the air from my lungs. As I lay gasping in the bottom of the boat, I felt it bob toward shore.

A string of lightning split the sky as Ishmael dragged me onto the sand, and by the time we reached the Try Pots the rain was not merely falling, but swirling about us, bursting against us. In the dark of the storm the inn was still and silent, the residents huddled by the fires in their rooms. I shivered in my wet clothes, and Ishmael took my hand and helped me up the stairs. Perhaps it was my destiny to be alone in a broken world, but I did not release his hand when we reached the landing, and I did not release it as I led him to my room.

He sat on the edge of the bed and let me kneel beside him to peel away his soaked shirt. He kept his gaze on the floor but dipped his soft curls against my forehead when I pressed my face into his neck and breathed in the scent of his skin. Despite the pelting of storm and sea, he smelled of sand warmed by the sun, of a pink-tinged rind of a fruit I had once been allowed to touch, but not open. He did not wait long to turn to me, to slide his palms beneath my ruined dress. As I held his face in my hands, I remembered Hosea—not his bones, but his countenance as he laughed when we lay together, the pinkness that spread beneath the rough blond waves of his beard. Beneath the fine brown silk on Ishmael's cheeks the same blush appeared. Delight— that was the youthful expression always in his face. At the scent of my chowders, as he stirred batter, as he rushed to sign his name to the *Pequod*'s rolls, and now at my touch.

We reaped what nearness we could from each other. When the storm subsided and we lay bare together, he tucked his fingers beneath the bone necklace that still circled my throat.

"You told me your name that first night we arrived, and I've yet to call you by it. Mistress. Mrs. Hussey. Evangeline."

As he said it, I felt a crushing weight. The cracks in my illusion split and spread, the web growing wider and finer, so little left to hold together.

~~~~~

THEY WERE SAILORS, and they would sail, as Elijah said. Ishmael and Queequeg began their work on the *Pequod* but informed me they would stay at the Try Pots until she sailed. They spent their days bustling around aboard the ship, stacking supplies and carousing with the rough men who would soon be their companions on the sea. Some evenings Ishmael regaled my lodgers with his expansive knowledge of whales, though they were creatures he had yet to see alive. Some evenings he spent in my kitchen, letting me guide his hand as he sliced cod flesh from bone, laughing with pride when he learned to pop clamshells and select herbs by smell in the dark larder, presenting me with a cake he'd baked on his own. Some nights he spent in my bed, spread with a clean white counterpane brought out from the linen closet and warmed beside the fire. Queequeg spoke little in those days but kept close to his friend, surrendering him only to me, and even then I saw the reluctance on his face each time he bid Ishmael good night and shut the door to their room, alone. I suspected that he, like me, could see more than most people. Perhaps he knew that when the day came, Ishmael would leave with him.

I awoke early on Christmas morning to prepare my chowders and found the young sailors dressed and waiting in the public room, their packed belongings stacked at the base of a table. Word had come the night before that the *Pequod* was to set sail. Ishmael could scarcely look at me, and he did not accompany Queequeg to Hosea's office to pay the last of what they owed for room and board. Queequeg placed a paper-wrapped bundle in my hand and leaned forward to kiss my forehead.

"You are a good woman, Evangeline," he said.

I dug my fingers into the rough paper and thanked him.

They did not eat breakfast. Ishmael seemed to hesitate at the door, but I could not ask him to stay. My attempts to gather prophecies had resulted in nothing but the assurance that I could not avoid being alone. I had let myself revel in his delight but never assumed I would keep it. Beneath the red porch lantern where I first greeted them, I bid farewell to the young sailors, and they did not look back at me. When I unwrapped Queequeg's bundle, I found more money than was due, and a gift along with it: a piece of scrimshaw unlike any I'd seen before, a sperm whale's tooth decorated with a simple engraving of the creature to whom it had once belonged. The whale was neither glaring malevolently nor in its death throes, as was often depicted, but floating peacefully, gently. I wrapped it back in the paper and stashed it in a cluttered drawer in my room, where I hoped I might forget it.

My days fell into their old rhythms of stirring pots and making beds and cleaning floors. I found routine to be a worthy way of holding back the pressure against the illusion that would not knit itself back together but, for a time, did not seem to grow worse. Mr. Davidson did not appear again in his purple shirt; no cousins or creditors came sniffing around. Hosea's name drifted out beyond the horizon again, and the days passed in a steady, undistinguished stream.

One afternoon, as I patted the cow and laughed over Freddy's muddy, giggling scrabble down the alley with his bucket of scraps, I realized I felt no chill despite my forgotten shawl. It was not spring, merely the first warm day of late winter, but I was surprised by its arrival. As I scrubbed dishes late into the night, my thoughts drifted to my young sailors, wondering about their lives aboard the vessel on which they'd sailed away, now two months gone. I felt a flicker of dread and refocused on a fleck of burnt cream. Their initial arrival had so disrupted me, I did not need to let them intrude again. Though I could barely admit it to myself, I was beginning to hope my life might not change as much as I had thought it would.

That night I dreamed of a great whale, white and furious. The shatter of a ship resounded in my head as I flew awake, but faded as I felt a sudden stir in my belly, the tiniest insistence of something new.

~~~~~

SHE WAS BORN in a rush of blood and water. I could not fight the pressure. I could do nothing but invite it, let it build in me until her cry split the air, shattered it completely, baring us both to the cold, bright world. I heard the entreaties of illusion in the back of my mind, the temptation to repeat the line *her father is at sea, he is coming home soon*, to make everyone believe it was true. But for once I could see the future: I could craft new lies and never stop struggling to hold them together, or I could finally face the real world in which I lived.

When I had cleared away the ruined counterpane and scrubbed us both with cool, boiled water, the girl and I rested together, her soft pink head so small against my breast, so easily broken. I bent my own head and whispered her name in her ear.

In the morning I carried her down the stairs. I could see the public room filled already with lodgers and visitors, waiting for me to put on the chowder pots for breakfast. Every man's face turned to me as I stepped into the room and the girl let out a wail.

"My name is Evangeline," I said, my throat still raw from my own cries. "This is my daughter. This is my inn."

And nobody dared ask me a thing.

Darkness fills the deep.

The sun hovers in an unseeable sky, its rays reaching out but never finding these waters.

Noise breaks the stillness, sounds that seem impossible in the sea—pelting hail, straining trees, a desperate knock at a door in the night—sounds that are felt as much as heard, fists and arrows into soft flesh. They follow a faint glow, a swirl of tentacles. And then the light and movement are gone, swallowed up. A flow of water follows something enormous.

Up, up, into the barest hint of twilight. A form emerges: sleek and dark, limber and long, twirling as it rises. It blends into the blue, until eyes and fins and flukes emerge.

A call erupts again, different this time, a reaching, a question, a name.

She is in the sunlight now, though she knows the depths so well. The sea is hers.

A sperm whale. The mother.

Part Two

RACHEL

Nantucket, 1856

Chapter 4

THE FIRST TIME I cursed my mother, I was six years old. I was playing at the top of the back stairs in the inn, and though she called for me, I did not respond. I heard her repeating my name. I ignored her, even as I could hear the worry in her voice. I knew she hated when I played on the stairs, but I didn't understand why. I was happy, distracted, amusing myself while she was occupied with the business of the kitchen.

"There you are," she said as she appeared at the bottom of the narrow stairwell. "I've been looking for you."

I wanted to continue my game, but I recognized the tone that meant she wanted me with her. I decided to stall, sliding down a single stair and grinning at her, knowing she might chase me up the stairs if she was in a cheerful mood.

"Rachel, come down this minute," she said.

I was old enough to hear her exhaustion, but still so young that I was certain I could push further, to convince her she did not need to interfere with me. I slid down another stair, and another.

Her face, usually so youthful, grew pinched, almost pained. "Rachel! You meant to stand and walk to me!"

I did mean to, didn't I? Even as I'd slid down those last two steps, all I'd wanted was to go to my mother. I leapt to my feet, descending the stairs with a grip on the handrail as I knew she preferred. Three steps from the bottom, I caught myself. I stood still, toes dangling, and I realized I did not have to go to her if I did not want to. And I hadn't wanted to. I had wanted to slide. I ran back up the stairs, tripping over my own legs and giggling at my cleverness. At the top I turned back to see her wringing her hands.

"I'm so sorry, Rachel." Her voice trembled. "I didn't mean to . . . to shout."

I stared at her a moment, trying to understand the strained look in her eyes, the tension in her shoulders. I had defied her before, though never so overtly—so why did she look frightened and exhausted, rather than angry? Why should I stop playing when she was the one so clearly in need of rest?

What horrors might have happened if I'd been able to conjure a phrase commanding her to obey me or let me do whatever I pleased. But I was a child, capable of mischief but too young for true malice, and I thought of all the times she had sent me to my room for a nap I didn't want to admit I needed.

"Remember, Mother, you said I could play while you took a nap." I threw all my will behind the words.

She wobbled, steadying herself with her hand against the wall.

"I've been so tired," she said, then climbed the stairs, kissing the top of my head as she passed.

My game on the stairs soon forgotten, I wandered through the public room, eating crusts of bread left on the sides of plates and gagging at the smell of congealing dregs of chowder. My mother's latest hired woman, Lucinda, tiptoed in soon after, her eyes red from chopping onions.

"Where's your mother got to, little miss?"

I sputtered through stuffed cheeks that she was asleep. Lucinda went to fetch her, and when Mother arrived back downstairs she kissed my head again, said she'd had a fine rest, and began to gather the dishes.

I could not comprehend why, exactly, my words had had such influence over her. But I knew whatever had happened, I had done it. Even as I gulped down the bread, I could taste the strength of the curse on my tongue, warm and metallic, the wind heralding a storm to come. I longed to try again, but I felt the ghost of her kiss upon my head and decided to shift targets. I feared Lucinda would tell my mother if I cursed her, the way she told her when she caught me sneaking bits of raw potato from the kitchen or dragging clean sheets from the linen closet to build nests and forts in vacant rooms. I could curse one of the regular guests (perhaps weaselly Mr. Coffin or one of the drunks or the stuffy old minister who grumbled over the presence of ale but could not resist my mother's chowders), but the public room during supper was rarely quiet enough for anyone to hear or notice me. I knew only two other people: my mother's friend Elijah, whose stories of horrible squalls and ferocious sea beasts endeared me to him, and Freddy.

Freddy Ross had worked at the Try Pots since he was a small boy. His father, like so many others, had been lost at sea, and his mother, Sarah, earned money by taking in the sheets and counterpanes from local inns to wash each week. She was a shy woman who spoke little and rarely ventured out of New Guinea, the free Black neighborhood on the edge of town, but when I was an infant her compassion for my lonely mother broke through her timidity, and the two became friends. She always greeted us with sweets, but still I fussed when forced to tag along on trips out to the Rosses' house. I knew it meant helping my mother haul clean laundry back, shaking the blowing sand from the fabric, and I knew Freddy would tease me every chance he got. He was seven years older than me, mischievous and clever, and it was easy for him to convince me to make a fool of myself searching for pirate treasure in the scrubland or waiting endless hours on the inn's porch to see our neighbor ride his new unicorn past.

Freddy was the perfect target for my newfound power. I knew he arrived early to milk Rosie, our cow, before he went to school, and I knew he liked to rest against her warm flanks when the pail was full.

The next day I awoke early with my mother, as I had done all my life. She heated a mug of chowder for herself and made a bowl of porridge for me, then set to work dicing onions into translucent flakes that would melt into the freshly churned butter she dropped into her largest pot. That part of chowder-making I enjoyed: the bubbling butter, the crackling bacon, the steam rising from the pot and filling the room. Mother handed me stalks of herbs to pick clean of their leaves as she chopped and stirred, then a rag with which to run out and wipe the crumbs and sand from tables (a job of which I was much less fond). I had noticed bitter-faced Lucinda always scrubbed them in my wake, and I figured she could do the work herself while I hatched my plan.

Freddy was where I expected him to be, his forehead against Rosie's side, the pail of steaming milk at his feet.

"Wake up, silly," I said, and his head jerked up.

I could see he hadn't been asleep, only lost in thought, but I'd startled him. Good. I'd plotted a simple test, something satisfying yet unlikely to draw my mother's attention. I steeled myself, anchoring my feet in the mud and balling my fists on my hips.

"Freddy," I said, "give me some of that milk."

I could see right away it didn't work. He snorted a laugh through his nose.

"Go play, sand flea."

I tried again. "I told you to give me some of that milk."

He did not even acknowledge me with an answer that time, just bent to wipe his forehead with the bottom of his shirt. I closed my eyes and remembered how it felt to curse my mother, the fusion of my will and my words. *Remember*, I had said. More than a simple demand.

"Remember you promised to give me some of that milk, Freddy," I said, my words sweet and calm, laced with power. "And tomorrow's cream besides."

The yard around us grew dark and cold a moment as the sun dipped behind a cloud. He rose, picked up the pail, and presented it to me. I dipped in a greedy hand and slurped the warm, sweet froth out of my palm. Wordlessly, Freddy allowed me to drink once more, then turned and stepped back into the kitchen.

The next morning he poured a splash of cream in my porridge. I smiled and licked the back of my spoon. The world, it seemed, was mine to command.

~~~~~~

AT FIRST, I only cursed people in small, selfish ways, as one would expect of a child. I overheard my mother scolding Freddy for spoiling me with Rosie's scant supply of cream, and I felt too guilty to ever curse my friend again. But I gleefully coerced candy from shopkeepers and warm bread from my mother's hired women. After Lucinda quit, my mother hired a woman who never spoke to me, only over me, and so I cursed her, imposing a memory that she'd agreed to do my chores when no one else was around. I tested whether I could command feral cats to let me pet them or demand mice leave the inn and live in other houses. (It worked wonders, though I never managed to make flies or spiders listen.)

But I told myself I would never curse my mother again.

I would not even tell her about the power I could hide in my words. Half my memories were of her warning me about the dangers of the world. Fretting over me and following me, reminding me to follow the rules, be cautious, pay attention. She worried less openly as I grew older, but I noticed the agony on her face when she bit down on reprimands and advice. Though I could see great use in the ability to command others as I wished, she might see my strangeness as yet another threat. I did not want her to be afraid.

When I entered school, she sat me down in the Try Pots' office with an inkwell and pen and taught me to write my name: *Rachel Evangeline Hussey*. My mother never called me by childish names; I

was only ever "Rachel," from the moment she first spoke it. She could
shape it into a thousand things, a whispered song in the moments
before I fell asleep, a hissed rebuke if I was reckless in the kitchen,
a shout that rose above the ruckus of the public room. She told me it
meant "ewe," like the sheep that wandered the island, and that Rachel
was the mother of the biblical Joseph, for whose prophetic dreams she
always felt a fondness though she was never one to regularly attend
(or be too warmly welcomed at) any of Nantucket's church meetings.

I did not know Evangeline was my mother's given name until I
was slightly older, as I entered the years in which a child realizes the
rest of the world is as real as her own family. To other people, Mother
was always Mrs. Hussey, ma'am, mistress, or nothing at all, simply addressed or beseeched or ordered. To me, she had always been
Mother. I suppose she put her name into mine as a seal, declaring me
hers when so little else attested to it. Elijah said I looked like another
woman's child from the very beginning, bony and long where my
mother was small and soft, my eyes brown to her light gray, my head
snarled with thick, dark curls against her wispy, straw-colored plaits.

I noticed no one ever said I looked like my father, either. Nantucket was crawling with Husseys—shopkeepers and doctors and
preachers, fine ladies who paraded down the street in their brocade
gowns, wild little boys who chased each other through the alleyways,
old women who stared from their windows as I passed. And of course
there had been Husseys on ships for as long as there had been ships
docked on Nantucket. Captains and cabin boys, mates and harpooners, every honor and rank and duty. People in town addressed me
as Miss Hussey, and so I assumed my father was Mr. Hussey, who I
knew had drowned two years before I was born.

A girl named Alice Chase informed me of this discrepancy in the
schoolyard when we were nine years old.

"A baby takes nine months, not two years," she said, twirling a
finger in one of the shiny blue ribbons her mother used to tie up her
perfectly cylindrical blond curls. "Everyone knows that."

Alice was a child who said many things with mock confidence (asserting regularly that her grandmother was a lost English duchess, though all the girls knew she was just a toothless old whaler's wife), but there was no bravado in her statement. I understood her intent clearly. My father was not my father. Everyone knew it but me.

I reached out and jerked the ribbon. I expected it to come loose, but it pulled tight around Alice's curl. She howled and, being an experienced fighter with her gaggle of sisters, spared no time in swinging her fist into my nose. The other girls shrieked, a sound of fear entwined with joy. Alice stood still, waiting for me to swing back, keeping our score even so she could claim she'd only struck me for striking her in the first place. A thin line of blood trickled down my cheek, but I ignored it. I felt anger flow like water down my arms, but I let it rush away. I had other ways of dealing with her.

"You're a liar," I said, my voice a scraping whisper. I found my strength as I repeated the words. "You're a liar."

Everyone was silent then, a shiver rippling through the crowd. Alice's hands went slack.

"My father is Hosea Hussey the innkeeper and you know it. You are a liar."

The girls murmured, sending dark looks my way as I stepped toward Alice.

"Remember that my father is Hosea Hussey," I hissed, leaning close so she was sure to hear the curse. "Remember you've always known it, and you were just lying before. And to say you're sorry, you're going to give me that ribbon, mine to keep."

Alice said nothing but began picking at the knotted blue silk with her fingernails. Only when it was coiled in my hand did the chill seem to lift and the girls spring back to life. Alice backed away from me, blinking, then turned and fled.

That Sunday morning as we made up beds in the Try Pots, my mother informed me she'd had an unexpected guest the evening before.

"Martha Chase tells me you and Alice have been talking at school," she said, not looking up as she focused on pulling the sheet tight.

"She sits by the window," I said, my mind finding something meaningless to say as I fumbled with a pillowcase in my sudden panic.

"Seems Alice has been telling some stories about your father. Hosea Hussey, she says he is? Called her own mother a liar for saying it was otherwise."

I dropped my head and nodded. She gave the sheet a last tug and sat on the bed, her face level with mine. I thought of storming out but was drawn in by her relaxed but watchful eyes, by her way of waiting wordlessly until I could no longer bear the silence.

"But everyone says Hosea is my father," I murmured. "Alice is a liar."

I wanted so badly for this to be true, I forgot to worry whether Mother would realize I had cursed Alice. I was desperate for her to say I was right and Alice was confused; I wanted her to say it was all a misunderstanding. Of course I knew who my father was.

She drew a deep breath through her nose, keeping her face locked on mine.

"Your father was a young sailor who called himself Ishmael. He was . . . my friend. A tender man. A restless man. He left this island well before you were born, and his ship sank far away," she said, her words plain and clear. "Hosea was my husband before Ishmael came, but he died. The Hussey name is yours because it's mine, and that is all."

Tears burned in the corners of my eyes. It was true, she had never said Hosea was my father. I'd simply assumed him to be. (Or imagined him to be.) I'd looked so many times at the daguerreotype she kept of him on her desk, framed in gold inside a sharkskin case that matched the rows of account books in the Try Pots' office, which my mother still called *Hosea's office* when she taught her ever-changing hired women the inn's daily routine. His eyes were wide-set and light, gazing at the camera as if his mind were somewhere else. His hair was slicked back from his broad forehead, and his wrists and hands poked out from the too-short sleeves of his jacket. I could imagine what his hands would have felt like on my forehead when I was ill, how they would have been firm around my shoulders when I was frightened. I could close my eyes and see his gentle face, how he would smile at me even when I dropped clean silverware or came home from school covered in mud. Sometimes I dreamed of him, though he was always sleeping in those dreams, strong and peaceful even in rest. He would have forgiven me for fighting with Alice—though I would not have had to fight if he had been my father. If he had been alive.

I shook my head, silent to hold in my tears, too distraught to see the open door she offered.

She stroked my cheek with her rough hand. "A lie is a fragile thing, Rachel," she said, her voice uncertain, as if finding a single word at a time, "but so is a heart."

The next day I snuck into the office to look at the picture of Hosea again, but I could not find it. Already I could feel his image fading from my mind, inked out by a faceless blot. Ishmael.

Chapter 5

MY MOTHER SPOKE no more of Ishmael. When I tried to conjure the comforting images of Hosea, I could only picture her face the day she told me the truth, her cheeks wan, the rings beneath her eyes seeming to deepen, her lips tight against her teeth when she spoke. She'd had no quiver in her voice, but I had heard the sorrow all the same. *A lie is a fragile thing, but so is a heart*, she had said. I went back to the words, trying to parse their meaning. Her voice was so soft, yet they felt like a warning. I had longed for a lie. I wanted it so badly, I spread it, forced it on another in a way my mother could not understand. In doing so, I had struck her in a tender place. Surely she remembered far more about Ishmael than the meager details she revealed. Maybe she was ashamed of him, or the pain lay in some false promise he had made to stay with her. I began to believe she had not told me more of the story because she couldn't bear to relive the memories.

I knew I could, if I desired, find the words to command her to tell me everything, but the incident at school had shown me the danger of my curses. I was haunted by the darkness in the other girls' eyes, the desperate way Alice had unknotted her ribbon. No one at school seemed to recall exactly what had happened, but they stayed even farther from me than they had before. I quit using my power for even small indulgences.

Besides, I did not believe I wanted childish things anymore. I wanted to know the story of Ishmael. I wanted to know why he'd come to Nantucket, where he came from, all he did on the island. I wanted to hear the conversations he had with my mother, to understand the friendship that led to me. I wanted to know why he left her. And I wanted to know what had become of him, after his ship sank far away. I decided the safest route was to learn what I could about him on my own, so I could determine what damage I might cause if I asked my mother more.

I searched for evidence of him in every drawer and desk and closet of the inn, apart from my mother's room, and found nothing but linens and dishes and sand. At school and in town, I kept my ears attuned for any hint of him. Nantucket was a small place, perpetually growing smaller, and there was often little to do but whisper. I caught enough gossip to conclude that Ishmael must have been aboard a ship wrecked so horrifically that people spoke of it only in hushed, veiled tones, as if saying its name too loudly would invite its terrible end on their own heads—the *Pequod*.

I gathered what scraps of the story I could. No one related details of the disaster, only muttered words of pity over those who did not return, and never deliberately in my hearing. Few people would confess to having a relative aboard the ship, or knowing any member of the crew at all. The mad Captain Ahab's wife had drifted away when word arrived that the ship was lost; she was a Nantucket-born girl, but her relations claimed not to have heard from her since she left. She had a son, a little older than me, but I never heard anyone mention his name. Just another fatherless child.

So, too, was Amos Starbuck, whose father had been chief mate of the doomed voyage. Amos attended the schoolhouse when I was small, and I remembered him as a sturdy, reserved boy with a serious face. He was fatherless and motherless; the babe that took his mother's life came seven months after the *Pequod* set sail, and it died as well. Amos set out to sea when he was fourteen on the first ship that would take him (the *Penelope*, one of the last whalers straggling across the Nantucket bar with what measly crew it could pull together). My old friend Freddy, no longer a wily kitchen boy but a strong young man, sailed aboard it as well.

"What madness would make someone orphaned by the sea go to sea?" I asked Elijah one afternoon as we sat together in the inn.

I was twelve, growing reedy but still skinny and soft-voiced, still a child though I believed my mind sharpened and quick. The old man was mostly blind by then, his good arm nearly as stiff as his bad one. His beard grew caked with chowder as he ate. I nibbled my bread.

"Thinking of sneaking aboard a ship, now, are you, girl?" he said. He grinned as he stuffed another spoonful lumped with clams into his mouth.

"You know I didn't mean that. It's all the boys at school talk about—sailing away to somewhere. Killing whales, or going to explore the Orient or to get rich in California. And a dozen of them have drowned fathers."

He patted his face with a cloth, missing most of the mess entirely. "What else have they to do?"

"They could be schoolteachers. Or shopkeepers or ministers. They could go to Boston or Philadelphia or Concord. Anywhere in the world other than the sea."

Elijah laughed his rasping laugh. "And spend their days walking the same streets, looking at the same skies, waking up next to the same tired woman each morning? When a man is born a sailor, he'll sail."

"Even if he'll die." I struck my palms against the table, but Elijah did not react other than to lose a bit more chowder from his spoon than usual.

"You're missing Freddy, girl? He'll be back."

I hated how well he could read me, despised his certainty when I felt none.

"You've said that. Mother's said that. You think you know so much?"

He did not grant me an answer, and fury rose in my cheeks.

"I suppose you said that when Ishmael left, didn't you? He'll sail? He'll come back?"

He cocked his head at this, letting his spoon slip empty into the bowl. At first I was satisfied I had made a mark, then alarmed—I had never spoken Ishmael's name aloud. Surely Elijah would tell my mother. He cleared his throat with a wet cough and leaned toward me, though it would not help him to see me any clearer. He found my hand with his and I let him grasp it, having always been comfortable with his blackened nails and split knuckles.

"I never said he'd come back."

"Damn your prophecies." I spit the words at him, but he gripped my hand tighter.

"I never asked for them, Rachel."

In my anger, a curse sprang into my mind, unbidden. He was old, weakened. My power could easily overtake him.

"Remember—"

With a wave of his stiff arm he sent his bowl and spoon clattering to the floor, shoving his chair back as he released me and stood.

"No," he said simply, pointing a finger in my face as if I were a disobedient dog. "No."

My mother hollered from the kitchen then, inquiring about the noise.

"Everything's fine, Evangeline. A spill is all," Elijah called. He bent and fumbled for the bowl, and I knelt beside him and nudged it into his path, an offering.

"I'll clean up," I whispered. He let me help him to his feet. I found the cloth beneath the table and mopped what I could from his shirt and beard. He leaned on the table, wheezing softly. I placed his cane in his good hand, and he allowed me to embrace him and sob an apology into his shirt before he turned to leave.

"You're your mother's child, Rachel," he said. "God only knows what that means."

Elijah spoke the truth. The *Penelope* returned home a month later. Freddy arrived at the Try Pots with a scrimshaw scene of a ship in full sail for my mother and a bag of molasses candy for me. He did not visit us long, for the voyage had found surprising success, and despite his paltry lay he had money enough to fix up his mother's old house in New Guinea, to find a girl to marry, to establish himself, if he wanted to. Freddy confessed that the *Penelope*'s prosperity had been hard-fought (six small whales over two years, rendering only the amount of oil two whales would have wrought a generation before, when the greatest beasts still roamed the seas). Two men drowned during hunts, one fell overboard in the night, one lost an arm, one deserted. And still he would have returned to sea at once, had the *Penelope*'s owners not decided to bank their money and retire, knowing they would not have such luck again. The captain and mates scattered to San Francisco, to New Bedford, to the war. Freddy, too, could not resist the pull of vast and roiling lands unknown, so he joined the Union army and left Nantucket once again. He wrote letters assuring my mother and me that he was content with his duty, but I heard rumors that caused me to lie awake at night, imagining him trying to sleep in rat-infested tents, picturing him freezing and hungry on endless marches.

On the morning word reached us that Freddy had been killed in battle, I rushed to tell Elijah and found him dead and cold.

~~~~~

AMOS STARBUCK, being an unusually stolid and traditional Quaker like his lost father, chose not to go to war—but neither did he return to sea. One of his fleet of uncles took him in at his dry-goods store, pleased to find someone young and strong willing to stay on the island. As the years passed, the boy who'd clung to riggings in raging storms and explored the glittering shores of distant islands became a man who spent his days shuffling from stockroom to shelf and back again.

On the mornings my mother sent me out to pick up flour or salt or spices for her chowders, I began to frequent Balaam Starbuck's store, despite the old man's gruff indifference toward me. On those errands I could not help but observe Amos, though all his actions fought against attention. He rarely spoke, content to let his uncle converse with customers and handle the transactions. He kept his face stoic, his deep blue eyes focused on his tasks. It did not escape my notice how his time at sea had sculpted him. (I'd seen other girls bunch together in the store under the guise of looking at fabric or shoes, whispering and giggling as he swept the shop's floors.) But I was far more interested in what his thoughts might hide. I'd spoken to no one about Ishmael since the day I nearly cursed Elijah, but I had not for a day stopped wondering. I knew Amos must have wondered about his father, too.

The spring I was seventeen, my mother sent me to buy candles one morning before school. I found Amos alone at the shop counter. He spoke a soft greeting to me but seemed to take no additional interest in my presence. As he tallied my purchases, the words filled my mouth, and I could not help but release them.

"I should like to speak to you about the *Pequod*."

Amos paused counting my change, his eyes skimming across empty aisles.

"Not here," I said. "I'll meet you at the Atheneum. This afternoon. Three o'clock."

He dropped the final penny into my hand and briskly, almost imperceptibly, nodded.

I rushed to the Atheneum after school. I had many fond memories of the building—the stately white exterior that belied the warm, lamplit rooms within; the Great Hall that drew crowds to listen to the latest great minds many evenings but stood empty and airy many afternoons; the cozy, well-kept rows of books I had often browsed with my mother or Freddy when I was a girl. But seeing Amos waiting on the steps, so clearly looking for someone, jolted me. Anyone could wander past, see us talking, and inquire about what we were discussing or why we were together, or report back to my mother or Balaam. The Atheneum was far too public.

I strolled past the building as if I had not seen him, knowing he would not be so bold as to wave at me. I circled the block into the quiet alley that ran behind the Atheneum, stopping to take inordinate interest in a small purple flower that hung through the low fence surrounding the library's garden. When I was sure no one could see me, I hopped over and edged up the side of the building, tucked into the shadows. Amos continued to watch the street as I hissed his name, finally spotting me when I had practically shouted it.

"Not here," I whispered as loud as I dared, before he could step toward me. "Shaw Mercantile, upstairs, ten minutes."

Shaw Mercantile was a tiny shop at the far end of downtown, somehow overstuffed with goods yet always out of what almost anyone needed. I was not sure anyone ever paid attention to customers until they insisted upon making a purchase, unlike Balaam with his ever-watchful eye. The proprietors were a pasty, indifferent man who rarely appeared, and a woman of indeterminate age who was either his daughter, sister, or wife (though I'd never heard anyone say for certain). I called her Miss Shaw, and she had never corrected me; in fact, she rarely looked up from her reading material to acknowledge me at all. I appreciated her for that, and for the fact that I'd never once seen her visit the Try Pots. Though I occasionally found a spice for Mother or an interesting object for myself among the clutter, the true pull of Shaw Mercantile lay up its derelict staircase, on its second floor. A roomful of books, a lending library of sorts for those who could not afford membership to the Atheneum or preferred not to return borrowed books for months or years at a time, if ever. The books were arranged in no order, and as many were piled upon the floor surrounding threadbare chairs as were on the shelves. Anyone who came into the library conscientiously ignored any other visitors, making it the perfect place to hide from my classmates, my chores, the stench of chowder.

I doubted Amos had ever stepped foot in Shaw Mercantile, but he appeared precisely when I had asked him to, clutching his hat in his hand.

He cleared his throat and cast the same nervous glance about as he had when I'd confronted him in his store.

"You wished to speak to me of my father's ship?" I noticed that he did not use the name.

"Yes. What do you know of it?"

The corner of his mouth flickered with a brief smile. "I heard you were demanding."

Of course I wanted to know who'd been talking about me with Amos, and why he'd been talking about me at all, but I was undeterred from my original mission.

"Do you remember your father setting sail? Did you ever visit the ship?"

He smiled no more. "I remember nothing. Neither him nor the ship."

He put his hat back on his head, turning as if he might leave.

I stepped toward him, once again feeling my words fill me up and spill out. "But don't you *want* to know?"

He turned to me, his jaw set. I could tell he was used to people shying away from him when he fixed them with such a look (one he'd surely honed facing down surly crewmates at sea), but I held his gaze. My mother had taught me to look a man in the eyes when I needed something from him. She said it frightened them.

Amos's teeth scraped across his lower lip and he let out a long breath through his nose.

"I do. I do want to know. I used to ask when I was small. No one would answer."

Excitement over this admission swept over me, and I caught him by his sleeve and dragged him deeper through the shelves to a small table tucked in a corner. I sat and he followed, dazed.

"There must be letters, records of some kind. Does your uncle keep a diary? Surely he must remember your father—perhaps they spoke of the voyage before the ship set sail. Do you think he'd tell you, if you asked? Have you ever asked?"

He shook his head, and I could not tell whether it was out of denial or bewilderment.

"You must never ask my uncle about any of this. Promise me. Please."

I rushed to promise, eager to agree to any terms as long as he seemed willing to help me. He nodded to acknowledge my reply but sat silent, staring at the table, until I had to grip the sides of my chair to keep myself from unleashing more questions.

Finally, he spoke, his words even and soft. "We'll not squeeze a word about that ship from anyone on Nantucket. But I think you will find what you are looking for elsewhere."

"And how would you like to look elsewhere, exactly?"

"When you asked me to meet you at the Atheneum, I thought you knew," he said. "I've heard talk in the store—a man's been writing whaling tales in a Boston newspaper."

I felt as if I were underwater, hearing his words from a great distance. His meaning drifted into my ears, and I forced my leaden tongue to respond.

"Tales of the *Pequod*?"

"He gives it another name, a fiction. But they say the stories concern a search for a white whale."

Like me, he seemed to struggle with voicing this news; he could barely wrench out the final words.

"And do they?"

"I've—I've not had the courage to read them," he said. "I hoped you would."

I INTERRUPTED MISS SHAW'S reading to inquire if the mercantile carried the *Spyglass*, the paper Amos said carried the tales, and she excavated
several recent copies from a pile of mail from Boston. Back upstairs,
Amos sat with his face in his hands, his fingers combing into his hair. I
pored through the stack of newsprint, already growing dusty and yellowed though it was only weeks old, until I had rooted out three editions
that contained the tales. I spread the earliest paper across the table and
began to read, my soft voice to our advantage, as the bell on the mercantile door rang to indicate late-afternoon customers.

The author called himself "Samuel the Sub-Librarian." Samuel
presented himself as a sophisticated gentleman retired from sailing,
reveling in the adventures of his greenhand days, but elements so
closely matched what I had heard of the *Pequod*, I knew he could mean
no other ship. As I read his reminiscences of coming to a place he
called Faraway Island in search of adventure on a whaler to alleviate
his festering, almost comical disquietude, I felt a wave of certainty. A
young sailor, my mother had said. *A tender man. A restless man.* Samuel
the Sub-Librarian had to be my father, Ishmael. He clothed his stories in fantasy that crept close to, but never quite touched, reality. The
Pequod became the *Perses*; peg-legged Ahab transformed into the one-
armed, vengeance-crazed Captain Asa. Samuel bestowed the whale
with ever-changing and exaggerated monikers: The Tahitian Terror.
The Demon Beast of the Southern Sea. The White Devil. He claimed
the stories had happened decades before, when Massachusetts whaleships ruled the globe, but I saw through his ruse. The tales were the
work of a man attempting to sort out the defining events of his life.
They seemed to have no particular order and varied between rollick-
ing narratives of chase and plodding explications of whaling terms,
peppered with moments of hilarity, rambling asides, eulogies for a lost
industry, and praises for the mighty, yet villainous, whale. Reading
the prose was simultaneously exhilarating and exhausting.

Amos's father appeared briefly in the second tale as Chief Mate Macy, and Amos lifted his eyes from his palms to watch as I read: *"Macy was no crusader after perils; in him courage was not a sentiment; but a thing simply useful to him, and always at hand upon all mortally practical occasions."*

I paused at the end of the scene to read Amos's reaction. Though he hid his mouth with his hands, I could see in his brow the hint of a smile.

"My uncle has said the same of him—he seemed to fear little which the sea could offer."

"You think this is all true, then?"

"Truth is a slippery fish," he said. "I believe the man he calls Macy is my father."

And I have no doubt Samuel is my father, I nearly replied, but dampened the words. I wondered if he'd heard the whispers about my origins. Did people say my father was Ishmael, or an unnamed sailor, or simply someone who was not Hosea Hussey? Would Amos, with all his Quaker demureness, refuse my company if I forced him to acknowledge my illegitimate parentage? He was the first person who had ever willingly spoken to me of the *Pequod*, and I could not risk losing him.

"Do you think there will be more?" I asked.

"There may already have been," he said.

The *Spyglass* printed only once a week, and the issues from Miss Shaw's pile were already several weeks old. The paper's arrival at the mercantile would likely be days or weeks after it reached the streets of Boston, depending on the reliability of the post office, the patterns of merchants and bankers coming to and from the mainland, and the attentiveness of Miss Shaw.

"We could tell Miss Shaw we like some other feature in the paper and want to read it as soon as possible," I said. "Or perhaps we could encourage your uncle to take a trip to the mainland someday soon and pick up copies. Are you short on any goods at the shop? I could make an order."

As I spoke, he gathered the papers from the table, folding and stacking them. I noticed a tremor in his hands.

"No. You already promised not to draw attention to our inquiries. We must not let anyone know we have interest in these tales, but especially my uncle."

"You said only we weren't to ask him about it! Surely he wouldn't forbid you from learning of your father on your own."

"He would, and he has. He is ashamed," Amos said. "Everyone is."

"I'm not ashamed."

I yanked the top paper from his arms. It was not an edition that contained one of the tales; still, I felt it important to demonstrate that this endeavor was not his to rule.

He did not reach to take it back, but his face hardened.

"What is the *Pequod* to you but a curiosity? You have nothing to lose."

So he did not make the connection to rumors about my parentage.

"I believe . . ." I wrestled with how much to reveal, what it might cost. "I believe my mother knew the writer of these tales."

"And you will run home to tell her you've read them?"

I could tell he knew the answer, and I found myself with nothing to say in reply. When I'd set out to learn more about Ishmael, I'd told myself that I would tell my mother when I knew enough. I did not know enough yet.

I sighed, though I did not return the paper to him.

"I will not speak of it to my mother, nor to anyone."

Chapter 6

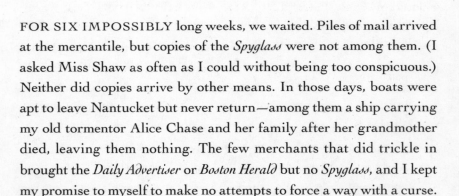

FOR SIX IMPOSSIBLY long weeks, we waited. Piles of mail arrived at the mercantile, but copies of the *Spyglass* were not among them. (I asked Miss Shaw as often as I could without being too conspicuous.) Neither did copies arrive by other means. In those days, boats were apt to leave Nantucket but never return—among them a ship carrying my old tormentor Alice Chase and her family after her grandmother died, leaving them nothing. The few merchants that did trickle in brought the *Daily Advertiser* or *Boston Herald* but no *Spyglass*, and I kept my promise to myself to make no attempts to force a way with a curse.

Amos and I did not speak in the interim, though I was embarrassed to dream of him, walking the quiet back roads of the island or working in the back room of the shop. On the days I stopped by the store, Amos was busy with his work and paid me no mind, not even so much as a nod or whisper. I spent most days at school, trudging through compositions and equations, drearily reciting the birth and death dates of the great men of Massachusetts, memorizing speeches until I could repeat them without considering the words, ignoring the other girls, who were only too happy to ignore me. I'd heard a woman ask my mother why she should send me to school when I could be more help around the inn, and she offered only a raised eyebrow and a turned shoulder in answer. In the days before discovering Samuel the Sub-Librarian, I had adored schoolwork, if not my schoolmates, but I found no joy in it when my mind was elsewhere. I had longed to know Ishmael's story, and now I had it, in his own words. I was pleased to find he was intelligent and humorous, full of adventure. No more was my father a faceless blot. I liked to imagine a vast sapphire sea, a man who looked like me calling *Land ho!* from the masthead as an island much more verdant than Nantucket rose on the horizon.

Finally, I stopped into the mercantile one morning (ostensibly to buy an apple for school) and Miss Shaw casually mentioned a large delivery was due that afternoon that included ten bolts of plaid cotton, a crate of ladies' gloves, and three more editions of the *Spyglass*. The moment I closed my schoolbooks for the day, I rushed to old Starbuck's shop. Amos was there, filling a cracker barrel as his uncle glowered at his account books behind the counter. I feigned interest in some crockery and searched my mind for ways to signal to Amos without alerting his uncle to our communication. I thought of how much easier it would be if I could simply curse Balaam. As Amos continued to pay me no mind, I landed on a solution and marched to the counter.

"I'd like a copy of the newspaper, please."

"*Inquirer*'s five cents," Mr. Starbuck mumbled.

"Oh, don't you have anything from Boston? I'd like to read news of the city this evening."

He looked at me over his glasses, his lip twitching toward a sneer. "What care have *you* about the city?"

Sure my signal was sufficient, I had no reason to continue.

"You're right, Mr. Starbuck. I've made a terrible mistake. I care nothing for the city. I'll be going now," I said, and marched out, swinging the door hard so it struck its bell repeatedly, leaving an insistent jangling in my wake.

I found Amos sitting in the upper room of Shaw Mercantile just before sunset, chewing his thumbnail. He hadn't yet fetched the papers from Miss Shaw, and I scolded him for it.

"You're the one who couldn't wait to get them," he said, flinching as he drew a bead of blood along the side of his nail. "Coming into my uncle's store and making such a racket—he already dislikes you, and he'll notice you forever now."

"Why should he? I was simply looking for a newspaper. What's there to notice?"

"And do you always stomp around yelling about Boston? Slamming doors?" He caught the rise in his voice and switched to a whisper. "You acted as if you had a mountain of secrets. Thank God he did not think they had anything to do with me. He just thinks you're preparing to leave the island. 'That girl's got her eyes on the mainland,' he said."

"I'm not leaving the island," I said, but as the words snapped from my mouth a thought bubbled to the surface of my mind. In Boston, I would not sit for miserable months waiting to read Samuel the Sub-Librarian's latest tales; I could purchase them on the street corner. Or directly from the offices of the *Spyglass*—where surely there would be someone to whom Ishmael had been sending his dispatches. Perhaps even someone who knew where he sent them from. Perhaps the man himself.

My reverie was interrupted by Miss Shaw appearing at the top of the staircase, newspapers in arm. "Saw you arrive," she said, and handed them to me with a curt nod.

I pushed them across the table to Amos, my mind too filled with images of the city to focus on searching the columns of text for a tale.

"None in this one," Amos muttered as I imagined myself striding into the offices of the *Spyglass*, declaring myself the daughter of Samuel the Sub-Librarian.

"Nor this one," said Amos, pushing the folded papers across the table to me as I envisioned an editor leaping from his seat, grabbing me by the hand and declaring my father a genius! brilliant!

"We've only one left, and I worry it will be empty as well," Amos said, snapping the third paper shut. "Where is your mind, Rachel?"

I grinned. "In Boston."

He cast his eyes to the ceiling. "Sometimes I do not understand you at all."

"Oh, come now, Amos," I said, unable to help myself from sweeping him into my fantasy. "Imagine it: We're standing right there before the editor of the *Spyglass*, and we say, 'We know the men spoken of in these stories! We are the children of Samuel the Sub-Librarian and Chief Mate Macy!' And he'll say, 'Of course you are! And have you spoken to the great tale-teller himself? I shall immediately send him a telegram and tell him his daughter has arrived!'"

Amos stared at me, unsmiling. "His daughter?"

"You complain about not understanding me, and yet you never listen! I told you after we read the first tale that my mother knew Samuel, remember? We have been drawn together from the beginning, in search of our fathers."

I caught sight of Amos's face, his sullenness of moments before lost as he watched me speak in the flickering lamplight. "We have always wanted to know the rest of the story. We could learn it in Boston."

~~~~~

THE STACK OF *SPYGLASSE*S in the mercantile's delivery did not contain stories from Samuel—but the copy that arrived by post the next week did. Miss Shaw left it upstairs where she knew I'd find it when I stopped by after school to read other things, as I did almost daily by then, but I attempted to abide by Amos's wishes for restraint and did not immediately go to the shop to inform him. I waited until after school, trailing behind a knot of other girls who turned out to be heading to the same destination. I took a breath before stepping inside and strolled through the front door the very picture of calmness (or so I hoped).

Old Starbuck did not look up from his work, but merely grunted as I walked in.

"And what do you desire today, Miss Hussey? News of New York? Paris, perhaps?"

"Oh, no," I said. "My mother hoped you might have some dried rosemary. She's trying a new chowder recipe this afternoon and she's run out."

She was not planning to, of course, but I knew simply leaving the herb in her kitchen would inspire her to and ensure I was not a liar. Besides, I liked the smell of rosemary, and thought perhaps it would temper the reek of clams.

Amos's voice rose from the back of the shop. "We have rosemary."

The other girls, who had been shuffling through some kitchen implements near where Amos swept, ignoring my arrival and exchange with his uncle, swiveled their heads to see to whom he spoke. I couldn't miss their glowers when they spied me.

"Thank you," I whispered, keeping my attention on the floor as I crossed to the shelf Amos indicated.

I meant to collect the herb for myself, but as I approached he opened the jar and placed the stems in my hand.

"Three should be enough," he said. "Come in tomorrow afternoon if you need more."

His signal was clumsy, but unmistakable. Three o'clock the next day in the upper room of the mercantile. He must have been too busy to meet right away. I could not stop my eyes from rising briefly to meet his.

"Thank you," I said, unable to discern whether it would be least suspicious to call him Amos or Mr. Starbuck or sir, settling on calling him nothing.

I exited the store in silence, feeling the weight of the girls and old Starbuck glaring at my back as I left.

Amos was at the mercantile the next afternoon as indicated, having already retrieved the *Spyglass* from Miss Shaw.

"It contains a tale," he said as soon as I stepped within range of our corner. "I've not read it yet. I'd like you to; you have a better reading voice than mine. That is, the tales sound more exciting upon your lips."

I noticed a bloom of red across his cheeks as I sat. I admit I had loitered a while on the main floor, checking to be sure the other girls in the store hadn't detected his signal as well. They had not (or if they had, they did not figure out our meeting place).

I took the paper, clearing my throat for show as I began: "*If the Sperm Whale be physiognomically a Sphinx . . .*"

Amos fidgeted throughout my reading, and I sympathized. While informative on the nature of the sperm whale's skull, the tale contained no story of our fathers. Though I suppose it said something more subtly of mine—of his obsession with understanding the creature that sank his ship and killed every other man aboard. As I finished, Amos took the paper in glum silence, giving me a moment to ruminate on Ishmael-called-Samuel. My mother had spoken to him, spent time with him, known him in a way that could not be revealed through his writing. I wanted to hear the real voice behind the performance on the page. He was entranced by the sound of his own words, perhaps, but also confident that his strange tales would be of interest to others. Did he write with the knowledge that some readers out there might spy the relationship to the true tale of the *Pequod*? Did he ever consider that my mother might read them, or did he think of her at all in nearly eighteen years? I knew she had thought of him, even if she would not tell me what she remembered. Surely Ishmael did not wonder if I could be reading; I was confident that the moment he learned of my existence he would acknowledge me. And I was certain, even more than before, that sitting about waiting for his missives to appear would do me no good. I had spun the idea in my mind for a week, and it had formed shape and substance.

"It's meaningless," Amos said.

"Yes, I suppose," I admitted.

"Still." He paused, letting out a breath. "I am glad to read it with you."

I felt as if my mouth had filled with wool; I attempted to swallow as he continued.

"Fred used to talk about you when we sailed on the *Penelope*. He said you were a tricky, spirited girl—insisting he sneak treats to you, bossing your mother's hired women around. He always laughed when he spoke of you."

I smiled, remembering my old friend, and Amos took this as encouragement to continue.

"I was charmed by you before I ever spoke to you. But still I think I would not have spoken to you had you not come into my uncle's shop to ask me about the *Pequod*. I had been so frightened to even think of it. Rachel, I am frightened no more."

My memory flew back to that first moment in the shop. What had I said to him? *The Atheneum. This afternoon. Three o'clock.*

"Amos, I—" But my voice was too soft to interrupt as he charged forward.

"I am sorry for my cross words to you last week." He reached across the table and clasped my hand, running the rough callus on the pad of his thumb across my knuckles. "These past days, all I have thought of is you—us. In Boston. We have been drawn together from the beginning through our fathers, as you said. We could remain together."

I realized how careless I had been, revealing my secret while I prattled on about searching for Samuel the Sub-Librarian in Boston. I had hardly listened to my own words. I'd grown comfortable with Amos, gotten to know him well enough to guess he would not reject me outright if I admitted to my mother's affair. Yet his eagerness felt like too much. I dashed through my memories, trying to understand the origin of his sudden passion. I had accused him of not listening to me.

I told you, remember?

I had not even considered what power I might have put into those words. And I must have dragged in all I said after, weaving a memory from a fantasy.

I stood, and he rose to match me. "We cannot do this." I scrambled for an explanation. "Your uncle would disown you. And what would you do in Boston? You have a job here. A life here."

"I would leave it all for you."

"You truly would leave Nantucket?" I said, though I knew the answer.

"I'd sail the world."

It would have been so easy to say yes, to share my plan to start in Boston and from there discover where Ishmael was hiding, to track him even if it meant crossing the globe. I did not doubt Amos's words. He was a sailor; he'd sail. He would be a good companion, with his gentle words and steady hands. He would go wherever I asked. But I was sure I had sparked his desire with a curse, whether I meant to or not. And a lie was a fragile thing.

"Amos, we can't," I said again.

One last chance. In the past, I had used my power recklessly, out of anger or eagerness, but I had never learned to use it well. Never again would I wield my words carelessly. A curse would be to me as a knife, cold and clean and sharp. If he would not release me, I would do the only thing I knew would set him free.

"We must."

I slipped my hand from his grasp. "Remember—"

The word felt wrong. I had caused all this by asking him to remember. I let my voice ring clear from my mouth, echoing through the dim and dusty shelves.

"Amos, forget you ever spoke to me."

~~~~~~

I CRIED NO tears as I scrubbed pots in my mother's kitchen that night, yet I felt as if I should. I scoured the caked-on cream until my hands grew red and raw, but I could not elicit the pain I felt I deserved for luring Amos into a trap without realizing what I'd done. Whatever care I might have felt for him—and I had been so consumed by learning about my father I had not fully entertained such thoughts—was now snuffed out by guilt.

By the last pot my knuckles cracked and seeped blood. My mother entered as I was blotting them on a kitchen rag. She retrieved ointment and clean cloths, wrapping and binding without a word. When the work was done, she spoke only to bid me upstairs to her room. I waited as she dressed for bed, an act I had not witnessed since I was small. She sighed richly as she peeled away the sweaty cotton, and I laughed at the sudden image of a lobster shedding its shell. She arched an eyebrow as she shook the sand from the dress and draped it over a chair, unfolding her nightdress and trading it for her underclothes. Freed from the smells and stains of her day, she sat in her chair by the fire. Its twin faced her on the other side of the hearth, and she waved for me to sit as I had done many nights before.

"I used to sit and talk here with your father," she said, watching the stirring flames. "He was a sweet man. Practically a boy, for all he knew of the world."

It was the first thing she had said to me about Ishmael since I was nine years old. I sat in silent shock, wondering why she had brought him up again, hoping she was about to offer up all her hidden memories.

"Amos Starbuck is a sweet man. A good man," she continued. "Miss Shaw is fond of a midmorning bowl of chowder, and she has witnessed some events she thought a mother should know of."

Miss Shaw. Of course. Not so wrapped up in her books as she'd seemed.

"It's not what you think."

"I suppose it's not. Why don't you tell me what it is?"

"We've just been reading together."

I wanted to leave it at that, but she waited, as she always did, for me to fill the silence.

"But today he said he wants to run away with me."

She huffed. "So like a man to think leaving is easy."

I understood much in those words, much I was sure she had not meant to reveal. I knew now that Ishmael was a good, if complicated, man. The *Spyglass* proved how much life he had lived after the *Pequod* sank, how many thoughts and adventures, and yet he did not return to Nantucket. He sent stories to a newspaper in Boston, but not a shred, that I knew of, to my mother. If she knew the tales existed, they must have felt like him leaving again and again. And what would she say if I told her I wanted to leave to find him? I imagined the pain on her face as I said the words. I could see her standing on the wharf as I sailed away, her figure growing smaller and fainter until it disappeared. I thought of her scrubbing pots alone, making beds alone, sitting by the fire alone. Turning me into a memory she couldn't speak about.

"I'm not running away with him," I whispered. It was not a lie, and yet it was, and I was sure she knew it.

"I see," she said. She laid her arms across her chest and rocked back in her chair.

In the firelight I could see the smooth lines of her temples, the soft curve of her chin. Her face was as it had always been, as I had seen it every morning and every night. In those weeks of waiting for Samuel the Sub-Librarian's tales, I had glanced at my mother mere seconds a day, yet she'd never stopped looking at me.

I knew in that moment what I had to do if I ever wanted to leave Nantucket. I told her I was tired and excused myself, leaving no chance of further discussion that evening. She did not mention Ishmael or Amos again in the days that followed, and I was careful to fill my time with nothing more than my usual routine.

On the night I left, I waited until she was deeply asleep before I packed my things. I snuck into her room and pulled open the drawer at her bedside table. There was the daguerreotype of Hosea. And there was an object I'd never seen before—a strange piece of scrimshaw, a tooth with a simple engraving of a whale. If she stored it by her bedside, it must have belonged to Ishmael. I left the picture, but took the tooth. If my plan worked, she would never miss it. She would never miss me.

I knelt by the bed and whispered her name. Her eyes opened in the dim morning light, darting from my face to my traveling dress to the whale's tooth in my hand. Before she could look me in the eye, I spoke softly but without hesitation, feeling the power flow out of me and into her, around us, across the island. It was the second time I cursed my mother.

"Forget you ever had a daughter."

Chapter 7

I WAS UNPREPARED for the sight of Boston. I had spent my life on Nantucket, a world contained on a crescent of beach, and here was a city that spread across the horizon and did not appear to stop. The streets crowding the harbor seemed a mass of doors and windows. It struck me as I gaped that everyone I had ever known would fit inside a mere handful of the buildings before me.

I clutched my bag as I departed the train and joined the throngs in the street. My day in the city was mapped clearly in my head. I knew I must first find someone to take me to the *Spyglass*; I had not planned for such a task to prove difficult. Men and women swarmed around me, all sure of their destinations, none of them appearing to care where anyone else was going. Looking down at my dress, I felt sure I stood out (I was neither so well dressed as the finer among them, nor so poorly dressed as those that haunted the edges of the crowd), but no one seemed to notice me. I took a deep breath and noted the familiar smell of a fish market, and stepped into the stream.

Before long I happened upon a team of horses pulling a long, enclosed cart. I approached the driver perched on the back before noticing the array of people piling in from all directions. The man stared down at me from beneath the shadow of his cap. "Ride's a penny, ma'am. Stops at the custom house, then on to the Common." I had brought a small amount of money but had not anticipated paying for anything; I had decided to clear my way to the *Spyglass* with curses. Yet I could not figure out what words to use to commandeer a cart full of people, and I felt their eyes on me as I hesitated, so I paid and boarded.

I was amused to discover I was not the only person gawking at the passing city—beside me sat a woman with feathery hair, so fair it was nearly white, neatly pinned beneath her hat, and she was even more openmouthed than me. She turned to me.

"Would you look at all this? My cousin told me Boston was a pretty city, but I didn't imagine this," she said.

I nodded; I did not intend to waste time on conversation.

She asked me if I would be staying in a boardinghouse, diving into a description of the place she was headed before giving me a chance to respond.

"Don't suppose you're staying there, too?" she asked.

I'd hardly caught the name, but regardless, had no such plans and said so.

"Ah, I shouldn't have hoped. Too many places to go to be headed the same way."

"Yes."

She grinned, revealing a wide gap between her front teeth. "You're a quiet one, aren't you? I'm Mary Hale, recently of Belfast. And you?"

"Rachel Shaw."

The name Hussey might mark me as a Nantucketer, and I had no intention of sharing my true origins. If anyone asked, I would be from Cape Cod, raised in some drab, unmemorable village. Let the name Hussey be a relic of the past.

"So, where are you going, Rachel Shaw?"

"I have business."

"Keeping it secret, are you?" She nudged me with her elbow.

It seemed I had reason to deliver a curse after all. I kept it simple and pointed: "Forget you wanted to talk to me."

Without comment she returned to admiring the buildings, and she said nothing else to me when we disembarked at the Boston Common and she disappeared.

I had memorized the location of the *Spyglass* office on a map at the Atheneum and knew I needed to travel west of the Common, yet it was much more difficult to gain my bearings on the ground than it was gazing at clean lines on paper. I resisted the enticing greenery of the park and instead found a boy hawking copies of a different paper beneath the shadow of an elm along the street. When he responded that he was familiar with the *Spyglass*—that he was, in fact, familiar with all of Boston—I reminded him how he'd offered to leave his post and take me there. I had trouble keeping up with him at first as he ducked and wove through the carts and crowds, but I soon found a rhythm. Everyone around me was going somewhere, but most were at least somewhat distracted by their companions or their pocket watches or the call of a bird from one of the innumerable trees. My boy thought of nothing but going where I wanted him to, and I had only to follow.

I had not presumed the *Spyglass* would have a grand office, but I imagined it might be something like the tidy storefront of Nantucket's *Inquirer and Mirror*. What I found before me could hardly be called a business at all, just a dark, smudged window and a deep green door with gold letters in peeling paint: THE BOSTON SPYGLASS, *est. 1858, Mr. Timothy Appleton, publisher.*

The boy began to glance around, eyes wide and glazed. As I had deployed my curses so infrequently in my life to this point, I was uncertain of their effects; I realized that, task completed, he might have been uncertain as to why he'd agreed to wander away with a stranger, perhaps even frightened that he would be in trouble with his employer. "Forget all this and go back to selling papers," I said. He turned and ran back down the alley with even more urgency than before. I decided I should have given him a penny for his time, but he was out of shouting distance, and I knew it would not trouble him. He disappeared around a corner, and I returned to the green door.

With a creak, the door nudged open at the force of my knock. I stepped inside. The dim, tiny room was cluttered with wooden desks and chairs, but only one was occupied. A man in red suspenders and a white shirt with the sleeves rolled to his elbows huddled over a piece of paper at a desk toward the back. He was tall, so tall that he had to sprawl his knees to the sides to fit them beneath his writing surface.

Though the scratching of his pen was the only sound in the room, the noise of the city seeped in from the street and rained from the floors above us.

I cleared my throat and said, "May I speak with Mr. Sweet, please?"

It came out a shout, and the man started so hard he knocked his knees into the desk. He rubbed them with his hands, wincing as he turned to me. He was younger than I expected, his face covered in freckles and framed by auburn hair that might earlier have been combed and shaped, but now fell haphazardly across his ears, held back by a pair of thick spectacles balanced above his forehead. He smiled with wide, curious eyes. Everything I had been sure I would say when I reached the *Spyglass* seemed lost somewhere in my head, the scene being so different from what I had pictured.

He glanced over my shoulder as if someone else were about to walk in behind me. I looked, too; the door was closed as I'd left it.

"Oh, damn it all," he said when I looked back. "I mean—pardon me, ma'am. How can I help you?"

"I'm looking for a Mr. Sweet. The editor?" I'd found the name printed in the *Spyglass* masthead; it was the only name listed, other than the publisher's.

"Nathaniel Norcross Sweet, at your service," he said, rising to his feet and lowering an inky hand to me—though I was considered rather gangly on Nantucket, he could easily have rested an elbow atop my head. "I apologize for my impertinence. I've one story left for this edition and it's due to the press in—" He patted his pockets and, coming up with nothing, shouted, "Clary, have you seen my watch?"

A woman's low voice called from a doorway in the shadows at the back of the room. "Not lately, unless you left it in my tool chest again."

That seemed to trigger something in him, and he rooted through a box overflowing with rulers and writing utensils until he retrieved the missing pocket watch. Flipping it open, he frowned and looked down at me again.

"Can I trouble you to sit right there for ten minutes?"

I had waited weeks for a single issue of the *Spyglass*. I could stand to wait a few moments in the office where it was made.

"I suppose so."

"Fifteen at the most. No more than that, I assure you. I'm already late."

He scribbled and scratched, and finally, after holding the writing up at his impressively long arm's length and muttering its words to himself, he gathered a stack of papers and flung open the back door, whistling sharply. A boy appeared, grabbed them, and rushed off.

Mr. Sweet crossed back toward me, unknotting his already disheveled tie. "Twenty minutes late. They'll print the *Traveller* first and perhaps even bump us after the leaflets. I'll hear no end of it from the boys in the morning."

He crumpled the silk in his hands as he dropped into the chair beside mine. "Now then. How can I help you?"

In the time I'd had to sit, I'd collected my thoughts and remembered the speech I'd been planning. I removed the whale's tooth I'd taken from my mother's bedside table from my bag, unveiling it from the scrap of black velvet I'd wrapped it in.

"I've read the tales of Samuel the Sub-Librarian, and I've come to tell you that I am his long-lost daughter. This belonged to him."

He smiled that odd, straight smile again. "You're whose daughter, now?"

"Samuel the Sub-Librarian."

"Ma'am, I'd be pleased to help you, but this is a newspaper, not a library, though I'd say that's rather obvious."

I put away the tooth and withdrew the tattered *Spyglass*es I kept in the top of my bag.

"Samuel the Sub-Librarian is the alias of a man who writes for your own paper, Mr. Sweet. The tales of Captain Asa and the white whale?"

He snapped out his long index finger and pointed at the papers. "Oh yes, right, right. Bit of an odd chap."

"So you know him?"

He must have seen the hope on my face, for he furrowed his brow and let his smile droop.

"I'm afraid I don't. I mean his stories are rather odd—all that business about whale brains and prophets' curses and all—and he can't seem to send his letters on a good schedule for publishing. But I haven't met the fellow."

Disappointment was like an anchor in my chest, but I was not yet out of options.

"But you receive letters from him, you said?"

He spun in his chair and began shuffling through the desk drawers.

"He sent an initial letter inquiring whether we might like to run his stories, but I can't seem to find it," Mr. Sweet said, returning to the box his watch had been in and thumbing through a stack of papers, coming up with nothing. "Clary, do you know where the first letter from that whale fellow went?"

"You moved it when we were attempting to tidy up last week," answered the voice from the back room. "Bottom right drawer."

"Oh dear, I've already looked there."

A loud clang erupted, and a moment later a slight Black woman in a trim navy dress, about my mother's age and blessed with the impeccable carriage of a person who was organized in every aspect of her life, marched into the main room, rubbing ink from her hands onto a handkerchief. She tugged open the bottom right desk drawer, and in less than five seconds drew a sheet of thin, crease-marked paper from among the chaos.

I leaned in, hoping to read it, but Mr. Sweet kept it folded in his hand as he and Clary bantered about his apparent tendency to misplace things and her apparent impatience with being relied upon to find them. It was clear they'd had the argument many times before, so often that Mr. Sweet seemed somewhat surprised when he looked up and saw me listening. He blushed, his whole face pink.

"I'm terribly sorry, ma'am. May I introduce the *Spyglass*'s spectacular illustrator and aspiring press operator, Mrs. Clary Tucker," he said. "And . . . I apologize, but I seem to have forgotten your name already."

"I never gave it," I said. "It's Shaw. Miss Rachel Shaw of Cape Cod." It felt a little easier using the new name, the new place.

"And you're new to the city, are you?" Clary asked.

I tried not to wince at how easily she had noticed.

"I arrived this afternoon."

She gave me a slow, skeptical look, pausing at the copies of the newspaper I still clutched. I was unused to being so directly assessed; on Nantucket, everyone had already decided what they thought of me when I was no more than a baby.

"You know, Nat," she said, a smile sneaking through her seriousness, "we could use another person around here. If you'd like to start meeting your deadlines, that is. And it seems she's already familiar with our little publication."

"I'd love to work here," I said, hardly giving myself time to think.

All I saw was the chance to study the trail Ishmael had left, to read new letters as soon as they arrived, to hope for the moment he would finally arrive to visit his editor. If I could not sail away with my father immediately, as I had hoped, the *Spyglass* seemed to be the best place to wait.

"Well then, that's settled," Mr. Sweet said. "Splendid idea, Clary. Would you like to start in the morning, Miss Shaw?"

"I would be happy to, sir. But first, if I may?" I gestured at the onionskin paper.

He looked down, pausing as if to remember why he held it.

"Oh yes, of course, the whale fellow!" he said, handing the letter to me, open and ready to read.

> *My dear Mr. Sweet,*
>
> *I read your paper at the home of my dear friend a month ago and have since concluded it to be a fine method of delivering my whaling tales to readers who will find them most fascinating.*
>
> *I shall take care that you receive regular letters for publication— still, with my travels, I can make no promises as to the reliability of their timing.*
>
> *You must pardon this brief note—I write fast.*
>
> *Very Sincerely Yours*
>
> *SS*

Mr. Sweet agreed to let me keep the letter but did not offer to find others; he was too occupied with informing me about my new profession as newspaper clerk and assistant to the editor. I forced myself to listen attentively, knowing I had bought myself time to ask more about Ishmael soon.

Though he'd asked me to start in the morning, it seemed Mr. Sweet wanted to tell me the entire history of the *Spyglass* without delay. His meandering flurry of details drew me in, so different from anything I'd experienced as a schoolgirl and the daughter of an innkeeper on Nantucket. He explained that Clary was working to repair a recently purchased small press that would bring the paper's printing operations in-house. Her father had been a printer at one of the abolitionist papers and taught her the trade before his death, and she'd sought out printing jobs of her own after her husband had been killed in the war. The press was woefully outdated and, even repaired, would be slow, but they were confident they could keep up with demand while saving the *Spyglass* a significant amount of money. But it would never get to being repaired, it seemed, if Mr. Sweet kept relying on Clary to do half of everything else as well.

Mr. Sweet confessed he was not particularly prepared for all the duties of an editor, a job he had undertaken barely a year before.

"I studied at Amherst, and newspapers seemed a romantic notion," he said. "I assumed the publisher might do most of the work and I could stick to writing my thoughts, but Mr. Appleton pays the bills and not much more. The paper's a bit of a vanity project for him, you see."

The publisher (a distant cousin of Mr. Sweet's, whom he seemed to only have met a few times) was from one of the old Boston families, fabulously wealthy, with a penchant for exploration. He had founded the *Spyglass* on the premise of bringing adventurous tales of the world to the people of Boston and enticing them to travel, and his involvement ended roughly there. When he hired Mr. Sweet as editor, the paper had not printed for a month, but it was of little matter because most of the advertisers had not paid for several, and the subscribers were all too fabulously wealthy and busy traveling to notice they had not received a new issue.

In his year on the job, Mr. Sweet had collected most of the *Spyglass*'s debts and restarted delivery, along with developing a small network of newsboys in an attempt to broaden the audience. He was uncertain how many papers were sold and how many simply abandoned, but it allowed him to brag of a circulation of two thousand.

"The advertisers like it," he said. "They appreciate my attempts to appeal to the common man. There are only so many makers of gilded mirrors and importers of fine liqueurs in the city, and fewer buyers. The fellows who sell shirt collars and tonics figure their customers are a dime a dozen, and they are willing to part with a few dimes to find a few dozen more."

He grinned at this practiced joke, and I couldn't help but smile in return.

For all his flightiness, I could tell Mr. Sweet would be an affable man to work for. Still, I did not entirely lose sight of the reason I had walked into his office. When he asked if I had any questions, I responded that I would like to read any other correspondence he had from Samuel the Sub-Librarian.

I read and reread the first letter while he wandered off to search for others, trying to glean from it any detail I could of Ishmael's life and personality. He was confident, a bit pompous perhaps, but his stories had proven to be popular as he had expected. He had a friend who lived somewhere close enough to Boston to receive the paper. He planned to continue traveling. Already he'd gone so many places; I had to hold out hope he would come somewhere near enough for me to reach him, or better, that he would return to Massachusetts.

Mr. Sweet returned, slightly dusty.

"There are others buried in the archives, but these are the most recent," he said, presenting me with two envelopes stamped from Honolulu.

"His tales have been popular with a rather eclectic set of readers," Mr. Sweet said as I opened them, careful not to tear the paper despite my eagerness. "The nostalgic types, of course, and the scientifically minded. Several readers have complained they're too odd, but they fill the pages. And they've found at least one fan, in you."

I scanned the letters and recognized them immediately as the last two stories Amos and I had read, with no additional notes or details.

"You're sure these are the most recent you've received?"

He assured me they were, and I began asking other questions before he had the chance to redirect the conversation again. All I learned, however, was that Samuel, as Mr. Sweet called him, left no forwarding address, nor had he mentioned exactly who his dear friend in Massachusetts was, nor offered any other indication of who he himself truly was and where he was going. Even when I revealed to Mr. Sweet that I knew Samuel's real name was Ishmael, he cheerfully brushed it off as yet another of the tale-teller's fabrications.

"You seek a charming phantom, Miss Shaw."

I DID NOT tell Mr. Sweet I'd made no plans for lodging in Boston. When I left Nantucket, I had only faith that I would stay briefly before being introduced to Ishmael, and I could commandeer the finest hotel room in the city if I so chose. When I left the *Spyglass* with the promise to come back the next day (and every day it took until I had reliably located my father, though I did not say so), I recalled what the fair-haired girl in the carriage had said to me. I repeated the nonsense syllables I remembered of the boardinghouse name aloud as I walked, finally concluding that Miss Hale had said she would be staying at "Miss Hand-writies'" house, or something near to it. I could not find my newsboy guide again, but when I asked the proprietor of a bookshop near the Common, he scribbled an address for me on a scrap of paper.

The boardinghouse had tall, narrow windows and an imposing black front door, its redbrick facade jammed against its neighbors in a way that made me reluctant to call it a house at all, especially in light of the grand homes on Nantucket. I swung the heavy iron knocker and a woman with wide-set eyes and even wider-set hips answered the door. I stumbled through the pronunciation of the name and she raised one bushy gray eyebrow.

"Miss Hanratty, do you mean?" she asked, in an accent matching Mary Hale's.

"Yes, ma'am."

"Well, you found it. I wasn't expecting any other girls this week."

"I didn't—"

But before I could attempt an excuse she'd grabbed me by the cheeks with her stubby fingers and set to twisting my head back and forth.

"This is a respectable house," she said. "A house of sound Christian morals. I'll not stand for any disreputable behaviors. No smoking. No liquor. No dancing. And absolutely no men."

She smiled then, still clutching my chin, and a peachy sweetness appeared on her face.

"Now then, dear, you've hardly brought a thing with you. Will you be needing bedclothes?"

I nodded, and without so much as asking my name she led me inside and up the stairs, stopping every few steps to catch her breath and explain the cost of boarding and the time of breakfast and the fact that no men meant *no men* and she wouldn't repeat it twice.

Chapter 8

WHEN SNOW FELL on Nantucket, it wrapped the town like a quilt, keeping the island's people inside to huddle around their hearths and sip hot drinks late into the night, telling stories and having grand arguments. On those nights my mother used to let me stay up and sit on her lap before the crackling fire among the crowd of men staying at the inn. They were apt to tell bawdy jokes that I didn't understand (and as I grew older pretended not to understand for the sake of my mother), and to lead each other in rounds of drinking songs and sea shanties. Elijah used to say that when I was barely four I brought a whole houseful of snowbound men to weeping laughter by singing a dozen verses of "Whisky Johnny," though I had no memory of this incident.

Snow in Boston did not slow the city down a bit. It fell as soft and white as it did on the island but soon grew sooty and dank, ground into horse dung and mud on the streets, trampled into slicks of ice by hundreds of rushing feet. A fellow boarder who had arrived in summer, Miss Smith from Tennessee, was entranced by the snow and attempted to draw the rest of us out to romp in the street, but most of Miss Hanratty's girls shared my mix of disappointment and annoyance at the weather.

In addition to Miss Smith, who always seemed rather lost among us, the boardinghouse was residence to Misses MacArdle, Kelly, and Hale from Ireland, who had come not only to Boston but to the country with the intent of starting a new life at Miss Hanratty's; and Misses Westover and Marshall, who were, like me, from Massachusetts hamlets—though they spoke eagerly about their hometowns while I deflected questions about mine. Miss Mary Hale, whom I'd met upon first stepping foot in the city, seemed aloof and unpleasant for several days after I first moved in, before I recalled that I'd cursed her, and her lack of greeting was in precise obedience to my command that she forget about wanting to talk to me.

One evening as she sat silently beside me, I passed her a tureen of potatoes and whispered, "Remember I'm your friend, Mary."

Her small spectacles fogged from the steam of the dish, and when they cleared she grinned widely and said, "You haven't said a word to me about how the newspaper business is going, Rachel!" as if I had been neglecting her.

I was unused to living in close proximity to so many other women. The bustle and noise of the boardinghouse reminded me of the inn, though I far preferred the smell of Miss Hanratty's fried potatoes and beef stews to my mother's wretched chowders, and there was never a grain of sand anywhere. We all left the house for work but spent the rest of our days together. I listened to their tales of home and their tittering about certain young fellows. I bobbed my head as they bemoaned the woes of their jobs, the cramped factory floors and damp air and lecherous bosses. At times I wanted to join the chatter, tell them about Mr. Sweet's endless stories and Clary's patient way of teaching me the skills of the office, but I kept quiet. Sometimes I told myself it was to avoid bragging about the excellent circumstances I'd found in the city. Other times I knew it was because I could not admit to them how eager I was to leave those excellent circumstances. I was wary of giving too much of myself to anyone, certain that I would soon receive word of Ishmael and have to leave them all behind. In those honest moments I remembered Amos's gentle face, glowing with adoration, growing empty and cold. I would not let myself picture my mother.

At the *Spyglass*, I spoke some about the boardinghouse and avoided all talk of my life before. I had made clear my aim to seek out Ishmael, yet Clary and Mr. Sweet eagerly accepted my presence for as long as they could get it. They shifted a mountain of daily responsibilities to me. My experience of work to that point had consisted of laundering and scrubbing and stirring, and I found I enjoyed a life of pen and paper. As soon as Mr. Sweet noticed my skill with arithmetic, he had me balancing account books, and my swift and steady hand earned me the task of taking dictation when he could not contain his thoughts well enough to put them to paper with any sense himself. As he was often too engrossed in his editing to deal with advertisers when they arrived unexpectedly, and as Clary was occupied with her press and illustrations, I soon took on managing their orders and requests as well. My days had never before passed so quickly. In the waning hours, when Mr. Sweet buttoned his long coat and donned his tall hat and said he was going home and I ought to as well, I often found myself nearly out of breath. Many nights I was too tired to tolerate the other girls' chatter during supper at Miss Hanratty's, and most nights I fell into a thick sleep immediately upon climbing into bed.

Some nights, though, I woke uncertain of where I slept, sweating beneath the quilt. I thought I smelled chowder; I thought I heard my mother saying my name. When my mind cleared enough to find my place, I could not settle in. My mattress felt thin and lumpy, the sheets scratchy against my skin. I could hear the other girls snoring, and it did not comfort me. The sound of horse hooves on the cobblestones, shouts of deliverymen at the nearby shops, and the scritching of mice in the walls coalesced into a harsh and unpleasant melody. When I did manage to return to sleep on these nights, I was often plagued by jumbled dreams of ships and sailors and deep black water.

THREE MONTHS WITH no letter from Ishmael stretched to six. Mr. Sweet was disappointed, enjoying the tales as he did, but could not match the impatience with which I pored over the mail. The fantasies I'd had of being whisked away by my father began to fade. The shimmering cerulean waters and lush islands I'd imagined grew muted and distant, but Nantucket felt even farther away. Ishmael was the only choice I had left. Even if a new letter arrived, it might not allow me to find him, but it was better than silence. I rushed out the door of the *Spyglass* office to meet the postman each day, and each day returned with another of my last crumbs of hope crushed.

Mary Hale wasted considerable vigor trying to cheer me up, though she assumed it was homesickness making me melancholy. She never waned in her attempts to convince me to join her for lectures or exhibits or strolls in the park, cornering me each Sunday after breakfast with an invitation I always declined. I did not regularly attend church (though I had been invited to Catholic, Congregational, Methodist, and Baptist), and more and more I retired to my room immediately after supper. The only place I frequented outside the *Spyglass* and Miss Hanratty's was the library; I had gained a taste for the drearier English novels, which often lulled me into dreamlessness.

One evening at supper I looked across the table and saw a girl I didn't recognize, and was primly informed that she'd arrived at the boardinghouse a month before, after Miss Smith was married— another fact I'd somehow overlooked. Miss Hanratty, whose motherly inclinations seemed limited to cooking and cleaning, gave me a sharp look, and Mary pulled me aside as we cleared our dishes to inquire if I was feeling well, which I assured her I was, though my sleep that night was brief and wracked with dark dreams.

The next morning at the *Spyglass*, I found myself distracted and weary rather than excited when I opened the mail. A cream-colored envelope with an intricate emerald seal caught my eye, awakening my attention. *Could it be?* I held my breath as I flipped the envelope over.

But no. I had studied Ishmael's letters so frequently I knew his handwriting well, and this was addressed to Mr. Appleton, besides.

In my exhaustion I found myself inadequately suppressing a sob. I contained it, but moments later felt Mr. Sweet's hand on my shoulder.

"Something seems to be troubling you, Miss Shaw."

"I'm tired, that's all."

He sat in a chair beside me, though he still had to slouch to look me straight in the face.

"Are you ill? I can finish the mail if you need to rest."

"I'm simply tired, Mr. Sweet. I'll make it through the day."

He pushed his glasses up his nose and frowned. "Oh yes, I nearly forgot. I have something that will help."

He crossed to his coat on the rack and, fumbling first in one deep pocket, then the other, withdrew two small oranges. He returned to his seat and dug his fingernails into the rind of one, peeling it in a slow, steady circle as the fruit's fragrance filled the air.

"I've been waiting for these for months," he said. "I know a shopkeeper who gets them on occasion from New Orleans. They're the best you've ever tried."

He handed me a segment, plump and dotted with juice. It tasted bright and clean, like my mother's kitchen when she'd scoured it to sparkling.

"Did you ever have oranges back on the Cape?" he asked, chewing a segment as he handed me another.

"Never as good as these."

"I've noticed you don't tend to share much about your home or your family," he said.

Over my months in the office Mr. Sweet had filled me with stories of his life—about growing up in Northampton and taking trips to the mountains and spending long nights with his schoolbooks at Amherst—but mostly he spoke of people. He regarded his parents as saintly: his regal mother, keeper of grand and abundant gardens, and his father, a preacher, stern but gentle. Both died of fever when he had not yet gone to college. He'd had a sister who died of typhus before he was old enough to make any memory of her, and a sprightly younger brother who'd been sent to live with an uncle. He spoke of scores of fellows from Amherst (and on occasion I greeted them when they burst through the doors of the *Spyglass* to drag him off to a tavern somewhere), and of an abundance of lovely aunts and cousins scattered across New England, good country people who didn't care to visit the city. Even Clary, when her attention could be pulled from the finicky press, would join his musings to recall her own fond memories, mostly quiet images: her father's large, ink-stained hands teaching her to sharpen a knife, her husband's room-rousing laugh, the smell of the air the first time she saw the sea as a child. All they knew about me were my desires for the future.

Mr. Sweet held the empty orange rind loose in his hands.

"I regret that a woman as clever and kind as yourself has such pain in her past."

"Oh, no, it isn't—"

But as I protested, pain washed over me. I was struck by the memory of my mother in her bed, the sudden blankness in her eyes in the moment before I left. I had given up my home and only family for a story I might never learn, a dream of a brighter, wider world that was not coming true. Yet I could not return. I would be a stranger to my mother—and if my curse had worked as I'd intended, no one on Nantucket would know my name. In that word, *forget*, I had imbued all the power I could; a wave into my mother's mind that I hoped would ripple across the island, erasing me from every inch of it. I did not know how to reverse something of such magnitude.

I took a breath and let the regret soak back into the depths of my mind.

"I left behind no one who misses me."

"In that case," said Mr. Sweet, "I shall have to know you sufficiently to miss you when you sail away."

Chapter 9

I DO NOT recall exactly when I began calling him Nat instead of Mr. Sweet, when I began arriving early to the *Spyglass* each morning to greet him, when instead of wrapping himself in his coat and bidding me good night, he began escorting me back to Miss Hanratty's, our path meandering through the Common and Public Garden, pausing by monuments, lingering in the light of cheery shopwindows. He kept a pocket of pennies to buy a paper from each newsboy we passed; he said he liked to keep up with the competition, but I saw the joy he took in any sort of well-written work and the diligence with which he sought it. One evening we stopped by the bookshop where I'd first inquired about the boardinghouse, and he bought me a fine, leatherbound copy of Charles Dickens's *Great Expectations*. After I told him I'd read it once before at the library, we began meeting there on weekend mornings. We strolled the shelves as he told me more of his stories and patiently suffered my lack of them, and often we did nothing more than read beside each other.

Once, I had thought it possible that I had loved Amos but had crushed my feelings when I cursed him. My time with Nat put that fear to rest. Amos could have been a friend, but I had always treated him as a means to an end, a means of escape. Nat opened doors I had not considered. My wish to find my father had grown threadbare, and I had no hope of returning to my mother. Why not replace my old desires with a warm, vivid picture of a happy future, a happy family?

We were married in August, a year after I'd arrived in Boston. He proposed the idea on a Friday afternoon at the office, and on Sunday we eloped. He waited outside Miss Hanratty's while I dressed (even bridegrooms were barred from the boardinghouse). I made no commotion or mention of my plans to the other girls, but Mary noticed him waiting outside and guessed. She insisted I wear a delicate ivory lace gown she kept tucked in the bottom of her traveling chest. "No one will know it's been worn once before, if I ever do get around to wearing it," she said with a grin. When she saw me in the gown, a bit too wide at my hips and several inches short at the hem but still the most elegant thing I'd ever put on, she looked at me with the same awe I'd seen on her face our first day in the city. Perhaps I should have remembered how I'd forced her to leave me alone that day, but the memory could not fight through the haze of bliss.

Nat and I said our vows as the bells rang two o'clock, with Clary and Mary sharing Miss Hanratty's handkerchief to wipe away their tears. Nat was behind on his editing, so we spent the rest of the afternoon at the *Spyglass*. When a boy arrived to deliver my bag from Miss Hanratty's, I felt the first and only pang of fear I had that day, realizing how little I had to bring to married life. I turned to face Nat. He was immersed in his writing, knees wedged against his desk, glasses and hair askew as they'd been the first time I saw him. I couldn't imagine anything but joy awaiting us.

That night I stood on the threshold as he lit the lamps in the room he rented on the top floor of the same building that housed the *Spyglass*. It was above us all this time, yet I had never so much as peered through the doorway. I was unsurprised by what the light revealed: a shelf cluttered with books, a table covered with folded newspapers, a picture in a gilt frame of a mustached man in a tall hat and a thin, freckled woman, and little else but a narrow bed. I laughed upon seeing it, imagining his long arms dangling off its sides, his feet hanging off the end. He blushed.

"We shall see about buying a larger bed tomorrow."

~~~~~

I SHOULD HAVE clung to each moment of those first months of our marriage instead of letting them wash over me. We kept on much as before, spending our days at the *Spyglass* and our evenings in the city, but at night we retired together to our tiny room, exhausted but fulfilled. Nat bought a four-poster bed as promised, and a cream-colored counterpane to go with it. I found myself opening my mind to him as we lay there in the moonlight. I recounted the plots of books I read, the details of my daydreams, the ideas I had for improving the *Spyglass*. We loved to imagine traveling to all the places the newspaper featured, planning what we might pack in our trunks and which landmarks we might visit in London, Florence, Cairo. Nat had an endless appetite for learning about new places, though he, too, had traveled little. He had never been to the coast south of Boston Harbor, so I spoke of the beauty of the land on which I'd grown up, the grassy shores lined with shingled houses trimmed in white, the creaks of old ships and the constant shush of the ocean. I let him continue to believe I was from somewhere on Cape Cod; I never repeated the lie, but I never corrected it. If I thought only of Nantucket's landscape, painted in cool colors, perhaps I could think of my former home as Nat did his: a lovely place preserved in the past.

Before we were married he'd left the topic of my mother alone. After, on those nights when he spoke of his mother teaching him to plunk out little tunes on the family piano though his fingers were too impossibly long to play with grace, or trailing behind her with a pail as she trimmed her flowers, he slipped in little phrases that let me know he wished I would not remain so reserved now that I was his wife. ("Surely your mother loved music?" "You know how mothers dote on their children.") But I had to accept what I had broken, and I could not speak of her without admitting what I had done.

I did not answer him, but his questions brought her to the front of my mind. I remembered her swooping chairs out of my path as I ran beneath the tables at the Try Pots, both of us whooping with laughter. I remembered her laboring in her immaculate kitchen, perfecting her chowders—the clam and cod she could make in her sleep, the unusual flavors she tested on her willing patrons, how she shrugged off my rejection of them all, spoiling me with fresh bread and porridge. I recalled her eagerness to protect me when I was a child, and the snippets of advice she later offered me as we folded sheets and made beds and scrubbed pots, even when I pretended not to listen. I imagined her sleeping deeply in the bed we had shared when I was very small. The more I thought of her, the more it felt as if she were gone, as if she existed only in the time before I abandoned her. It became easier to miss her, and for the first time I allowed myself to.

I thought of her all night when I learned I would soon be a mother. I had never been close with another woman, and my few friends did not have children, so I had no reference against which to gauge the enormous emotions that filled me, body and soul. Did everyone experience this union of joy and terror? It dawned on me that my mother would have felt these sensations alone, knowing my birth would be received with pity or disgust, knowing the immense difficulties the future held for her, and for me. No wonder she did not unfurl her past like a banner for me. Perhaps it was a mercy I took those moments with me when I left.

Nat was overjoyed to become a father, switching the subject of our evening conversations from memories of the past and musings about the world to conjectures about what the child would look like, what he or she would enjoy doing, where we would go together. When winter came and I piled quilts on my expanding belly to ward off the chill air that threaded beneath our room's thin windows, he declared it high time we lived like a proper family. He had a small inheritance from his father and grandfather in the bank, and by the end of the week he had purchased a house near Beacon Hill, tall and thin as he was. We would rent out the lower levels to lodgers (I imagined Miss Hanratty's horror if she knew that we allowed both men and women, though it was common practice elsewhere), and we would have a full suite of rooms above, among them a tiny nursery.

"We'll fill it with books," Nat said as we stood in the room, which for the first months of our residence remained empty, as did the parlor adjoining the kitchen, while we waited for the boarders to appear and the next issues of the *Spyglass* to refill our purse. "We'll prop up the cradle with them when we run out of shelves."

"It will be some years before the baby learns to read."

"I'll read aloud," he replied, bending his body as if he were sitting in a tall chair. "I suppose we must start with fairy and folk tales, but we'll get to Dickens before long, and I'll work my way up to Frederick Douglass."

"And Emerson, I suppose."

"Of course, Emerson! And Miss Austen, perhaps. *It is a truth universally acknowledged, that a single man in possession of a good fortune, must be in want of a* . . . What is it now?"

"How should I know? Her novels always put me to sleep too quickly."

"A wife!" he declared, leaping to his feet and wrapping me in his arms. "And look at us here, right out of the end of a storybook."

~~~~~~

WE NAMED HER Margaret Jane after Nat's mother, but the first time I held her in my arms I called her Mara. It seemed a happy name, a sleepy morning sigh, a deep-throated laugh. I stroked her head and imagined her in a few years, her hair curlier than mine and as red as Nat's, her face freckled, her legs skinny and long as she ran across the park in a white dress, Nat and I strolling behind, calling out her name. It felt like a vision of the future.

When Mary came to visit I informed her of the nickname, and she plucked the baby from my arms and cradled her against her chest.

"I'll call her Margaret, thank you kindly," she said. "Don't you know your scripture? Mara means bitter." She tipped her nose against my daughter's and smiled. "And you're no bitter child, are you?"

The first year of Mara's life passed as if in a thick, incessant fog. I am certain those months contained distinctive moments—the first time she smiled at the sound of her name, or scooted across the floor, or waved goodbye—but I could pinpoint none of them. I read books; I could not remember which. I must have eaten and slept, but the rhythm the *Spyglass* and the boardinghouse had brought to my life in Boston was lost in the haze. I was Mother now, but she could not say the word. She could only cry, and she did so for hours each day.

I do remember that cry: low and moaning at first, rising to a piercing shriek, then a ragged wail that paused only when she gasped for breath. I remember holding her at arm's length and watching her writhe, her cheeks scarlet and mouth a hollow maw, her legs kicking the air. I remember letting her scream in her cradle as I curled up in the middle of the four-poster bed, hands pressed to my ears. Nat rushed home each night and paced the floor with her, tracing a path through rooms that remained mostly empty, her body draped across his long arms. He shushed and rocked through hours of her cries, until finally they faded to whimpers. Often he continued to pace long after she fell asleep. And always she woke before long, crying again. Needing me.

I considered cursing her. I whispered the words as I stood in other rooms while she raged. *Remember you're a happy babe. Forget how to cry.* One day I thought of my mother at the base of the stairs in the inn: *You meant to stand and walk to me.* The way I'd instantly stood and obeyed, at first. The horror on her face, the way she apologized for shouting at me. I realized finally what it meant, but I was too exhausted to do anything with this knowledge. I let it dissolve into the endless crushing waves of regret and loss I already felt.

And then, like rays of sunshine, moments broke through the fog. Mara's first steps, just after her first birthday, her arms held out to me, her face alight. The first time I set her on the grass in the park and she pushed her chubby fingers deep into the soil. The first time she greeted Nat with a delighted shriek of *Papa!* when he arrived home (though still he shushed and swayed every time he carried her). We built a new routine of songs and games and long walks, and Nat began to read to her before bed each night, as he'd promised.

Once my days had shape again, I found I missed the *Spyglass*. Nat kept me informed of developments—Clary had sold the cumbersome old press and invested in a new one, allowing them to take on additional printing projects and even hire an assistant; of course Clary insisted on another war widow. Circulation had increased to almost three thousand, and Nat had hired two young men, Amherst boys like himself, to keep up with clerical duties and help him with editing. They continued with the publisher's mission of bringing the world to Boston, printing steamship timetables, reports from the news services, and essays by world travelers, but more often, now, the paper included news about events in the city. "We bring the world to Boston, but we should bring Boston to the world as well," was Nat's new philosophy. The winter before Mara's second birthday, the old publisher died and left the *Spyglass* in its entirety (and a good deal of money besides) to Nat. The world was open before us.

~~~~~~

I AWOKE ONE gleaming spring morning with a book on my chest from the night before and Mara stretched beside me, Nat having silently slipped out to work. I watched her sleep for a moment, red curls damp with sweat and stuck to her face, her arms flung above her head, the picture of perfect rest. She was nearly two, full of words and expression, eager to explore, becoming the child I'd imagined. I could see cloudless sky through the window and began to plan a long walk. She was strong enough to toddle beside me around the neighborhood, but I still had the carriage that Miss Hanratty and the girls of the boardinghouse had pooled together to buy when she was an infant, and I had a longer journey in mind.

I let Mara lead me through the Public Garden as I did on usual days, leaving the path to follow a squirrel around a beech tree and watching sparrows bathe in the dust beside a pond. I convinced her to climb into the carriage with the promise of roasted peanuts from a street cart; she chewed slowly at first, then attempted to grab the entire bag from my hands.

She dozed as we left the park and wound through the familiar streets to the *Spyglass* office. I did not bother knocking—I hadn't knocked on that green door since the day I arrived. The young man at the front desk raised his eyebrows in surprise at my entry and asked if he could help me. I felt a surge of ambivalence, unsure whether to laugh that this silly boy didn't know this was my place or to accept that it was not so much my place anymore. Another wave struck me when I opened my mouth to introduce myself and did not know whether to inform him I was the woman who had last held his job, or to introduce myself as Mrs. Nathaniel Norcross Sweet.

Mara solved my problem, shuffling in her seat and blinking until she spotted Nat and cried "Papa!"

Nat, who was absorbed as usual in his work, had not noticed our arrival until then, but sprang across the room to greet us.

"Goodness, Arthur, why didn't you tell me my family was here?" he said, swinging Mara out of the carriage and onto his hip. "I suppose you haven't gotten to the billing yet, either?"

The boy at the desk looked mortified, but Nat laughed.

"Don't look so flustered, now. My good wife here can man the desk while you finish up."

He turned to me. "You don't mind, do you? William's out on an errand and is taking his precious time."

"I suppose I could," I said, attempting to dampen my eagerness, though I was sure he could read it on my face. I shooed Arthur to another desk and resumed what had been my usual post while Nat and Mara trotted off to interrupt Clary.

I had organized my desk the way my mother ran her inn and

Clary kept her pressroom: clean and efficient, everything in its place. Arthur was slovenly. On one side of the desk, a puddle of ink from a leaking fountain pen soaked into an account book, which was mercifully empty. A pile of unopened mail sloped down the other side, intermixing with notes on scraps of paper and empty envelopes. I opened the first letter in the stack, a brief note from a Mr. Beauregard reporting that his tour of the Mediterranean was going splendidly and he intended to give a lecture on it when he returned in August, and found a piece of stationery on which to compose a reply. I could find no pen other than the leaking one, however, and began to search through drawers. The first was even more shocking than the desktop, packed with crumpled paper, grease-streaked sandwich wrappers, and spilled pipe tobacco. The next was completely empty, and I decided to pull Arthur aside later and suggest some improvements to his organizational methods.

The final drawer was the only tidy one, and it contained a small stack of envelopes, opened neatly and worn at their corners. The top one was addressed to *Mr. Sweet, The Spyglass*, in a familiar hand.

My body went cold, a bloom of ice that started in my shoulders and ran down my back, seizing my breath. I glanced to be sure that Nat remained out of the room and Arthur was occupied with the bills, then slipped the first envelope out of the drawer. The note inside read, *I hope your readers have been enjoying my tales, Mr. Sweet, as I have quite enjoyed writing them. I remain with my dear friend Don Sebastian in Lima and intend to stay for some time more, so you may continue to expect my dispatches with regularity. SS.* It was dated February 4, 1872—just months before.

I continued to read but was interrupted by the sound of Nat's and Clary's voices and Mara's delighted laugh. I scooped up the stack of letters, clutching them in my hands a moment before tucking them away in my bag.

I walked swiftly back to our house, both to lull Mara to sleep and to buy myself as much time as possible to examine what I'd found. As soon as I'd put Mara to bed, I sat by the window in the parlor, where

I could see Nat approaching on the street below if he came home early. I read through Ishmael's brief and cheerful letters and devoured his tales, each as strange and scattered as the ones I'd read those years ago in the upper room of Shaw Mercantile. There were ten, each arriving in Boston three or four months apart, all with some indication that Ishmael was living in Peru. The earliest was labeled *Chowder*, a tale of Samuel the Sub-Librarian and his companion Koqueeg finding a room in an inn before setting sail on the ill-fated ship *Perses*. There, clear and raw on the page despite Ishmael's veil of fiction, was my mother. *"Come on, Koqueeg," said I, "all right. There's Mrs. Folger." And so it turned out; Mr. Isaiah Folger being from home, but leaving Mrs. Folger entirely competent to attend to all his affairs.*

Reading each word felt like heaving a great weight, yet I could not stop. Here was a memory of my mother through the eyes of my father. His words revealed no apparent affection, and he garbled my mother's tongue with a ridiculous mock-Nantucket accent. Yet the scene rang true—in busy moments at the inn I had often known my mother to greet men with shouts of "Clam or cod?" and though I despised the taste of chowder, Ishmael's delight in describing it brought me back to the steamy, salt-scented warmth of my mother's kitchen when I was very young.

I looked again at the date on the letter. Ishmael had simply used the notation *Wednesday*. But on the envelope, I found a small note in Nat's hand: *received August 13, 1869.* The day he asked me to marry him.

~~~~~~~

IT WAS NOT difficult to find a ship to leave on; the *Spyglass* ran the timetables and advertisements, after all. The clipper *Flying Star* promised swift passage around Cape Horn and a stop in Peru, and a berth was mine with one curse. I gave myself no time to change course.

I planned to leave while Nat was at the *Spyglass*. I would say nothing. I would not lie, and I would not curse him. He would have to contend with the truth of my departure on his own. I told myself he would know where I had gone; he would not have hidden Ishmael's letters from me if he didn't realize what would happen if I found them. If I started to tell myself that it had been years since I truly believed I would find Ishmael, that my life had changed, that I had put away my childish dreams, I rekindled my resentment by imagining the day Nat received that letter and tucked it away without a word to me, and how he had repeated the sin, again and again. I fed my anger with the knowledge that he had lied to me. Had, in proposing, sought to keep me from discovering I had other choices.

I intended to leave Mara as well. A sea voyage was no place for a tiny child. I would feign illness and beg Miss Hanratty to mind her for the day, where she would be happy until Nat realized I was gone. For all he had taken from me, I could find no fault in his love for our daughter. I assured myself I would see her again. I considered sending for her after I found Ishmael, or returning to her with Ishmael in tow. I imagined so many possibilities they could not be contained in my body; my lungs and veins and insides felt as if they were trying to escape my skin as my mind whirred with bigger and brighter visions, fueled by the hope I had smothered, hidden, or diverted for years. At the height of my confidence, I was sure I would find Ishmael and he would tell me everything that had been hidden from me, and it would make my whole life make sense. I would bring him to Boston and Nat would fall at my feet in confession and relief. I would take Ishmael to Nantucket, find a way to unravel my curse, and reunite with my mother. My leaving would not break another family, but instead would heal two. (In lower times, I let myself imagine that I might search for Ishmael without finding him and in doing so could choose a new life in which I wasn't responsible for anyone at all.)

The morning of my departure, Mara woke crying from a dream she did not yet have the words to describe. I was brought back to her infancy, to those long, howling days, and her voice was like a string tied to the base of my brain, pulling me to her. I could not leave her, even if I swore to return. I let her cling to me. I knotted my fingers in her hair and felt her tears soak through my dress. In my hurry to pack her things, I left behind the box containing most of Ishmael's letters to the *Spyglass* and the whale's tooth I had taken from my mother, all the evidence I had of him, save for the letter with the story about my mother, which I'd tucked into my coat pocket.

I rarely let go of Mara on the ship. We spent most of our time pressed together in our narrow bunk, close as we had been when she was a baby. My trip from Nantucket to Boston was insufficient to prepare me for the open ocean, and I heaved from the incessant rocking, but she seemed unbothered by the waves. She never cried, yet I thought again of the time when she seemed to do nothing but cry. I discovered that while I would never wish to return to those days, I didn't regret them. They were part of her, this child I could not leave behind. When I was too tired to hold her, she paced our tiny cabin, singing nonsense songs to herself. When she grew restless or asked about her papa, I held her hand and struggled to remember the fairy tales Nat used to read to her, any story I could tell to make her smile.

I read and reread Ishmael's tale of my mother to myself, but as we sailed on, it grew difficult to think about anything beyond the confines of our berth. My mind grew scattered, fevered. Because I rarely left our cabin, I didn't know whether it was night or day, and the hours crushed together, squeezing and stretching into meaninglessness. I slept at random, sometimes in brief bursts, other times in deep stretches that felt like days, interrupted only by Mara's needs.

One night I woke delirious, imagining I was in the bed I once shared with my mother, certain I would roll over and find myself tiny against her side. Instead there was a girl, my own little girl, deeply asleep, sure she was safe in her mother's arms. How had I taken that from my mother? From myself? I had let myself miss her, but I had never grieved for her. I tried to picture her—still cooking her chowders and running her inn, unaware of what I had stolen—but I could not.

The storm hit off the coast of Brazil. A roar shook me awake, followed by shouts and the sound of water lapping at the walls of the room. The lantern had been wrenched off its nail, so I grasped in the dark, panicked, unsure of what I could find to help us, if anything could. My hand found the soft collar of my coat, and I wrapped Mara in it, clutching her to me as the sound of gushing water drove us out and up. We joined a mass of activity on the deck, lost among the ropes and screams and waves. I turned to retreat to our cabin but found our way blocked by a black pool. The ship jerked and swung; the planks beneath my bare feet seemed to flow like water. In the brief illumination of a lightning strike, I saw a sailor before me, his mouth hung open in surprise or warning.

The moment froze and a thousand memories flashed across my mind, each thread of my life tangled with the next: Freddy, Mary, Amos, Clary, Elijah. Nat in his overcoat and tall hat. My fingers in Alice Chase's blue ribbon, my hands opening Ishmael's first letter, my foot hovering above the step in the inn, my arms holding newborn Mara. My mother's nightdress, billowing and white. The smell of scalded milk and fresh fish. A flicker of firelight across a face I wasn't sure I could remember anymore.

The crash of thunder yanked me back into the chaos of the storm, the shouting men, the rending waves. I could not see the future, but I could feel it rising to meet me. As I felt my feet lose purchase, I grabbed the sailor's sleeve, thrusting Mara into his arms. I could make Mara forget me. I could rip myself away, again. But what kind of life is one torn in two? I could not force another such sacrifice again. I could only give myself.

I poured all my strength into my words: "Remember you promised to keep her safe."

I heard the wave coming but could not see it. *Remember*, I whispered as it sucked me in, my dress and hair twisting around me as the churn of water and wreckage replaced the sky. *Remember.*

The mother and daughter float in the boundless blue, water above, water below, water upon water upon water. Their great noses point to a sky that is little more than a shimmer of light through the sea, their tails wave above shadowy depths. Their immense mouths rest, teeth and tongues hidden inside narrow, speckled smiles. A trio of silver fish pass, leaving a glittering ripple in their wake. The whales sleep.

A ribbon of bubbles escapes the daughter. Her eye blinks open, no longer hidden amid the wrinkles of her head. She awakens slowly, bobbing, twisting. She ascends in a smooth arc, a breach that breaks the surface into white splashes. Her exhalation interrupts the air.

Full of breath again, she dives. She finds her mother still suspended in the water, still asleep. She swims a loop, her mother's body so long and large the smaller creature's currents do not disturb her. The daughter approaches the mother's side, her soft pearly nose brushing rumpled gray skin. She nudges again, and the mother's flukes wave, the enormous muscle of her body slowly bending.

The mother swims and the daughter follows, blowing and breathing, glowing like polished stones in the sun. The mother slows and calls a name, and her sister responds from a distance. Their family has returned from the deep, greeting them with tentacles streaming from their teeth.

The daughter skims her mother's side, pleading. The mother swoops, flipping so her mottled belly gleams. The daughter dives, her slim jaws scraping skin as she gulps thick braids of white milk. Satisfied, she leaves to greet her grandmother, to prod her cousin into a chase, to bask in the warmth of the sunlit sea, to watch while her mother dives deep, her form fading into the cloudy blue far below.

Part Three

MARA

Rio Grande do Norte, 1872

Chapter 10

I REMEMBERED MY father's face, his crooked ears, his round bright eyes, his left eyebrow just slightly raised, always on the edge of a smile or a question or a delighted surprise. He kept a thin mustache that resisted his attempts to trim it neatly, and his waves of red hair would not submit to comb or style. In my first years of life, new wisps of gray appeared at his temples. Many mornings I rested on his feet as he shaved, scraping his cheeks pink, his freckles showing through. His forehead showed the slightest hint of a furrow, and then only when he could not find something, whether in his desk or in his mind. He had a small scar, faded white, extending from the corner of his right eye. When I was a tiny child I stared at the ceiling at night and thought of that face, cataloging its features. Ears, eyes, eyebrow, mustache, temples, cheeks, forehead, scar. I thought of his smile, which spread straight across his face. He only showed his teeth when he laughed, and he loved to laugh at me. His front teeth crossed, just slightly. I often forgot to think of his nose, as it was not so distinctive as the rest of him, but I never failed to remember it when I wanted to. I never failed to remember anything. Even my mother's face, falling away from me into the sea.

~~~~~

THE SAILOR KEPT me tight to his chest, both of us soaked through, my mother's coat a sopping weight on my back. At times he ran his fingers through my tangled hair and shushed me as if I were his own child. Another sailor stood beside him, shouting over the storm at Sister Maria Josefa. I did not speak the language then, but I did when I was a bit older, and I pieced together their conversation. My memory kept it flawlessly, impossibly, as it keeps all things, and I had plenty of long, sleepless nights to mull over the indelible moments of my life.

Her mother was aboard our ship, the sailor said. *There was a storm, a terrible storm.*

And her father? the old nun said, her voice muffled as she shielded her face from the pelting rain.

We do not know. Only the mother was aboard our ship. She fell overboard. But where is her father?

The sailors leaned close to each other, their words stifled by the collars of their coats and the rush of the wind.

He is dead, sister.

Very well then. We will take her.

I have thought on this conversation for many years. What if the old woman had not pushed for an answer, if the sailors had not lied to ensure she would keep me?

He paused a moment before releasing me, his fingers tucking a curl behind my ears.

She will be safe here?

So safe, she said, rocking and humming as I curled into her warmth. *So safe.*

In a candlelit room that smelled of straw and oil, Maria Josefa placed me atop a table and attempted to peel me from my mother's coat. I resisted, thrashing and kicking, and she knocked her open hand against my cheek to still me. She said nothing, knowing I would not understand her, only pointed a bent, brown finger a hair's breadth from the tip of my nose. I could see no more than a hint of her features, concealed by the shadow of her veil. I was too small to wonder who or what she was, and yet clever enough to know her gaze would be fixed upon me, her mouth stern and unmoving. I stared back, my tiny fingers clutching the wet fabric a moment longer before relenting. A rush of cool air struck me as she draped the coat over a nearby chair. I wore only a thin nightgown, puckered against my cold-mottled skin. She slowly backed away, keeping her finger aimed at my nose, until she disappeared through a dark, arched doorway.

I did not consider running. Where would I have gone? The chill overtook me, a shivering that started in my gut and spread into my chest, down my legs. I tucked into myself, my stomach churning as my fingers brushed the gooseflesh on my arms. My vision blurred, though not from tears—I had been bathed in salt water and rain, but I had not had water to drink for hours.

Maria Josefa reentered, slow and deliberate, a swath of fabric draped across her arm. She lifted me by the elbow and in two swift movements slipped the nightgown over my head and replaced it with the dry dress. It was far too large for me, the sleeves drooping over my hands and the hem puddling against the table, but immediately the chill receded. My stiff joints softened enough to allow me to sit, and I let my head fall against my knees. Before my hair could drip onto the dress, the old sister turned me and lifted the curls off my neck, twisting them into a braid so only a thin line of water dribbled down my back. Her footsteps were soundless, but I felt her leave and return once more. She turned me to face her again, lifting my chin and placing the rim of a cup against my lips. I attempted to gulp but she pulled back. The trickle of water that found its way down my throat was the sweetest I ever tasted, then or after.

She lifted me, cradling me like the baby I had so recently been, and stepped into the dark room. I could see nothing, but her steps were sure. I let myself rest against her, breathing in the dampness and sweat of her warm habit until she stopped and released me onto a slim straw mattress. She extended her finger toward me again, this time letting it press against the skin of my forehead, where she scraped the sign of the cross with her thick nail.

When she was gone and my body finally stilled, the sounds of the strange room in the strange country washed over me: the chattering of an unknown bird, the rush of rain from the roof, a distant, steady rumble that I could not discern as ocean or thunder. Through it cut the soft rhythm of breathing. I emerged from myself enough to realize there was another person in the bed with me, a body not much bigger than my own, wrapped in a rough blanket. I nestled myself against her, as I had so many nights with my mother on the ship or in our large bed at home, and she did not stir. Finally, I fell asleep.

~~~~~

IN THE MORNING I woke to a pair of large, black eyes rimmed with a thick fringe of lashes, open so wide they seemed to have no lids. The girl was not smiling. She stared, saying nothing, not blinking, barely lifting her chest with breath. I had not spent much time around other children, but in the moments I had, I had learned not to trust those who were slightly larger than me. Those who were much larger ignored me, as did those of my own size. But the ones whose chins brushed my forehead were apt to push and punch, to swipe toys, to pull hair. I thought of one round-faced boy in particular who had shouted in my face, flecking my cheeks with spit, as his mother waited behind mine at the library. This girl did not look as if she were about to shout, but she certainly did not appear friendly.

She blinked, slow and deliberate, let her face rest in its frown a second more, and spoke.

What is your name?

I did not understand. She spoke again.

What is your name?

When I still did not respond, she rolled her eyes. *You're stupid.*

But her response was premature. I did not understand the language she spoke, but I had been hovered over by a multitude of ladies in the park and had had my cheeks pinched by my parents' friends, and I knew the question they always asked first. They smiled when I chirped the answer in my tiny voice.

When she resumed her stone-faced staring, I whispered, "Mara."

The girl lowered her eyebrows, which were as thick and dark as her eyelashes and the braid that draped over her shoulder.

Maré?

I nodded. I did not know the word meant the "tide" to her.

You smell like it.

I nodded again, assuming she was saying something kind, as the adults who asked my name always did.

She rolled her eyes again, then pointed at her face. *Otávia.*

I formed the syllables carefully, my mouth still growing accustomed to words, though my head was full of them. "Oh-tah-via."

It's not my real name, though.

I nodded.

Is that all you do?

When I began to tilt my chin again, she flung out her arms and pushed me off the bed.

My teeth cracked together when I hit the hard tiled floor, and I shrieked. Once I started I found I could not stop, all the fear of the previous day pouring out of me in a crescendoing wail as I remembered again that my mother was gone, taken by the sea, and I was lost, far away. Otávia leapt off the bed and knelt beside me, patting my cheek and rushing through whispered shushes, more desperate than soothing. When I failed to quiet, she slapped me with her small hand. Unlike Maria Josefa's smack from the night before, it did not shock me into calmness, but distressed me further. Otávia slumped to the floor and cried as well.

A woman strode through the doorway. She was taller and thinner and paler than Maria Josefa, the hem of her habit striking her mid-shin, the face beneath her veil younger, but still plain and weathered. She ignored Otávia, scooping me up, her arms as thin as bird bones against my back as she swayed and hummed a song I had never heard. I wriggled, gasping for air between screams, but those weight-less arms were stronger than they felt. She finished the first song and began another. By the time another person appeared, a bronze-complexioned older girl whose tunic was far too large, Otávia had quit crying and returned to the bed, where she buried herself in the blanket, leaving only enough of a gap to peer out.

A baby? Where did she come from? the new girl asked, her voice over-powering my faded, whimpering cries.

The rocking woman did not stop her humming.

Did you find her in the forest or something? Come on, tell me. Her tone grew demanding. *Sister Dorotéia, tell me!*

Dorotéia held the final note of her song, then let out a sigh that shook her thin frame and echoed into mine.

I have no idea where she came from, Rosi. All I know is that she is here. Didn't you hear the commotion last night? Ask Maria Josefa.

Rosi flung her arms up, the loose sleeves of her tunic sliding to her skinny elbows. *I've been looking for her all morning!*

My protector hummed a few bars of a new song before replying. *Isn't it Friday? She has gone to see Father Matheus.*

How am I supposed to know what day it is with all this noise? Did Otávia bite her or something?

I already told you, I don't know. Why don't you take Otávia and go start breakfast?

Rosi stomped across the room and extracted Otávia from her den. The girl did not protest, but gave me a dirty look on her way out of the room.

Otávia is not one for surprises, Dorotéia said, stroking my back as my last hiccupping sobs subsided. *There now, are you feeling better?*

She placed me on the mattress and sat down beside me, tucking her legs to the side so she could hold her face near mine. "*Bom dia?*"

"Mara," I said, and she knit her eyebrows.

"*Buenos días? Bonjour?*"

"Mara," I said again, slower, confused as to why she was not responding to my name and slightly concerned that she, too, might push me out of the bed.

"Good morning?"

"Good morning," I said, forgetting my confusion and responding instinctively.

She laughed, mouth open. *Thank God. I don't know what I would have done if you were French!*

She switched back to my own language. "Good morning, little one. My name is Sister Dorotéia. Your name is Mara?"

"Yes, ma'am."

"How old are you, Mara?"

I held up two fingers.

"You are two! That is good. I hear you came to us late last night. Where is your mother?"

The image of her face in a flash of lightning streaked across my mind. I pushed it away, pressing my face into the blanket.

Poor dear, Dorotéia muttered. *Poor baby. Poor girl.*

She waited, rubbing my back, and when I did not begin to wail again she asked another question: "You speak like an American. Are you from America?"

I had heard the name but did not know what it meant. My world before the ship had been our house, the park, Papa's work, the library, places we met my parents' friends. I could not even begin to know where to look in my memories to understand what to call this collection of places. I knew only that I was not there, and I had traveled farther than I had ever been before. I did not know how to answer, so I voiced instead my most pressing thought.

"I'm hungry."

She laughed. "We will eat breakfast soon. Do not worry," she said, fixing the hair my morning had disheveled. "You are safe here."

Chapter 11

EVERY MORNING OTÁVIA and I fed the hens, scattering scraps as the birds tussled and chittered, picking at the food and each other. The sisters of the Recolhimento de Nossa Senhora dos Navegantes were frugal people by nature and requirement, and they wasted no withered onion stems, no stringy stalks from the bottom of a bunch of greens, none of the leftover tapioca pancakes that I rejected at breakfast, day after day. The chickens turned up their noses at nothing.

In the two years since I had arrived at the recolhimento, I had learned which hens to fear and which to love. Branca cared only about food and would peck bloody anyone, chicken or human, who tried to swipe it from her. Amarela was mellow, an excellent layer who was fond of sunbeams but took no interest in my attempts to stroke her soft, yellow feathers. Vermelha was unpredictable, friendly one day and ferocious the next, so I kept my distance. My favorite was Cinza, so small she fit neatly in my arms, where she was content to rest while Otávia gathered her tiny, glistening eggs. Otávia said Cinza was spoiled. She preferred Brilhante, the biggest hen, who watched us warily. She would not hesitate to peck if we rushed too near her, but Otávia plied her with pea fronds and whispers until Brilhante consented to let her pat her blue-black wings.

In the same way, I spent those first years deciphering the women who lived in this whitewashed, run-down, half-empty structure at the edge of the brush-filled forest. Each day after prayers and chores, the sisters sat in the yard weaving fishing nets or palm baskets to sell in the village. I tried to imitate them, but my hands struggled to shape the fronds, which nicked my soft fingers with a thousand invisible, stinging cuts. Otávia tried to lure me away to play in the garden, but I preferred to sit and listen. Sister Dorotéia, who spoke several languages, had taken on the task of instructing me in Portuguese, and my mind snapped around each word and phrase. Even when I could not entirely understand their conversations, I observed their preferences and dislikes, their moods and dispositions.

Dorotéia, long and angular as a heron, held a library of ideas in her head but doled them out slowly—a snippet of poem here, a string of song there—preferring instead to focus on facts. Each day she led me through the rooms and grounds of the recolhimento and down the dirt road to the church to light candles, explaining the proper sowing time for different garden plants, guiding my tongue to recite simple scriptures, nodding sweetly at the people we saw and informing me of pertinent verbs in Portuguese: to walk, to eat, to ride, to sell, to wait. When I was very young, I saw her break routine only once, when she was enticed into dancing at a rowdy wedding party, her thin feet keeping perfect time to the guitar and accordion.

Rosi often wore a habit, but the nuns did not call her "sister." She was young and fickle, at times full of energy and eager to chase Otávia and me around the garden, at others prone to sulking, even raging. Otávia said Rosi and the chicken Vermelha were cousins, pink and red. Every few weeks Rosi would insist that she was leaving the recolhimento, never to return, sometimes going so far as to pack her scant belongings. But I never saw her travel farther than the church, and I never saw her speak to anyone other than Otávia, the sisters, and me, not even Father Matheus.

At last there was Sister Maria Josefa, the eldest, august and aus-

tere. She participated in the daily life of the recolhimento the same
as the rest of us, scrubbing floors and repairing clothes and cleaning
fish, but she did so with an air of solemnity, as if each task was laden
with secret wisdom she could gain by paying sufficient attention to
detail. Her hands were gnarled and cracked, but her fingernails were
always clean. She spoke no more than a few words a day to me, but
sometimes at night she would ease her body onto the end of our bed
and let Otávia and I curl into her arms.

I lived among them in those first years, but not with them. I was
still waiting for my father to arrive. I always imagined it would happen during a storm, like the one that had brought me. I fell asleep each
night cataloging his features, revisiting the last day I saw him. That
morning he had kissed me and told me to be a good girl and to think
about what story I would like to hear at bedtime, as always. My final
memory was of his smile as he shut the door behind him. Why would
he leave as if it were a normal day, when it so clearly was not? Only
hours later my mother would pack my things and lead me to the ship
that took us away. I was still too young to understand that my father
had not known we were leaving, that he had indeed expected to put
me to bed that night. I assumed he had said goodbye knowing he
would have to travel far to bring me home.

I did not understand how far. Sequestered in the tiny room on the
ship with my mother, I could not conceive of the days and distance we
traveled. Even if I could have parsed more information from my memories, I was not willing to experience them again. When the image of
my mother being swept into the sea arose, unbidden, in my mind, I
refused to remember a second more.

At first I waited cheerfully, a good girl as my father had asked,
but fear found me as the months and years passed. On rainy nights, I
would wake to the sound of my voice calling out for him. More than
once I sprang from bed, awakened by a flash of lightning, and rushed
to the front door through the black hallways. Always one of the sisters
would hear my frantic footsteps and rise to whisk me back to bed.

One night, I clawed and screamed when Maria Josefa found me, sure that my shouts of "Papa, Papa!" would draw him in from the darkness. She set me on the table and prodded me with her finger as she had when I had first been delivered into her care. "He is not coming," she said. "You must understand this. He is not coming."

The memory of the night I had arrived flooded back then, the whip of wind and rain, the feel of soaked cotton against my chest, the weight of my mother's coat. *He is dead*, the sailor had told Maria Josefa. I did not think to ask how he could have known. I had been so sure my father was coming, yet I had seen nothing, heard nothing, in more than four years. He would never have forgotten me. If my mother could be swept away, so could he. It only made sense that he was dead.

I had no choice but to make the recolhimento my home. Though my life before remained clear in my memory, I pushed the thoughts away, giving myself over to the routine of prayers and lessons, meals and Mass, walks to the church, feeding the chickens.

"I like it here," I said to Otávia one day as we folded clean laundry outside. I had just turned eight; she was unsure of her birthday, but the sisters said she was ten.

"It's all right," she said, focused on her hands as she attempted to line up the corners of a sheet. "I won't stay much longer."

This was the first I had heard her speak of leaving. "Are you going with Rosi?"

Otávia was capable of many different laughs, and the one she gave at this was short and dismissive.

"She'll never go. She's too scared. But I won't be, when he comes."

"When who comes?"

"My father."

My first feeling was of jealousy, followed by confusion. I realized I had never before considered that Otávia had a father or mother. No one had ever commented on her presence as the only small child in the house, before I had arrived, and it seemed to me that she, and the rest of them, must have always lived at the recolhimento.

"When is he coming?"

"I don't know. But he is. He told me he would."

I had never seen her father, or did not know if I had. Perhaps he was among the travelers that passed through the village? Or one of the farmers or fishermen who came to Mass? I thought of Maria Josefa's clear insistence that my father was not coming for me; surely Otávia had reason to hold on to such hope.

"When did he tell you that?"

"When I was a baby. I know he's coming back for me."

"Where did he go?" I thought of my father, smiling through the doorway.

"To the city. He said he would get money and come back for me." She dropped the towel she was holding. "You're asking too many questions today, Maré."

"Sister Dorotéia says it is good to ask questions."

Otávia kicked over the basket of laundry, sending my clumsily folded linens and her immaculate ones tumbling into the dirt.

"From now on, I'll tell you when you can ask me questions."

~~~~~

FATHER MATHEUS WAS OLD, and not just to my child's mind. His earlobes drooped to his chin, his leathery forehead and hands were splotched with violet liver spots. He wore glasses thick as my thumb, though it was unclear whether he could actually see through them. But his voice was rich and low, soft but not weak, like the hooting of an owl. The church in the village seemed made for his voice with its tile floors and high wooden ceiling, the arches above the altar and the sanctuary's white walls angled to amplify each gentle word. Like Maria Josefa, Father Matheus was a person who spoke little, but the two seemed to have the most to say when they were together. He called her "daughter," and she did seem to be a daughter to him—and not only because of his advanced age. She protected him, worried over him. A young widow from the village cooked his meals and cared for the tiny shack in which he lived, but Maria Josefa was known to drop in unexpectedly to inspect her work.

"Relax, Maria," Father Matheus would insist when Maria Josefa would glare at a layer of dust on the mantel or frown at a bite of undercooked beans. "You look for a hair in an egg. It is fine. It is good enough for me."

"You are a man of God," Maria Josefa would say, at which Father Matheus would simply nod and shuffle off.

I had infrequently been to church before coming to the recolhi-mento, though I remembered pillars and spires and steeples, the sand-colored stone and towering windows of the churches I had passed in the city where I was born. I understood by then that I was from a country called the United States of America, as Sister Dorotéia showed me on a small, tattered map. When I wished for a moment that I could locate the city I remembered in that land to the north, find a way to sail back to it, I reprimanded myself. My mother was dead. My father was dead. I had nothing to return to.

In the village where Father Matheus preached, there were only fishing boats and a scattering of small houses and the one little church. I was always nervous when I went into the village, on edge at the ever-present roar of the ocean, but I found some solace in the church, where the chorus of intonations drowned out the sea. Most women in the village attended Sunday Mass, as did a handful of pious men who were not out fishing. The adults were warm to me, admiring my red hair or tickling my chin, winking and babbling at me when they thought I could not understand Portuguese or their native languages. Their children filled the wooden pews as well—youths dozing with their palms folded against their faces as if in prayer, babies bawling through the Pater Noster, little boys squabbling on the floor. Though a few of the children were close to my age, they rarely spoke to me. Only about me.

"What is an orphan?" I asked Dorotéia on our walk home one Sunday.

Ahead of us Rosi swung Otávia on her back, both of them shouting and laughing, but the lingering image of the sneering girl behind me during Mass kept me from joining in their fun.

Dorotéia frowned. "A child with no mother or father."

I pondered this a moment, cringing as I saw the last image of my mother in the storm, and tried to refocus on my final glimpse of my father. *Ears, eyes, eyebrow, mustache, temples, cheeks, forehead, scar.*

She reached out a hand to draw me nearer to her, her fingers tangling into my curls. "It is nothing wrong with you."

I wondered why she would say that. The girl at Mass seemed to think being an orphan was a shameful thing. I did not know how my father had died, but I could not forget my mother's death, no matter how I tried. I wondered, for the first time, why she had taken me aboard that ship. All I could remember from our life before was love and safety and comfort. I thought of a day not long before we left, when my mother had taken me for a walk in the park and to visit my father and his friends at his office, a day full of laughter and sunshine. I thought we had been happy.

I was a child, and like a child I assumed the blame lay with me. Could I have done something to anger her, to make her want to tear me away?

"Are you sure there is nothing wrong with me?" I asked Dorotéia.

"It is simply what is. And it is why you live with us."

"It is?"

She smiled. "Of course. What do you think the recolhimento is for? To care for little girls with nowhere else to go."

It was true. I thought of the room where Otávia and I slept. The sisters had dragged in a second small bed and placed it across from Otávia's, but the space could have held four more. Each of the sisters had her own room, and still so many rooms stood empty that Otávia and I had transformed them into our own imaginary landscapes. The room filled with sheet-draped furniture was "the City," the dirt-floored space beside the kitchen "the Darkest Jungle," the hall with intricate peach-and-gray tilework "the Palace." Before it became the recolhimento, the building must have been a grand home, owned by someone too rich to stay in the middle of nowhere.

"But where are all the others?" I asked.

She laughed again. "Oh, the Church has not sent us any in a long time," she said. "Since before I arrived, actually. You were our gift from Our Lady."

"So it is just Otávia and me, then?"

Dorotéia's smile wilted, her eyes grew serious. "Otávia is not an orphan. She has a mother."

Otávia had never mentioned a mother, only her father, lost on his journey.

"She does? Where is she?"

"Otávia is special to us all the same."

I pulled my hand from hers and stopped, listening to Rosi's and Otávia's fading shouts as they disappeared farther up the road. No matter how angry my mother was at me, I was sure she would never have left me behind on purpose.

"But where is her mother?"

"Oh, you do not have to understand now," Dorotéia said. "She is gone."

~~~~~

EVERY SUMMER OF my childhood in Brazil was sweltering, but the summer I was ten and Otávia was twelve was hotter than I had imagined the world could be. The sisters woke us before dawn each day to care for the gardens. While they wove, we hauled water from the dwindling creek to soak the beans and okra. The corn was stunted, the tomatoes shriveled, the yam leaves crisped by the sun, but still we watered and weeded, and the sisters worked wonders with those measly vegetables, mixing them with fish and shrimp the villagers traded for their baskets, and eggs when we could get them. The chickens scraped the earth for insects in the morning, retreating to their coop the moment the sun hovered above the trees and refusing to budge. Most of the chickens from my first year at the recolhimento had died, but Brilhante remained, aloof as ever, continuing to lay even as the other chickens dozed. "You're my wise girl," Otávia said to her on the many mornings we found nothing in any nest except hers. "You know what we need."

When the temperature began to rise, we hid inside like the chickens. I liked to press my forehead against the chipped white plaster walls, wishing I could save their coolness for later. Dorotéia was perpetually pushing cups of coconut water at us, chanting *drink up, drink up*. Rosi refused to wear her tunic, going through her chores and prayers in her cotton shift, and the others did not reprimand her. Otávia even swore she had caught Maria Josefa fanning herself with her veil when she thought no one was looking. For hours every afternoon the sisters would retire to their rooms, leaving Otávia and me on our own. Usually this was the time we would race the halls of the recolhimento, immersed in our adventures, but the weather was too much even for restless little girls.

Instead we stripped to our underthings and lounged in our beds or on the shady floor of our room. If we were not too listless, we played cards or Cinco Marias, or sorted through our collections of feathers, stones, and trinkets. Mostly I let Otávia talk. She was a brilliant storyteller, her mind full of wild beasts and impossible quests. When she pressed me to take a turn, I usually picked one of the Bible stories in the primer Dorotéia used to teach me to read Portuguese—Daniel scratching the lions' great manes after their jaws were shut, the angel appearing to Mary, Christ feeding the thousands with a few skinny fish from a boy's basket. Otávia appeared to listen, but I always knew her mind was weaving what she would say next.

One afternoon she insisted she was out of ideas, and I would have to entertain her.

"Please, Maré," she said. "I'm melting. My guts are mush."

I started to tell of the Israelites wandering in the wilderness and praying for food, and she flung out her arms and groaned.

"Enough with the stupid old people in the desert. Are you trying to make me more miserable? Tell me a cold story."

"But I don't know any."

"Make one up. Think of something, or I'm going to turn into a puddle and leak through the floor and stain the tile and Maria Josefa will make you scrub it out."

I closed my eyes and opened my mind. *Something cold.* I thought of wet bare feet in the darkness, the rip of lightning and thrashing of the sea. I flinched, fighting the image. *No.* I reached farther and found frost curling up a window, a low fire, my father's arms around me, a book draped across our laps.

"OK, I have one," I said, and I told the story of the Little Match Girl.

When I finished, Otávia lay silent, staring at the ceiling, her fingers worrying the end of her braid.

"I didn't know someone could die in the snow," she said.

"Snow is cold. Terribly cold. It hurts to touch it."

She tilted her head toward me, arching an eyebrow. "How would you know?"

"It snows in America," I said.

She flopped back to face the ceiling. "But you don't *remember* it."

"I do," I said, feeling the echo of cold flakes scraping my fingertips, the crunch beneath my boots on the street in front of our house.

"Stop telling stories."

"I am not. I remember what it was like when it snowed in the city where I lived."

"You don't even know what that place is called. Besides, you were a baby when you got here."

"I know I was."

She propped herself on her arm, staring straight at me. When we were that age, she usually treated me as a friend, but sometimes my behavior or misunderstanding frustrated her to the point where she spoke to me as if I were a much smaller child.

"No one remembers being a baby, Mara."

"No one does?"

She didn't respond, and my fears flowed to fill the silence. Could it be true? Could people lose months of their lives, years? Couldn't everyone unfold their memories like a map? Didn't everyone spend their nights begging some to leave? It could not possibly be.

"But you said you remembered your father. You said he left for the city when you were a baby."

Her face transformed from annoyed to angry. "I never said anything like that."

"No. No."

I could not control the quiver in my voice, the terror lacing my insistence. I had accepted, perhaps, that my father was dead. I had accepted, for now, that the recolhimento was my home. As much as I longed to forget the scene of my mother's death, the memories I carried of the time before she ripped me away assured me that I had once had a home, a city, a history—a place I might someday return to, if only I knew the way. If I could forget, what would I have left? Surely Otávia was wrong.

"You *did* say it once. We were folding laundry and you said you were waiting for your father to come. You said he went to the city to make money and come back for you. And you got mad at me and kicked the basket over. You must remember!"

She stared at me, her cheeks stone, her eyes coals.

"I don't," she said, clipping each word. "I don't remember that."

I started to cry then, pressing my face against my pillow. After a moment I felt her climb into the bed beside me, leaning on the wall to keep space between us so we would not make each other even warmer. Her voice broke through my sobs, in the clear tone she always used when she told a story.

"My father was a rich man. He had gold teeth and gold rings

on his fingers and golden hair that sparkled in the sun. His horse
jingled when it walked because its saddlebags were full of gold. My
father could whistle and make birds appear. When he laughed, cashew
apples fell from the trees all around him and pineapples sprang up
from bare earth. His horse was born the same day he was, and he
learned to ride before he could walk. He trained his horse to run
backward as fast as it ran forward, and to kill snakes with its teeth
and spear fish with its hooves.

"When I was born, my father picked me up and got on his horse
and rode around the village, lifting me toward the sun so I glowed.
When everyone in town had come out to see me, he brought me back
here. When he walked through the garden, all the manioc plants
bloomed like roses. The chickens sang a hymn. And he put me in
a basket of clean laundry and whispered to me my name. It wasn't
Otávia. It was a better name, a stronger name. A name that could
shake mountains and drain seas. He said with my name I would be
Queen of Brazil.

"But that night, while we slept, a snake came into the house. It
stole my father's gold rings with its tail and wore them on its body. It
used its forked tongue to lick the gold from his teeth. Its scales turned
his hair gray. And when it was done, it crawled back outside. The
horse was too tired from riding around the village, so it didn't wake
up and kill the snake when it stole the saddlebags and slithered off
into the forest.

"In the morning, my father wept. All his gold was gone. How
could he care for his one and only daughter? How could he make
her Queen of Brazil? So he put me back in the laundry basket and
told me to wait. He would go to the city and make his fortune again
and come back for me. But he couldn't have me shaking mountains
and draining seas while he was gone. I was just a baby. So he took
my name. He wrapped it in a handkerchief and put it in the pocket
of his vest. Then he got on his horse and rode away. And someday
he'll be back."

I had stopped crying and rolled over to watch her. She shut her eyes tight as she spoke, letting the words leave her lips and fill the room. I believed, then, that it was true most people could forget, that their memories could be more imagination than reality. Her stories were all lies, I knew. I ate them up like manna.

Chapter 12

SISTER DOROTÉIA CONTINUED our schooling, determined to revive the recolhimento's long-faded mission of educating orphan girls. She taught me to read Portuguese, and I taught myself to read English by laying the sisters' Bible side by side with one left behind years before by an American missionary, winding through my favorite books in both languages. I picked up scraps of a native tongue from Maria Josefa, who rarely spoke it in my hearing but sang songs in it while she worked. I loved the mechanics of language more than the art of it, and I enjoyed the reliable outcomes of arithmetic and geometry and delighted in Dorotéia's mathematical puzzles. I knew the names of stars and constellations, and despite having no real interest in them, could list generations of monarchs from Portugal, Brazil, France, Spain, and England, along with all the popes. We had few books in the house, but I devoured those I could find dozens of times. Sister Dorotéia's primer began to split at the spine, and she hid it from me on a high shelf.

Otávia could read but claimed to dislike it, preferring instead that I read aloud to her—or, better, listen to her tell her own stories. Dorotéia never forced either of us to attend lessons, so Otávia bobbed in and out of the classroom, only reliably attending our daily walks to the church. When we visited Father Matheus, he let us read his enormous book of saints. He often regaled us with tales of unlisted martyrs and monks and wonder-workers, stories he had collected from generations of parishioners and travelers, and from his mother, who he claimed was a saint herself. Otávia loved the stories of his mother best, and she pleaded with Father Matheus to tell her more about his childhood. He shared plenty, none so fantastic as the stories Otávia told, but still replete with treacherous explorations, youthful spats, and minor miracles.

She begged for the same from the sisters, but with less satisfying results. Maria Josefa simply ignored the requests most of the time, redirecting us to chores and prayers, but a few times curtly replied that she was not obliged to tell us anything about herself that we could not see with our own two eyes. Otávia believed this meant she had dark secrets. Having come to accept that most people's memories diminished with time, I argued that she must not remember. Rosi would only tell one story, of a time when she was a small girl in the city and a woman in a fine gown gave her a coin and she took it to a bakery and bought a delicate French pastry, the sweetest thing she ever tasted. If we asked her any other questions, she never answered, and sometimes grew angry or cried. I learned early not to ask. But Otávia, who loved and loathed Rosi as if she were an older sister, could not help needling her at times, though it often ended with them both in tears.

Sister Dorotéia was more likely to indulge us, but Otávia was less interested in her answers. Dorotéia grew up in Recife, the daughter of a wealthy plantation owner. Her early life involved tutors and governesses, ruffled dresses and elaborate dances, carriage rides with her mother and gifts of horses from her father, all described as if they were nothing but wonderful—which Otávia, of course, did not believe.

One afternoon when I was thirteen, on a day when the rain was too relentless to wander the garden, Otávia attended lessons but spent the whole day staring out the window. As Doroteia described the brief courtship of Ferdinand and Isabella, Otávia interrupted her.

"Have you ever been in love?"

Doroteia lowered her gaze a moment, then looked back up at us, seated side by side at two of the dozen wooden desks that filled the room.

"I have," she said. "I was married."

Otávia's eyes grew wide, and I knew she had not expected an answer at all, let alone this one.

"*Married*?" she said. "To who?"

Doroteia's mouth pressed into a line. Though I wondered if she regretted answering Otávia honestly, I also could not resist a new story.

"To who, Sister?" I echoed.

"His name was Joaquim."

"You only have to tell us about him if you want to," Otávia said, her voice soft.

I had never seen her relinquish a line of questioning so easily before—and whether she had planned for it or not, her gentleness worked.

Doroteia sighed. "I have not spoken about him in many years," she said. "But I suppose it would do no harm for you to know."

He was the third son of an aristocratic Portuguese family who sent him to Brazil to watch over their landholdings. He had an eye for business, and soon after arriving he sold the land to Doroteia's father and invested in a sugar factory, buying and selling more land with his earnings. He worked his way up, and with his increased status came invitations to the family home. Doroteia fell for him immediately, watching him across the dinner table, admiring his serious face and expressive hands as he spoke of shipping schedules and market prices. Her tutors and governesses had told her little about love. She spoke nothing to him until, months later, he requested her hand from her father.

Dorotéia's face at this point in the telling was radiant, reflecting the innocent infatuation of the girl she remembered being. But it soon lost its luster.

"It was a business deal, I believe now," she said. "But I could not have seen it then. I loved Joaquim. I would have followed him anywhere, done anything he asked."

They were married shortly after her seventeenth birthday, and her father built them a house on his estate. Little of her life changed other than where she slept, and with whom she slept. She offered us no details of her marriage bed, and at that age I was unable to imagine such things.

"Was he horrible to you?" Otávia asked Dorotéia, her relish too obvious.

She paused. "No," she said. "He was never cruel. He simply paid me attention when he had attention to spare, and ignored me the rest of the time. He traveled often. It was not such a bad life. I had time to read, and one of my tutors still brought me books. I learned to sew."

"But you never sew," I said.

It was true; Rosi made all our clothes now that Maria Josefa's fingers were too stiff.

"I never said I liked it," she said, her smile returning.

Otávia was not about to let us meander too far from the primary story. "So what happened? Did he die?"

Dorotéia's expression faded once more. "He did not. He is still alive, as far as I know."

Otávia leaned forward in her chair. I tried to restrain myself, but I admit I shared her curiosity.

"Then how did you end up *here*?" Otávia asked.

Dorotéia twisted her fingers together. Had she meant to reveal so much to us? I wondered if she had even spoken this story aloud in years; I could never guess what the sisters discussed in their private moments. But she submitted to finishing what she had started.

"Joaquim and I had been married for five years and still I had not given us a child. I prayed for one, but—" She clenched her hands in her lap, breathing a moment. "But it was not God's will. And then my father died."

Joaquim stepped into a greater role in her father's company then, not only as a skilled manager, but as heir. Again, little changed in Dorotéia's life, but one day Joaquim announced he had a deal to make in Barbados and wished for her to accompany him on the journey. The ship's captain turned out to be a drunk, and when Joaquim declared he would sail no farther with such a man, they went ashore in the village near the recolhimento. From the village Dorotéia saw the church, and she went alone to pray while Joaquim decided on a course of action. When she finished her prayers, the ship and her husband were gone.

"The sisters took me in. I was sure it was some kind of mistake. Perhaps one of the sailors told Joaquim I was resting in my cabin and he did not realize I was not there until it was too late to return for me without completing his business. But we received word months later that he had our marriage annulled, as if it had never happened in the eyes of the Church," Dorotéia said. "So I suppose I was wrong in telling you I had been married."

"But you were in love?" Otávia asked.

Dorotéia glanced toward the door, and I knew her openness had reached its limit.

"I was," she said. "I am tired, my girls. Let's continue our history lesson later."

Otávia sprang from her desk, meeting my eyes in the urgent, silent way she had of letting me know she was desperate to go to our room and talk. I followed her toward the door but lingered a moment. Dorotéia flipped idly through her book of European history. I had never considered before that Dorotéia could be like me. It seemed to me she had always lived in the recolhimento, when in fact she had been forced here, left here, just as I had been. I did not understand how she could remain so calm, telling us such a terrible story. Could she have forgotten Joaquim in a way I would never be able to forget my mother? I put a hand on her arm, wondering, and as I did a string of images entered me: *A man with a waxed mustache, a hint of wave in his hair, somber eyes. The same man standing beside a window, coat draped on a chair, untying his tie. The man at the prow of a ship, his face turned toward the sea.*

I leapt back, and Dorotéia looked at me quizzically.

"Did you have a question, Mara?"

I shook my head and stepped away from her, but remembered what I had planned to say.

"I am sorry, Sister. You should not have been abandoned."

She examined me with no expression, then nodded once, slowly, and turned back to her book as I left.

Otávia waited cross-legged on her bed, chewing the tip of her index finger as she often did while deep in thought. I draped myself onto my own bed—as I had descended the stairs from the classroom, a heaviness had overtaken me, my limbs leaden, my head pounding.

"Well?" Otávia said after a moment.

"Well what?" My mind was so fogged I could barely make my mouth form words.

"Did she tell you more? Is that why you stayed?"

"No," I said, my eyelids drifting shut.

"What were you doing then?" She sounded far away, as if she were shouting from the other side of the garden. "What's wrong?" She was so far away.

~~~~~~~

WHEN I AWOKE Otávia was sitting at the end of my bed. She noticed I was conscious and slid her body beside mine, putting a hand on my forehead.

"Finally," she said. "I was about to go get Maria Josefa."

My lips were light again, the headache gone. "How long was I asleep?"

"Less than an hour, but I had to feel your back to make sure you were breathing. What was that all about?"

In my exhaustion I had had no time to think through what had happened in the classroom with Dorotéia, but my rested mind found an answer.

"I think I saw her memories."

Otávia's shoulders stiffened. "Dorotéia's?"

"Yes. I saw a face—Joaquim's face, I think—when I spoke to her after you left."

"That's all you were doing? Speaking to her?"

"I touched her arm. And I—I was wondering. I wanted to know whether she remembered him."

Otávia arched away from me. She sank to the floor, kneeling beside the bed, her fingers barely on the edge of my mattress. "Did you tell her? Did she know?"

I shook my head. "I do not think she noticed anything."

"This hasn't happened before, has it, Maré?"

I tried to reach for her hand, but she tucked it beneath the bed.

"No," I said. "And I hope it never happens again. You said yourself you were worried I had died. I felt like I might."

Otávia bit her lip, her eyes fixed on my forehead as if she were trying to pry it open and parse its contents. "You're wrong. You should do it again."

"Why, so you can find out everyone else's dark and terrible secrets?"

"Of course not," she snapped. "You're already smarter than anyone I know. Who knows what else you can do?"

I sat up, flipping myself with my refreshed strength so that I knelt on the bed, leaning over her. "Then let me touch you."

"No." Her voice trembled just slightly.

I was fascinated by her fear and found myself greedy to wield my newfound power. In all our childhood, I had never had the upper hand. It was always Otávia commanding me, coaxing me, entrancing me.

"What are you so scared of, Otávia? Scared I will find out who your father is? Scared I will see your mother? Scared you will have to remember everything? You spend so much time begging for everyone's secrets and you will not even tell the truth about yourself."

I did not want to hurt her, only to prove to her that she could not dismiss me. She could not dominate me. We were not little girls anymore, and I deserved for her to face me, as her equal.

"How about this—I will try it again, but not on you. I will try it on Rosi and Maria Josefa and Father Matheus, on everyone in the village if I have to, until I find out every lie you have ever told me."

She leapt to her feet and I braced for her to strike me. We had not fought in some years, but each moment of Otávia's girlhood rage flashed in my mind.

But she extended her open palms. "You want to take the truth from me? Take it. It's yours." She pressed her hands against my collarbone. "Go on."

I had no response. I had roused myself for battle, a chance to prove myself her peer, and she had fully disarmed me with her surrender. I could not tell if the trembling that resounded in me was from her still-shaking hands or my own exhausted body.

I dropped my head. I did not understand how I had managed to pull the memory from Dorotéia. It satisfied my curiosity in the moment, but I hated the feeling afterward—and worse than that, I hated the knowledge that I had stolen something. I wanted none of this power. Instead I leaned forward and let Otávia embrace me.

～～～～

MOST DAYS I told myself the moment with Dorotéia was a misunderstanding, a well-timed burst of my own imagination. I was aware that I had an incredible memory, though I did not recognize how extraordinary, and I believed I could not possibly see another person's experience. I remembered clearly touching Dorotéia's arm, the images of the man replacing the dreary classroom, but I told myself I was simply exceptionally observant and longing to relate to Dorotéia, to share the pain of abandonment. It was no wonder that my mind concocted a story. Still, I did not ask her about Joaquim again, nor did I try to re-create the moment with anyone else.

Otávia was unwilling to go on as if nothing had happened, though she sensed my wariness. She was sure the moment was the result of something far greater and more mysterious, something from within me. She never said so but I could hear in her voice how desperately she wanted me to attempt to use it—how, though she feared my power, she wanted to know truths she could not reveal on her own.

"There is no one in the world like you," she would whisper from her bed at night.

Most times I simply laughed at this in a mixture of delight and disbelief. Sometimes I argued.

"What do you know of the world? You have never been beyond the village."

"Enough, Maré," she said. "I know enough."

Chapter 13

AS I GREW older I began to understand the fragility of our life in the recolhimento. By the time I was sixteen, Maria Josefa's feet had become so gnarled that she could no longer walk the road to Father Matheus's house. The priest, who had been old as long as I could remember and now was by far the oldest man in the village, had not traveled the route himself in many years, so he commissioned a small cart with large wheels that could navigate the ruts and bumps. The recolhimento had had an ancient donkey when I was small, but she had not survived one of the hotter summers and we could not afford to replace her. Rosi rarely left her room, let alone the recolhimento, and Otávia and I agreed it would not be right to allow Dorotéia to pull the cart—she, too, was beginning to slow. So Otávia and I took turns each Friday pulling the old sister to town, while the other stayed behind to manage chores.

Maria Josefa usually napped on these trips. She did not sleep well at night—I often heard her labored steps in the hallways in the earliest hours of the morning—but was soothed by the fresh air and rattle of the cart. This left me alone with my thoughts for the rough, drawn-out walk. I knew I had to imagine a life beyond the women who had raised me, my mind tracing the possibilities. What would we do if Dorotéia's willowy back bent further, if Rosi would no longer leave her room even to eat, if Maria Josefa's milky eyes went fully white? Would they die, one by one, until only Otávia and I remained in a cold, empty building? Or would we remain at all? Love of the sisters—and lack of other options—held us there, but we had made no vows of our own. Dorotéia had urged us both to consider the path of postulancy, but Otávia rejected her, so I did as well. When we were alone, Otávia said she could live without a man, but not with the vow of poverty. "I'm going to find buried treasure digging up manioc one of these days, and when I do, I'm not living like a nun," she said. "We'll buy a big house in the city and eat pastries covered in gold, and we'll pay people to clean our toilets and scrub our floors and rub our feet."

Though I loved God, my own mind would not let me imagine the vow of chastity. None of the sisters spoke to us about sex, so the extent of my knowledge was based on the whispers of the village children and observations of animals, but my body understood on its own. Lust blossomed everywhere. I still grew shy in the village, but I lingered to watch the men on their boats, strong backs and lean arms backlit by the morning sun. The shopkeeper who sold us cloth and rice had perfect teeth, shining eyes, a calming voice. Each time I picked up an order, he called me *minha flor*, my flower, and told me what a lucky man my husband would be someday, and I blushed so hard I could barely breathe. At church I no longer listened to Father Matheus's homilies but spent the time gazing at the people in the pews: the altar boy who brushed his hair from his forehead with graceful hands, the round-hipped rancher's daughter who sat in front of me and smelled like vanilla, the solemn young fisherman whose chiseled face I studied when we were supposed to be praying. The people who had teased me when I was a child were kinder now, but still I rarely spoke to those I watched.

I dreamed of them all and of countless faceless others. When I awoke one night in a cold sweat, I found Otávia sitting up in her bed, stifling laughter—I had been crying out in my sleep. She whispered to me that I did not have to leave such feelings to dreams, then explained how to awaken them whenever I wanted. "Just don't tell the sisters," she said. "Even though I bet they've all done it, too."

Otávia's technique, though pleasing, did not fulfill the restlessness in me that longed for something more. On those walks pulling Maria Josefa's cart, the thing that occupied my thoughts more than anything was marriage. Like sex, it had never been a topic of discussion in the recolhimento, save Dorotéia's unexpected confession. From my limited contact with the outside world, I knew marriage was no simple solution to the desire for love—my own parents' story, from what I could understand of it, seemed to prove that. I still comforted myself with memories of my father, but over the years my mother had grown monstrous in my mind. No matter how often I revisited my childhood memories, I could find no justification for her leaving with no apparent announcement, no discussion. If my father had known what she planned, surely he would have tried to stop her, or come with us. But I grew certain she must not have given him the opportunity; she had been swift and silent and cruel. I no longer blamed myself, at least not entirely, but I came to believe she had left to hurt him. And I came to believe our leaving was what had killed him.

Yet I imagined that marriage would not carry such strife for me. It promised possibilities beyond a rotting building filled with the ghosts of the women I loved, beyond a distant city I remembered but could not find, beyond the wild, impossible dreams of Otávia's stories. It would mean a home, a companion, a future. I set my hopes at the feet of an unknown man.

~~~~~

WHEN THE DAY came that Father Matheus could barely hear the sound of his own voice as he delivered the homily, he wrote to the bishop in his shaky, spidery hand and requested a seminarian to serve as his assistant. Jonas reached the village before the bishop's reply, on a boat up the coast from Olinda. I had just finished carting Maria Josefa to the priest's house when he arrived. It was midmorning and already the day was hot. Sweat plastered my hair to my face and dripped down my back, between my breasts, down my legs. I leaned against the outer wall of Father Matheus's shack, fanning myself as he and Maria Josefa conversed inside. I saw a man's shape appear on the road but paid no mind to it, figuring it was someone coming to light candles in the church.

As he came into focus, I noticed he walked quickly, long arms loose at his sides, his chin slightly raised as he scanned the landscape before him. I had never seen a man from the village who carried himself in this way—all were bent under some sort of work or age or care. Even the strongest fishermen seemed to wilt on land, but this man moved as if the ground would never be anything but sure and steady beneath his feet. He drew closer and I stared, unabashed. His dark hair was trimmed short and slicked against his head so it shone, his face clean-shaven and square-chinned, with a hint of boyishness in his golden cheeks. He wore the whitest shirt I had ever seen. I did not turn away when his eyes met mine.

He stopped at the edge of the rocky border that marked Father Matheus's yard, resting his hands on his hips.

"I was told Father Matheus lived here," he said, his voice crisp and rich with an accent I had never heard among the country men.

"How do you know I'm not Father Matheus?" I called back.

"Oh, you are far too young," he said.

"And too beautiful as well?"

His smile was wide and warm. "I shall have to judge for myself, once I meet him."

Maria Josefa put Jonas to work without delay, sending him out to cut kindling even though it was too hot for a cooking fire. I waited in my patch of shade a bit longer before circling to the back of the shack to watch him. He seemed never to have handled an ax before but was not clumsy, only untrained. I did not think he noticed me until he sank the blade deep into the chopping block and turned toward me, laughing.

"The sister says I have soft hands," he said. "I didn't want to believe she was right."

He held out his palms, smooth and unmarked save for a thin line of blood on the pad of one slender finger. He noticed it and rubbed his hands together.

"I was testing how dull it was," he said. "For an old man, your Father Matheus keeps his ax sharp."

"That is all Maria Josefa," I said.

He crossed his arms, careful to avoid the white of his shirtsleeve with his still-bleeding finger. "I've studied the ways of the church since I was a boy and have never met a sister who gives orders to priests."

I felt a sharpness cross my stomach like a cut. No one in the church or the village ever questioned Maria Josefa in such a way.

"She does not give orders," I said, my voice rising. "He listens to her because she is right. Everyone does."

He broke into a grin, his teeth even and white. "She's already ordered me to come fix some windows at the recolhimento, anyway. And remove cobwebs and replace the roof of the henhouse and add a new fence for the chickens. Father Matheus told her no, but she kept right on with it."

I heard Maria Josefa call from the front door, ready to return home before the day grew any warmer.

"I suppose I will see you soon, then," I said.

"You live at the recolhimento?"

"I do."

"Preparing to take vows?"

"No."

The sun lit up his deep brown eyes. "That's unfortunate. I can tell you are very good."

The way he said the word *good* sparked a new feeling in my stomach, hot like the cut of anger, but brighter.

"I am very good," I said back, trying to match the tone, though it came out more like fear.

Maria Josefa called out again, and I turned to leave.

"You are more beautiful than Father Matheus," he called after me.

I pressed my hand to my mouth and ran to the cart, where Maria Josefa was already nearly asleep in her seat. On the walk home I hardly noticed the shaking of the cart or the ache in my arms; I felt as if I had a piece of ripe mango in my mouth, cool, juicy, and sweet, and if I held it still on my tongue I might taste it forever.

~~~~~

ON SUNDAY, Jonas assisted Father Matheus during Mass, and I could not keep myself from watching him. He smiled and blushed and accepted kisses and blessings from a line of elderly villagers afterward, but I stayed with Otávia, conversing as if it were a normal Sunday, attempting to pretend he was not there. I looked over once, just before we left, and caught his eye. I wondered if he had been looking at me, or if it was merely a lucky accident. He smiled before leaning down to allow a woman with a passel of children at her ankles to clasp his face and pray for him.

On Monday I sensed him coming before I saw him. I was weeding the front garden of the recolhimento when I heard the change in the birdsong, the snap of unworn shoes on the stones of the road. Through the tangle of bromeliads and tree branches I saw the white flash of his shirt. It was early still. Maria Josefa was praying while Dorotéia prepared breakfast and Rosi slept. Otávia was out back feeding the chickens. I had not said a word to her about Jonas, other than to confirm that I had seen Father Matheus's helper arrive.

I found myself worried that he would shout to me and she would hear and come see what was going on, so I rose to my feet and stepped out into the road.

"Good morning, Brother Jonas," I said, careful to keep my voice just loud enough for him to hear me.

"Good morning, Mara," he said.

I had learned his name by listening to Maria Josefa's conversations with Dorotéia, and I wondered where he had learned mine.

We stood in the road a moment, both of us smiling but unspeaking, for some reason unable to re-create the confident joking of before. I could not bear the silence and decided to fill it with business.

"I will show you to Maria Josefa," I said. "She will want you to start on your tasks early."

My own chores kept me from watching him, but I could hear the thumps and crashes of his work on the henhouse—they did not teach construction at his school in the city, I presumed. When we sat down to eat, his shirt was smeared with dirt, one sleeve torn. His left thumbnail was bruised. He did not complain. He responded politely to the sisters' questions, recounting a brief life history that began with being given up by his impoverished parents to be raised by the church, followed by a strict education. He did not brag but made it clear his teachers had considered him intelligent; he knew Latin and Greek and spoke of complex politics. Otávia was mostly silent, eating quickly, but when her plate was cleared she interrupted his description of the seminary's trimmed and tidy courtyard.

"Mara speaks English," she said. "She can read it, too. And Portuguese."

I gaped at her, unsure what to say.

"Do you speak English?" she continued.

He responded he did not.

"That's really too bad. Nobody speaks Latin outside of the church, and everyone from ancient Greece is dead."

Jonas tilted his head, addressing me for the first time. "Maybe she can teach me."

Dorotéia folded her hands in her lap. "When is Father Matheus expecting you home? It will be too hot to work soon, and we take our quiet time."

"If it is all right, I would like to stay," he said. "I'd like to see the rest of the recolhimento. Perhaps Miss Mara and Miss Otávia could give me a tour while you rest?"

Dorotéia looked to Maria Josefa, who nodded.

Otávia stood up. "I'm tired," she said, and left before anyone could speak to her.

In the abandoned rooms where Otávia and I had played as children, I led Jonas through a maze of dusty furnishings and faded walls, across cracked tiles, through dark, empty rooms. In the room we had called the City, I guided him past the sheet-draped skeleton of a piano—which I had tried to play only once before discovering it was inhabited by generations of mice—and to the window through which he could see the back gardens and the chicken coop, and beyond into the deep green thicket of the forest.

As I leaned out to point through the trees toward the village, I felt his fingers rest on my hip. I stilled and he pulled back. For all of my longing, I had never been touched by a boy before, and I did not know how to tell him I was not upset, he did not need to pull away, I wanted more. I turned to face him and saw the same uncertainty in his face, his hand still poised before him. I took it in mine, tracing his fingers with the tips of my own, easing it toward me, leaving it to rest again on my hip. He tilted his chin and I rose to meet him, surprised to find the sensation of kissing was not what I had imagined—softer at the lips yet sharper from the presence of our teeth, louder with the sound of our breath, less graceful with unpracticed hands. I did not care. I had found the path I desired.

Chapter 14

HOW WAS I to know we were children? My life did not look like a child's in so many ways—my days at the recolhimento were filled with labor and study, along with a growing and pervasive sense of responsibility toward the elderly sisters. The only other child I spent time with was Otávia, and we no longer wrestled, no longer climbed trees, no longer drew Dorotéia's chastisement by returning from hauling water dripping wet. We had grown up, and we were beginning to grow apart. In the weeks after Jonas arrived, Otávia told fewer stories and asked me fewer questions. She often disappeared for hours, coming home smelling like the seashore I still avoided. In our beds we often fell asleep in silence, my mind on Jonas, hers somewhere unknown.

Jonas's childhood had been brief and disciplined. He was seventeen but seemed to me to speak and think as if he were older, to express himself more intricately than any of the grown men I knew—though admittedly I knew few. The school and seminary in Olinda were filled with more books than I could dream of, and he often lamented the sparseness of Dorotéia's library. I did not hear rudeness in these statements, but rather a true sense of loss. He, like me, adored the complexities of language. He persuaded Maria Josefa and

Dorotéia to let him stay during the afternoon rest each day, with an agreement to teach me Latin and Greek in exchange for English. We did as promised, yet so much more.

This, too, was an education. We learned to kiss, to caress. We grew less clumsy, and for some weeks the novelty of touching was enough. We had been raised by people sworn to celibacy, isolated from sex; intimacy had been revealed to us only in glimpses of men and women in public, and it was a joy to discover what could be done behind closed doors. This is not to say that we were unaware of limits: Jonas, having lived in a city, raised among boys, had heard women's bodies spoken of in filthy terms, had learned of desecrated women and the sinful men who wasted themselves with them. We knew, too, that priests did not marry, were not supposed to be with women, tried to keep it secret when they were. Jonas had until then obeyed his superiors' commands to resist the temptations of the flesh. I assured myself that if I could decline to become a nun, surely he could decline to become a priest. Whenever uncertainty arose in my mind, his lips and hands extinguished it.

One afternoon, as he pressed against me in the corner of the empty classroom, he said he had had a revelation. He had been praying, thinking of me, and he understood in a flash that our bodies were holy.

"Holy?" I said, laughing, thinking of the sprinkled water in the church, the doves carved into the walls.

He repeated the word, kissing my shoulder so I laughed even more. "Do you remember it in Greek?"

Of course I did. *"Hieros. Hagios."*

"Hagios," he whispered. "Different, distinct. Set apart. I've never felt anything like I feel when I'm with you. It must be holy, do you understand?"

I met his eyes and saw fear in them, as if he did not believe his own words, which seemed so carefully practiced.

"I do."

I was willing to say anything to keep him, anything to comfort him, anything to convince him to continue what we had started. Whatever it took for him to be as filled with me as I was with him, I would agree to it. If he wanted holiness, I would give him ecstasy. Otávia had taught me to elicit it from my body, and I would elicit it from his.

When my fingers found him he gasped. He did not pull away but sank his chin to his chest, gaping at my hand clasping him. I hid my own surprise at the warmth and softness of his skin, at the feel of something I had until then hardly been able to imagine.

"We are holy, remember?" I said.

He whispered *yes*.

The recolhimento was large, so much of it empty when the sisters took their afternoon rest, so much of it never visited by them. Rosi never left her room, Maria Josefa could not climb stairs, Dorotéia's days were spent caring for the other two, and Otávia showed no interest in my whereabouts, so the upper floors of the building belonged to no one but Jonas and me and whatever quiet ghosts remained of the girls and women who had lived there and left long ago. At the end of a dusty hallway we discovered a tiny room Otávia and I had ignored when we were younger, a gray-walled cell with no windows and no furnishings save a narrow mattress on the floor. Perhaps, once, a serious nun had spent her hours there contemplating the great mysteries of faith, but Jonas and I thought only of each other. Jonas's declaration of holiness and my response had removed his fear, and he shied from nothing. Jonas never begged or coerced or forced. He enjoyed what I enjoyed, and whether ignorance or youthful eagerness drove me, I found every touch pleasurable. We were doing what humans have done for all our existence, but it felt like discovering a new world. In the breathless dark when we finished for the first time, I wanted nothing more than to return, to lose myself in that strange land.

HOW WAS I to know what would surely happen? My education had been not merely limited but deliberately so, under the direction of women who loved me but knew no other way, who either believed I was innocent or feared they would destroy my innocence if they told me the truth. But perhaps I should have known; perhaps I did know. For all my flawless recollection of conversations and faces and stories, my memories are shaped by the person I was when they occurred; when I think of those days I cannot separate the joy I experienced from the lies I must have believed to make it feel so real. I loved Jonas, worshipped him, and he me. We were holy. Naked in the shadows, sweating in the afternoon heat that had no way to escape our tiny room, I asked when we would marry, and he promised to write to the bishop that night, explain everything, leave the path to the priest-hood, cleave to me. We would live in the village and continue to care for the recolhimento and Father Matheus. When those duties ended, we could go wherever we wanted. Neither of us had seen a city other than the ones in which we were born. I felt I no longer needed my lost city or anything that had been in it; I had detached myself from my past. I would go where Jonas went. Soon, soon, the whole ripe world would be ours.

When the rains came, Dorotéia insisted Jonas take a break from his work at the recolhimento, and often the road was muddy and impassable, besides. I told the sisters I was studying but spent hours in bed, my body aching from what I thought was his absence. I lost interest in food, able to stomach little more than the tapioca pancakes I had once despised. I had read of women grown weak with love, and I told myself it must be this.

One morning as I lay in my bed, under a blanket despite the warmth of the day, my legs tucked to my chest and my hands pressed over my eyes, I heard Otávia come in from feeding the chickens. I could feel her presence as she stood above me. We had not talked beyond necessity in so long, and I felt sure she was about to laugh at me, to gloat at my pain and her strength, as she sometimes had when we were small.

Instead she stroked my forehead with her dry hand. "You little fool," she said.

"Something is wrong," I said. "I have a fever."

"You're cool as ever," she said. "Only more stupid than usual."

I wanted to sit up, to yell at her, to strike her, but any movement caused waves of pain from my churning stomach. I curled my body tighter. She sat beside me, her hand still on my forehead.

"When was your last blood?" she asked. "Two months?"

I could not remember.

I started to cry. "Am I dying?"

"Maré, Maré," she said, her voice the singsong she used when telling stories. "I love you, but you are a fool. I know you've been fucking that priest."

I did not understand the word she used but I could feel its vulgarity, the way she spat it out. I managed to speak from behind my hands.

"I love him. He is not a priest and he is never going to be. He wrote to the bishop."

"You think the bishop will bless this?"

"What are you saying?"

"Oh, Maré." She peeled my hands from my face. I shut my eyes at the intrusion of light as she wrapped my hands in hers and drew them to her warm shoulders. "Listen to me. I know you can."

The ability I had shut out came flooding back. I could not help but wonder, and so I could not help but see. The images came in flashes, moments, as they had when Dorotéia's memories entered me: *A boy with one palm on Otávia's neck and another reaching under her skirt, the scrape of her fingernails across his cheek. Rosi, younger, crouching in a dark room, something small and still and silent slipping from her. The shopkeeper who called me his flower looming over Otávia in a corner beside his stockroom, saying words like none he had ever said to me, words terrifying in their specificity,*

their lewdness, their violence, their insistence. He did not seem to care that she
turned her face away.

I crumpled away from her, my nausea overshadowed by new exhaustion. Why had she shown me such things when I was weak and ill? Why would she respond to my love for Jonas with these wretched memories? I was too faint to move away from her or tell her to go, though I longed to. She sat beside me, let my head drop into her lap, and told me a story.

"Once there was a girl made of ice. Her hair was ice, her skin was ice, the soles of her feet and the back of her neck and the skin between her fingers were ice. The ice was clear and pure, finer than any glass. You could see right through her.

"When the ice-girl's mother died, she wandered through the night weeping tears of sleet until she happened upon a cave. A family of wolves was curled inside, and they let the lost ice-girl in. They gave her cool water that dripped from the cave's ceiling and made her a bed on the smooth stone floor. When she awoke and rose to leave, they swirled their soft tails around her so she would not go. They were frightened she would melt in the sun, or trip and shatter on the jagged ground. They swore they would protect her. They spread their sleek, furred bodies before her and begged her to stay.

"For a while, the ice-girl did. She learned to speak like a wolf and play like a wolf. The wolves brought her all the coldest foods they could find, thin slices of papaya and thin silver fish and cold-blooded lizards. These made her grow taller, her icy features more delicate by the day, but more fragile as well. The wolves stirred at night, fearful of what might happen if their ice-daughter wandered away.

"One morning when the wolves had grown tired from their vigil, the ice-girl woke early to walk outside the cave in the chill morning air, and she saw a human boy. He beckoned her and she followed, forgetting about the wolves. She had not been touched by anything other than the soft paws and tongues and tails of her protectors, so she was surprised when the boy reached out a palm and it rasped against her, sending a shimmer of frost into the air. She was so intrigued by this new thing she let him touch her again. He stared into her clear, bright eyes and she thought she saw some ice in him, too. She did not notice the flakes falling until it was too late. She looked down at her feet and saw a little child made of snow."

I lay still, cold with the truth of her words. *A little child made of snow.* I had been a fool.

Chapter 15

JONAS WROTE TO the bishop, as he had promised. Instead of a response, the bishop himself arrived, on a sailboat on a Friday morning. Otávia and I had taken Maria Josefa to see Father Matheus together that day; in the early days of my pregnancy we always did, as I was too weak to pull the cart alone but could not shirk my duty. Otávia had quietly stepped back into my daily routine, designating herself as a sort of protector. We knew the sisters would discover me before long, but Otávia was willing to help me extend that time, though she did not specify why. The only times she kept away from me were the rare days when Jonas visited the recolhimento. I had not told him of our child. I did not know how. In the brief moments in which I felt refreshed, we still stole away together, and I was certain his hands would notice my rounding belly and spreading hips, but he was too lost in pleasure to recognize these changes for what they were. More often than not, I told him the dreary, humid days were leaving me weary, and he believed me.

Otávia and I were sprawled in the cool, damp grass outside Father Matheus's shack when a child from the village ran down the path to deliver the news of the bishop's arrival. He did not tell us directly, but shouted it so loudly to Father Matheus that we heard. We crept to the back of the house and crouched beneath the unshuttered window. I knew the bishop must have come because of Jonas's letter, and I let myself hope that he was set to release Jonas from his obligation and bless our union. Perhaps he would even perform the ceremony himself—why else would he come in the flesh rather than sending a letter? Otávia, I knew, did not share my optimism, but she said nothing, only knelt beside me and waited.

We heard the hooves of the borrowed horse; we heard the bishop telling the man who led it to return in an hour. I had met no clergymen other than Father Matheus and so I was shocked by that voice, loud and commanding, an edge like a sword. I lifted myself once to peer through the window as the bishop was stepping through the door, and was surprised by his appearance as well: his broad shoulders shaping his dark cassock, his thick fair hair, his sharp chin. I had read about Portuguese military commanders in one of Dorotéia's history books, and he looked as I had imagined they had. He did not smile as he greeted Father Matheus.

"The old woman must wait outside," he said.

"Marcos, please," said Father Matheus. "My friend does not walk as well as she used to. It does no harm if she stays."

"You would do well to address me as my rank commands, Father."

I could not see Father Matheus but could hear both the irony and irritation in his voice.

"I was unaware any but God commanded me, Your Excellency."

"I am not here to debate."

We heard shuffling, the door opening and closing, then nothing, until Maria Josefa sighed softly behind us. I nearly screamed in surprise but Otávia caught my mouth. Maria Josefa tapped her lips with her clawed hand, and together we listened as the bishop listed our sins. That metallic voice dragged a litany of them into the light. As far as the Church knew, the recolhimento had been shuttered long ago. Father Matheus had not only failed to report the continued existence of the sisters of Nossa Senhora dos Navegantes; he had, in fact, reported fifteen years before that Maria Josefa had died, that Doro-téia had gone to Portugal, and that no others remained. The building, too remote and expensive to maintain, had supposedly been aban-doned to the forest—and then the bishop receives a report that it is not only inhabited, but taking in orphaned girls? And allowing them to distract and deceive a pious, intelligent young man, the bishop's star pupil, whom he thought he was sending to help an elderly priest in a distant village, not to be made sport of by women? The bishop knew he had to deal with such a disaster in person.

In my astonishment at the bishop's revelations, I did not notice how black the clouds were growing, how heavy the air. As if in con-cert with his words, lightning slashed the air. A gush of warm rain arrived with the thunder, and Otávia and I leapt to grasp Maria Josefa's arms, half for her safety, half for ours. We had nowhere to go. Otávia took Maria Josefa's elbow and led us in a chain to the door of the shack, neither pausing nor knocking as she entered. The bishop turned away from where he stood over Father Matheus, a sneer blighting his handsome face. His eyes traced my body, my light dress soaked by the rain and clinging to the unmistakable shape of me.

"My God," he said, "it's worse than I thought."

~~~~~

AFTER THE RAIN CLEARED, we began the long, dreadful march from Father Matheus's house to the recolhimento. The bishop watched us from the yard until the path entered the forest, though he did not allow Father Matheus to join him outside. Once the black-robed fig-ure had faded from our sight, Maria Josefa spoke.

"Dorotéia and I decided we would protect you and the child," she said. "We have never questioned how Our Lady delivers our little ones to us."

With that, the secret Otávia and I thought we held fast was revealed to be no secret at all. Maria Josefa said nothing more, only drifted to sleep in the cart as she always did. I could not understand how she could rest, given what loomed ahead of us. The bishop had handed down our sentence swiftly and without conversation. The recolhimento was to become in reality what it was on paper: dismantled and abandoned. Maria Josefa and Dorotéia would be reassigned to a convent in Olinda. Father Matheus would be forced to retire and move to the city as well, to let his days dwindle away in the company of doddering old priests and monks. "I shall decide what to do with the girls when we arrive," the bishop had said, his tone making it clear that he had no pleasant options in mind. As we walked, my mind gnawed on what those options might be. Was I too old for an orphanage? If I were forced into a convent, would they tear my child away from me? Could they leave us on the streets? I tried to pray but found my words aimless and absent. When my hands began shaking too hard to help Otávia with the cart, she marched wordlessly as I trailed behind and cried, and Maria Josefa slept.

I did not realize until we neared the end of the trail that Jonas was yet unaware of the morning's terrible events. Father Matheus had sent him to a farm far outside the village to visit an ailing parishioner— and surely as soon as he returned and discovered the bishop's plan he would rush to explain himself, to claim me, to rescue us. I exclaimed this with joy to Otávia, who turned her face toward me and stared. The muted sunlight following the storm illuminated the smooth curve of her neck, the sharp corners of her eyes, the fullness of her lips despite her flat expression. She wore her hair out of her usual braids, a loose black tangle tumbling around her face. With a rush I saw my friend had become beautiful. I saw, too, the rage and fear and love she held for me. I waited for her words, already hearing the voice in my head declaring that Jonas would not come, he would not help us, I was a fool. But she said nothing, and I knew the voice was my own.

~~~~~

DOROTÉIA AND ROSI seemed to have prepared for a moment such as this, their faces stoic as Maria Josefa listed the bishop's commands.

We finished the day with prayers and chores as usual. I was mortified that they were not making plans to plead for mercy, to beg to keep the only home they knew, the only home I knew, but I could not think of anything to say to them. I went to bed early, letting myself weep so I would not have to think about what might happen next. I did not expect to sleep, but my exhaustion overwhelmed me. Sometime in the night Otávia arrived and, instead of resting in her own bed, lay down with me. I awoke once, my face sticky with sweat and tears, to the feel of her warm hand on my stomach, her breath soft on my neck. As I had on the first night I spent in the recolhimento, I rested against her and fell asleep.

A low, keening wail woke us. Downstairs we found Maria Josefa kneeling at the open door to Rosi's room, her face pressed to the floor. Otávia ran to find Dorotéia as I dropped to the ground, close enough to hear Maria Josefa's muttered Hail Marys.

"Sister? Maria Josefa, what has happened?" I barely dared to whisper above her words. "Where is Rosi?"

She did not respond. The morning seemed quiet and empty, her prayer the only sound in the dark hall. The energy that had charged through me upon waking plummeted, and I rested my aching body on the cool tile beside her. Her voice began to break and rasp through her repetitions, and neither Otávia nor Dorotéia had returned. And where was Rosi? As the question entered my mind, Maria Josefa shuddered, a sob interrupting her prayer. I reached out and touched her shoulder, and in the shadow of her face against the floor, I saw her eyes open and dart to me. *Rosi so young and so skinny, too skinny, her hair in clumps and bare feet bloodied, curled in front of the door to the recolhimento. Weeping in her bed, her belly now swollen. Weeping again beside a tiny box and an empty grave. Laughing, the same age as when I first met her, her face full and healthy. Her body thrashing, her voice raw with screaming, as Maria Josefa's hands wrest a knife from her fist. Her body unmoving, her face to the wall, as Maria Josefa bathes her in a tub of cool water.*

Running footsteps interrupted the vision. Dorotéia swooped into the space between Maria Josefa and me, cradling the old woman, whose voice had gone too weak to pray aloud. Otávia's strong arms reached beneath mine and she guided me to our room.

"She's gone," she said. "She left sometime during the night. She didn't take anything with her."

"She must not have gone far—surely someone will find her on the road, help her get home. Can we go to the village? Borrow a horse?"

Otávia hung her head. "She wouldn't have gone by the road. And she's never coming home," she said. "She just decided to leave before the rest of us."

Chapter 16

JONAS ARRIVED WITH the bishop that afternoon. I rushed to
the road and threw myself at his feet. I had planned an appeal to his
love and mercy, but I could not make myself speak. I looked up, sure
that the sight of his beautiful face would spark the words I could not
find, but it was blank. His jaw seemed slack, his eyes pink-rimmed
and drooping. The bishop dismounted his horse and I watched as the
older man stepped over me and strutted toward the doorway where
the sisters waited. Otávia was nowhere to be found.

"Ignore the girl," the bishop snapped.

Jonas obeyed without hesitation, moving as if under a spell, leaving me prostrate on the ground.

"The little whore is a liar as well," the bishop said, his voice booming across the garden, though it was unclear to whom he spoke. "Jonas
says she coerced him into writing to me, and when he came to his
senses he prayed daily that his letter would alert me to the dire situation in this . . . place."

He stood before Dorotéia and Maria Josefa, eyeing them as if
they concealed the bodies of devils beneath their habits.

"I suspect dark forces at work, though the boy is too softhearted to make such accusations. He wishes me to believe the girl is with child by a traveling storyteller or some such poetry, trying to snare him out of desperation. But he is ignorant of women and what troubles they invite when left to their own devices."

Upon finishing his speech he finally seemed to notice who stood before him.

"Where is the other one?"

One? But two were missing. Dorotéia moved as if to speak, and I saw Maria Josefa tap against her sleeve.

"She is working in the garden," the elder sister said. "Sister Dorotéia, please fetch Otávia. Come in, Bishop. Would you like coffee?"

I remained on the ground, watching her in horror. Hours before she had been inconsolable over Rosi's disappearance, and now she was offering to serve the very source of the evil that had overtaken us. I could not at first see the strength it took for her to hold together the illusion of calmness, to replace the shattered lies with the new ones we needed to survive. She would have gained nothing by pleading or fighting, for the bishop's power far exceeded her own. She had to protect what shards of her life, and ours, remained. One of those shards was Rosi, whom the bishop never mentioned in his list of admonishments. I did not know what had happened to the older girl who seemed so torn between loving and hating us, why she had arrived beaten and pregnant at the door of the recolhimento when Otávia was small, why she had chosen to walk into the forest rather than face the Church. But I knew Maria Josefa gave her a final gift of dignity, of choice, by hiding her existence from the bishop that day.

I knew Otávia was not weeding the garden, though I did not know what she was doing, other than avoiding the contempt of the bishop. I feared how she would react when Dorotéia dragged her inside. I imagined her swearing, spitting, pushing, turning again into the ferocious thing she had become when wronged as a child. But when she finally joined us, she seemed distant, almost indifferent. I noted her reaction only briefly—my attention was focused on Jonas. I sought to catch his eye, to detect something in his expression that would reveal hope for us. I could see the tension in his body, the work it took for him to avoid me. It was the only sign he gave me that our passion had not been an illusion. Still, whatever love he felt, or had felt, for me was not enough to overcome whatever the bishop had threatened to do to him. We had been too young to see the fragility of the future we had imagined for ourselves, and it could not have taken much for the bishop to destroy it.

And yet I felt more than desire or desperation for Jonas. Resentment sprouted in me like a sinewy vine, twisting around what I thought was unshakable love. Yes, he had been pushed into a corner by our situation—but he could pretend his sin was not his own. He could stay holy. I was trapped, laid bare. I felt nothing could wash me clean again.

The bishop gave us until the next morning to pack our meager belongings and prepare to board the ship to Olinda. When he and Jonas left, I knelt again in the mud of the road, waiting for Jonas to look back before they disappeared around the bend. He did not. It was the last time I saw him.

As Otávia and I stuffed our clothes into burlap sacks, Dorotéia arrived in the doorway and beckoned us to follow. She led us to Maria Josefa's room, which we had never before been allowed to enter. It was less sparse than I expected—though the floor held nothing but a blanket, mattress, and a small chest, the wall was decorated with a large painting of Our Lady, its frame trimmed with bright feathers and small carved figures hanging from the corners by strips of patterned cloth. Maria Josefa sat on the blanket clutching her worn wooden rosary, her back against a pillow on the wall.

"You leave at dusk," she said. "Father Matheus paid a man who is trustworthy. He will take you as far as Natal, and from there you will be on your own. I cannot tell you where to go, but I know you will find a home. Our Lady will care for you. She loves you more than even I do."

"You mean *we* leave," Otávia said. "We leave together."

Dorotéia shook her head. "We would only slow you down. We are too old to avoid the path ahead of us, my darling. Your path remains open, and we will give what we can to help you find it."

She crossed to the chest and drew out a bundle of faded blue felt—the coat my mother had wrapped me in the night of the shipwreck. I had fought those memories so fiercely, I had never allowed myself to wonder where it had gone.

"Perhaps it will protect you once again," Maria Josefa said as Dorotéia placed it in my arms. It felt lighter than I remembered.

I noticed Otávia was looking at the floor.

"Your mother left you with her strength, Otávia," Maria Josefa said. "You will need to use it well."

Otávia rushed to her side, kneeling beside her and pressing her face into Maria Josefa's tunic. I remained at the end of the bed.

"I am sorry," I said. "I am sorry I did this to you. I am sorry I sinned. I'm sorry—"

I began to cry before I could say more, and Dorotéia embraced me.

"We forgive you, my love," she said. "And we beg your forgiveness as well."

When I knelt to say my tear-choked goodbye to Maria Josefa, she patted my cheek with her hand. "Do you remember?"

Too frightened by our circumstances to fear my own power, I let myself see: *Two shaken sailors clutching a bundle in a storm. A child from so far away. The feel of my wet hair in her fingers. The prayer she said after she tucked me into bed. The pain of telling me my father was never coming, flooded by the warmth of knowing she could give me a home.*

"Thank you, Sister," I whispered. She reached up and scraped the sign of the cross on my forehead with her nail, as she had done the night I arrived.

Their parting gift was money, more than I had ever seen.

"Father Matheus says it is not stealing. It is simply helping the

bishop remove you from this place," Dorotéia said with a gentle curl
of a smile.

By then it was closer to dark than light. I had never walked the
road to the village at night before. As we left the recolhimento I looked
back once at the sisters standing in the doorway, then forced myself to
focus on navigating the ruts, on listening for movement in the trees,
on clutching Otávia's hand. I desperately wanted to run back, to cling
to Maria Josefa and Dorotéia, to refuse to leave them, but I could not
reject the gift they had given me.

When the light of Father Matheus's shack appeared in the distance, Otávia stopped and grabbed my other hand

"I trust you with my life," she said. "I need you to trust me
with yours."

"I do," I said. "I have always trusted you."

"You can't, because I haven't let you know me. I've lied to you."

"You have not," I said, squeezing her palms, suddenly terrified
that she would abandon me. "You told stories, that is all."

I could not see her face in the dimness, but I knew she smiled
at me.

"Stories are just pretty lies. But I want you to know me, Maré.
All of me."

She did not speak in her storyteller's voice or use the beautiful
words of her usual tales. She spoke plainly, directly: how her mother
had left her at the recolhimento in the early hours of dawn, thrusting
her into Maria Josefa's arms, too panicked to explain anything before
she disappeared into the forest. Otávia did not remember her mother's
face; she did not know who her mother was or where she came from
or why she was running. The sisters listened for reports of a runaway
woman and child but heard nothing, and they feared asking, because
they feared whatever the woman was running from. She knew nothing of her father. The snippets of memory that remained had been so
terrible she had pushed them away as a girl, replacing them with the

tale of the magical father who had gone to the city and would someday return for her. She had hated her mother for leaving her. It had
seemed to young Otávia to be a brutal abandonment, though the sisters had always insisted her mother must have loved her very much.

"I understand it now," she said. "What she did for me."

"What about your name? You always said your father stole it
from you."

She laughed. "It's all I have of her."

I heard her voice catch, and she pulled my arms around her. "It
was her name, too."

～～～

DOROTÉIA HAD SAID the bishop lacked imagination. He would rest
well that night, confident that we were defeated, that we would wail
and await our fate, and he would not return to the recolhimento until
late the next morning. By the time he realized we were gone, we would
already be in Natal, seeking a ship to take us elsewhere. The cheesemonger Father Matheus hired to deliver us seemed nearly as old as
the priest himself, tiny and wizened, as was the donkey that pulled
his wagon. The man did not speak, but patted our heads as he tucked
us beneath a threadbare quilt, weighting the edges with cheeses and
stacking the top with the sisters' palm-frond baskets to disguise our
presence. Otávia and I wound together, waiting for the rattle of movement to signal the beginning of our journey. When it did, we remained
silent, listening to the squeak of the wagon wheels, the gentle mash
of the donkey's hooves, the lilting melody of the cheesemonger singing, a sleepy song I had heard Maria Josefa sing sometimes as she
folded laundry. His voice was pleasant, and he seemed not to fear the
road at night, though it lay between the vast shadowed forest and the
vast shadowed sea. I could hear the waves roaring in the distance,
and my mind recalled my mother's last moments, splashing the vivid
scene before me. I thrust my palms against my eyes, but it was no use;
the memory was fresh as it had been fourteen years before, and no

amount of reliving it eased the horror. I saw my mother shout to the sailor, though I could not hear her above the tumult of the storm. I felt her shove me into his arms. I watched her fall, her mouth and eyes open wide. She was falling forever in my head, but I knew she would have hit water and sunk down, drowned amid the remains of the ship.

"What are you thinking about?" Otávia's voice sounded far away though her face was inches from mine.

"I have not been on a ship since I was a baby," I said.

I did not have to say more. She knew my story.

"I'll hold onto you," she said. She tilted her chin to kiss my lips, and I trusted her.

Sometime in the night I fell asleep, waking to muted sunlight through the quilt and the cheesemonger's warble—a different song than the evening before, a brighter tune, a morning song. Otávia was asleep beside me, snoring softly with the rhythm of the wagon. My hips ached, but I shifted slowly to keep from waking her, rolling onto the bag that held my clothes. At the sudden sound of paper rustling, I held my breath. Once I was sure she remained asleep, I returned to the sound. What could have made it? Leaving behind the books in the recolhimento's tiny library felt like leaving behind old friends, but I had packed none, nor any notes or letters. Gently I pulled the opening of the bag to my side and reached in. My stomach heaved as my fingers found the smooth fabric of my mother's coat, then something concealed within it. I drew out a faded envelope, the edge of which had crumpled beneath me.

In the muted light I read the sprawling handwriting among the scattering of stamps and postage marks: *Mr. Sweet, The Spyglass, Boston.* A different, smaller script I immediately recognized as my father's listed the date of receipt at the bottom. And on the back, a name written in my mother's flowing letters, traced over and over: *Ishmael.*

The memories came in a cascade, jarred loose by that name. I do not know whether I had hidden them from myself deliberately or whether they had simply been overshadowed by the memory of my mother's death, but they arrived as vivid as anything I remembered. I saw her bent in her bunk on the ship, a letter in her trembling fingers, this same envelope on the bed beside her. I felt her take my hand, steadying me as we stepped onto the ship. I was so distracted by the polished planks of the deck I barely heard her voice: "Up you go, Mara. We're off to see Ishmael."

My mother never spoke of her past within my hearing. And beyond that statement when we boarded the ship, she revealed nothing to me about the reason for our disastrous voyage. I had concluded that our leaving was some sort of punishment for me or my father, but I had not given myself room to consider that she may have been doing more than running away. That there could have been something, or someone, she was heading toward. *Ishmael.*

A wave of sourness rushed into my mouth, and I forced myself to swallow, feeling it burn on its way back down my throat. *Ishmael.* She had deserted my father for him. She had stolen me to search for him. She had died without finding him. For my whole life, I had thought of my mother only in terms of my story, my life, my loss. Here was proof of how little I truly knew about her. Here was a name I could attach to nothing other than my mother's death, but which had meant enough to her that she was willing to give up everything.

I reached out to wake Otávia and tell her about my discovery. I should have anticipated her question: "Aren't you going to see what's inside?"

The paper was wrinkled and dried, but the flap of the envelope was not anchored, only tucked in. I would not even have to tear it. I knew Otávia wished for me to explore my mother's story, the way our final hours in the recolhimento had allowed her to revisit hers. We could weave our futures together, learn to accept what had happened to us as children, contemplate the wonder of how our mothers' flights had brought us together from across oceans. I imagined telling the tales to my child someday and was struck by a surge of awe and terror.

I was somebody's mother. The rocking of the wagon suddenly seemed too much, too like a ship swaying at sea. My mother had not meant to die, and I pitied her for her terrible death. But I promised myself I would never, ever let my own child go so easily. Not for anything or anyone.

"You don't have to be scared," Otávia whispered.

I stared at that name on the envelope. *Ishmael.* I was not scared. I was enraged. The lifetime of effort I had put into suppressing my memories of my mother transmuted, bloomed into hatred for the faceless man she chased.

I tightened my fist and felt the flakes of paper crumble into my hand.

"Knowing more about her won't make you be like her," Otávia said.

"I will never be like her," I said, the words ripping from my chest in a rasp, a growl. "I will never care about this man. This *Ishmael.*"

The name was bitter as a curse in my mouth. I never wanted to speak it again.

I crumpled it all, the letter and the envelope, and reached for the edge of the quilt hanging above us. I expected Otávia's eyes to go wide, for her to insist I stop, not sacrifice this last fragment I had of my mother, but she held my steady gaze as I found the edge of the wagon and flung the paper out.

~~~~~

WE HELPED THE cheese seller set up his stall in the marketplace in Natal, then stepped into the crowd. Otávia used some of Father Matheus's money to buy fresh fruit, roasted peanuts, rice and bits of dried beef wrapped in palm leaves, all of which she tucked into her bag, refusing to let me carry anything. I left to ease my bladder and returned to find her waiting with a plate of tapioca pancakes.

"They're not as good as Dorotéia's, but I thought you would enjoy them. And who knows whether they'll have them, wherever we go. Did they have them in America, when you were a baby?"

My stomach rumbled at the smell. "I don't remember."

She arched an eyebrow, smiling. "You know that's a lie."

She kept smiling as I devoured them. She waited until I was licking my fingers clean to speak again.

"I was thinking we might go to America."

"Why would we? I have nothing there."

She shrugged. "We have nothing anywhere. We don't have to stay there forever. We can go anywhere you want to go, once we're gone from here."

I loved the thought of being gone, being somewhere else, being anywhere else. I loved the thought of being with Otávia, and of having the world and the rest of our lives before us.

"America, then. The first ship we can find."

We set out for the harbor. When Otávia asked a man about the destination of the first ship we encountered, he glared at us. "No women." The second man made a lewd gesture, and I had to grab Otávia's hand to keep her from slapping him, even as I reeled at the shock of such rude treatment. The third would not even speak to us.

After two more failures, Otávia insisted we needed a break. We hiked up the shore until we found a sun-bleached log in a quieter place, perching on it to share a chunk of melon, Otávia peeling and slicing with a sharp knife she had removed from its hiding place in her dress. She caught me staring at the blade.

"The world is going to be tough for you, Maré."

"What is that supposed to mean?"

She shook her head and handed me the last bite of melon.

"Nothing. Let's get back to work. We're looking for a ship to America—so we need to find an American captain. It's about time you put your English to some use."

Back among the sailors I breathed deeply through my nose, held Otávia's hand, and began asking everyone we encountered if they spoke English. My initial entreaties were met with more glares and nasty words, but finally we found a young boy carrying a length of rope who grinned widely, revealing missing front teeth, before replying, "American?" At our enthusiastic response, he bolted, gesturing for us to follow.

He scrabbled through the maze of the harbor despite the weight of the rope, and we hurried to keep up with him. Even as the ache reappeared in my hips and my lungs burned, it felt good to run. He led us to a tangle of sailboats, then to a large one painted sky blue, the name *Margaret* in bright white letters across its hull. The boy jumped aboard, pounding at the door of the cabin, shouting "Sir! Sir!" until the door creaked open and a man appeared.

His wavy, ruddy hair fell past his crooked ears; his eyebrows were wispy, his cheeks hidden behind a beard, his furrowed brow tanned by the sun. But I knew my father's face.

A crowd of whales simmers and swirls, their chorus of whistles and clicks resounding through the sea. In the center a rusty cloud of blood disrupts the jewel-blue ocean. A tail emerges, disappears, reappears; a slack, supple body follows. A baby is born. The granddaughter.

Her skin is a swirling blend of soil-brown and oyster-gray, barred with bolts of white, still creased from her curl in the womb. The oval of her opaline head is unmarred. Her flukes droop like late-summer petals, not yet strong enough to swim. She stretches her mouth wide and feels the flow of water against her tongue.

Her mother slides her nose across one silky side, pushes the dome of her head beneath the lithe ribbon of her child. The others join, jostling the little body to wake, to move, to wave in the water.

The granddaughter releases her first sound, a cry like a thin tree bending in the wind. A clatter answers, a cacophony, a symphony she will learn to imitate as she grows, babbling at first until her patterns grow clearer, until she can speak her name and her mother's and her clan's.

The great form of her grandmother passes above, a silhouette against the glare of sun. It is time to go up.

Her mother lifts her again, her great-aunt urges with a gentle nudge, her cousin nips the soft tip of her tail to drive her skyward. The crowd boils beneath her, pushing up, up, up.

She breaks the surface with a gush, white rivulets rushing from her sides, her blowhole stretching as her lungs inflate, as she takes her first breath beneath the endless sky.

Part Four

ANTONIA

Florence, 1900

Chapter 17

THE DAY I learned about Ishmael, Grandfather asked if I wanted to go for a walk and get breakfast. Mama had already left for work and I was supposed to be conjugating Italian verbs, so I told him I'd better ask Tia. He waved the idea away like a fly. "No need to interrupt her," he said. "We'll bring her back a pastry. She'll like that."

I couldn't argue. Tia Otávia always loved something unexpected, hard as she was to surprise, and I knew she was focused on her writing. Grandfather and I had always liked to take walks in the morning, and he seemed well enough. So I said yes.

He waited until we were in the street to announce that he didn't want to go to our usual neighborhood bakery. Mumbled something about their bomboloni being too dry. He strolled off in the opposite direction, thumping the cobblestones with the cane he'd started using. It didn't take me long to catch up with him, even though his stride was twice mine. Soon we were out of sight of the apartment, the bells of the Duomo ringing at our backs, heading away from the heart of the city.

We'd lived in Florence nearly a year, and I was sure I knew every street within a half mile of our apartment. I was good at finding my way in unfamiliar places. And pretty much everywhere was unfamil-

iar. We were always in a new city, a new neighborhood. I was born
in Boston but we moved to Europe before I could walk. We'd lived
in seven countries, eleven cities. A flock of flats and apartments and
rooms. Mama said we could go where we pleased, but I'd noticed how
she never seemed pleased to be in any place for long. She said we were
made to move. She could teach Latin or Greek or English anywhere.
Grandfather could find a newspaper or magazine to edit for. Tia could
write her plays. All I could do was follow along.

As I followed Grandfather through Florence, I noticed he'd managed to find a street I'd never been down before.

"Where was it you wanted to go, Grandfather?" I asked.

"Oh, somewhere new. Somewhere interesting, I think you'll find."

I was thirteen, old enough to know there was something he wasn't
telling me. Old enough to guess that he was probably too sick to be
wandering around. Young enough to want to go, anyway. He took his
time along the wider streets, pointing out pottery and fancy dresses
in shopwindows and nudging me to practice my Italian by reading
signs. He turned down alleys and shuffled up stairwells. We must
have seen a dozen places with baskets stuffed with pastries, but he
passed them all by. Once I was so distracted admiring a glistening
display of marzipan fruits I almost missed Grandfather turning onto
a narrow pathway nearly hidden in the shadow of a church.

I was old enough to know better than to whine. But I was getting
hot and hungry.

"Nearly there, Annie, my love," Grandfather kept saying.

The sun glared from the bare blue sky. Sweat was starting to drip
down my shoulders when we entered a piazza with no streets going
out but the one we came in on. A fountain with four lions roaring
toward the four directions dribbled out a narrow stream of water.
Grandfather glanced around. I spotted a dim shopwindow, an open
door releasing the smell of yeast.

"Oh, splendid," he said.

The bomboloni were fresh, light, crusted with a thin layer of sugar like frost on a puddle. Grandfather knew I'd make a mess inside the café, so we sat on the rim of the fountain to eat them.

"How'd you hear about this place?" I asked, my mouth stuffed with pastry.

"Now, I never said I'd heard of it before," he said. "I only said I wanted to go somewhere new."

"Then how'd you know how to get here?"

A smile stretched across his cheeks. They'd gone thin a few months before. Haggard. But they were pinker, healthier, than I'd seen in months. He brushed the sugar off his hands.

"To tell you the truth, Annie, I had no idea where I was going. None whatsoever. That the bomboloni materialized is a pleasant stroke of luck for us both."

I glanced around the piazza. It was empty except for a small band of pigeons waiting to clean up our crumbs. A fat yellow cat basked on the warm stones of the street. Someone was whistling from an upper floor, but I couldn't see where. I was old enough to know we were lost.

Grandfather patted my shoulder before I could say anything. He always could read whatever I was feeling, no matter how well I hid it on my face.

"Don't fret. We will make it home in plenty of time for lunch."

"How are we supposed to make it home? We were walking for an hour!"

He rested his chin on his hands, his hands on his cane, his cane on the fountain. I could tell he was more tired from the journey than he was willing to let on. He leaned toward me.

"Do you remember the albatross?"

"What does that have to do with anything?"

"Be patient and you'll see. Do you remember?"

How could he want me to be patient when we were about to spend another half the morning trying to find our way home? If we ever made it home at all? But I supposed it was better to indulge him than start to panic.

"Tia told me about it once, I think. Something about a marionette at a street fair when I was little."

"When we were living in Lyon. You were three." He ran his hand through his hair. His forehead wrinkled as he called up the details. "You had on a red dress. It should have been so easy to follow you in the crowd. But we were enchanted by that bird on its strings and wires. Do you remember?"

An image leapt into my mind. The marionettist making an albatross dance through the sky, dipping its wings in the breeze. It snapped its beak. Bobbed its head. I remembered how badly I wanted to stroke its silky feathers. How I followed the marionettist into the crowd at the end of his show.

"Your mother thought you were with me, and Tia thought you were with your mother, and I thought you were with your tia," Grandfather said. "And we found each other all at once, and realized we all were wrong. You were gone."

He let the statement hang in the air. Trying to draw me further into the story.

"I'm not sure this is a good time to get sentimental about being lost," I said.

His laugh was edged with a wheeze. "These days, I find I get sentimental all the time. But I don't mean only to recall a memory of my own. I want you to think a bit. You didn't stay lost after you followed the albatross, tiny little thing though you were. Go on, see if you can remember what you did."

I closed my eyes and hints of the moment fell into place. The flurry of carts and people. The streets cluttered with booths. The marionettist stopping to buy a meat pie and sitting beneath a tree. Twirling the bird into a still pile of feathers, snuffing out its magic. I wasn't frightened, only disappointed. I realized I was alone, so I turned back to the street and walked back the way I'd come. The path was as clear to me as a line on a map. In the square where I'd first seen the albatross, my family rushed to me, hands and voices shaking.

"I didn't know why you were so scared. I never was lost," I said.

My eyes were still squeezed shut, but I felt Grandfather lean toward me.

"I knew exactly where to go. I knew where I had been."

"Yes. Yes, that is what I thought." His voice was barely a whisper.

"In the same manner, you will take us home today. Then I will need to rest and gather my thoughts. Tonight, I have to share with you something I have kept to myself for many years. A mission for you, my dear. And it begins with a story your mother has forbidden."

~~~~~~

I CARRIED THAT word with me like a stone the whole way home. *Forbidden.* Grandfather was right that I could get us back without a problem. It took less time than I'd thought, too, even following the odd path he'd taken. Every time I thought I wasn't sure where to turn, he told me to stop thinking. Just know. And I'd find the way again, imagining the city like a map. In the moments I stopped worrying about finding the path, I remembered the word. *Forbidden.*

Mama was a person who kept secrets, I knew. She didn't like other people knowing too much about our family. She always had some story or another to tell about who my father had been, who Tia was, where we'd come from. I knew the truth of all that, of course. And I understood why she didn't want other people to. But until Grandfather said *forbidden,* I didn't know she'd kept anything from me.

The word grew heavier and heavier as the day went on. We stopped down the street from our apartment to buy bread and prosciutto. Ate lunch with Tia, who was pleased with the pistachio cornetto I had brought from the distant bakery. Grandfather told a funny story about something I'd done as a little girl, entirely unrelated to the day. He winked at me when Tia wasn't looking and excused himself to his study to rest. He stayed there after Mama came home. Through dinner. By the time we all retired to our rooms, the idea that my mother had hidden something from me, lied to me, forbidden me to know something, felt tied to my neck, dragging me toward the ground.

I found Grandfather awake at his desk, writing on the satiny paper he reserved for letters. His hand moved slowly. The loops and curves that had once come easily to him had become exhausting. I attempted to read the words as I tiptoed toward him, trying not to break his focus. All I caught was *Mara has spent her life running from every memory of her mother* before he folded the pages together and turned to me.

Of course I was impatient to learn the forbidden story. But his appearance disrupted me. He didn't look ruddy and bright as he had that morning. He didn't have the spirit he'd had to hide how tired he was. I could see his lower eyelids sagging, a thin line of red. His cheeks gone from thin to hollow. He lifted his lips into a smile I knew was genuine. For me.

"You know that I am very ill," he said.

I'd known for a long time. It stung to hear it said out loud. I was old enough to know that death followed everyone around like a darting sparrow. No one wanted to admit they could see the tips of its wings. But everyone could.

I nodded, feeling the burn that comes before tears crawling up my throat.

He braced himself against his desk and stood. Slowly moved to the high-backed green leather armchair we always kept in his study, one of the few things we took with us from place to place. When he was settled, he tilted his head against the wing of the chair. He'd always been a tall man, but for a minute he seemed smaller. Fragile even. He motioned for me to sit at his feet, as I had many times before.

"A man in my situation tends to review his life. His triumphs and failures. I have done uncommon things in my life, to be sure. But I cannot ignore that I have made many mistakes."

I slid closer to the chair. When I was little he would pat my hair while he talked, but I'd grown too tall. He rested his long fingers on my shoulder.

"You know I searched many years for your mother after she was lost at sea, and I've shared with you the best of the places I went in that search."

I loved his stories of watching dancers in Japan in their winglike kimonos, plucking bananas from trees in Tahiti, climbing the mast of a ship and looking out over nothing but green water. He'd always portrayed it as a grand expedition, a noble voyage. Maybe the forbidden story was something more scandalous. Pirates. A beautiful maiden on an island somewhere.

"I thought I had many years left to share the rest, but it seems I do not."

He reached down, grabbing my hands. I could feel his pulse through the skin of his palms.

"I tried hard to confuse you this morning. I walked until I was sure we were lost, then walked further until I spotted the bakery. But you took us home. Even on streets where I'd sought to distract you, you took my hand and you knew the way."

I couldn't deny it. Even if I didn't know what to do with that fact yet.

"I am sure now of what I believed about your remarkable perception, and it is more astonishing than I had even imagined. I wish I had noticed it sooner. I think you can see what I need you to. I think you can find what I never could."

His voice was eager, but something else I couldn't quite read. Reckless? Afraid? Bile rose hot in my chest. What did the albatross, the bakery, his journey all those years ago have to do with something Mama had forbidden?

"But you found Mama."

He gripped my hands tighter. "She was not all I sought. I think you can understand if you see it—and I think you can see it. Close your eyes, Annie. Can you see where I've been?"

I closed my eyes. All I could think of was the rattle of his breath in his ribs.

"Imagine it, Annie. Before Florence, we lived in Vienna. Before Vienna, Frankfurt. You know the path. Follow it."

I imagined the globe we kept in the parlor, a gift from a museum curator whose sons my mother had tutored. A globe so big my arms couldn't wrap around it, held up by wrought-iron rings. Hand-painted continents floating on seas of pale blue. I'd adored it for as long as I could remember. Spent hours staring at it. I knew the shape and color of every country so well, I could pick up the globe in my mind and spin it, exploring the world.

I felt Grandfather's hands, dry and warm, so much larger than mine. I imagined us in the third-story apartment in Florence, as if I'd lifted off into the sky. The streets and buildings of the city swirled together as I rose higher, melting into the green shape of Italy on the globe. I followed our path backward: Florence, Vienna, Frankfurt. Before that, Brussels, Madrid, Seville. Berlin, Zurich, Milan, Lyon. Paris, where we first arrived on the continent. Scenes of each city buzzed across my brain. Churches and train stations, bridges and gardens, the door to each flat, my mother standing in each doorway.

I imagined us floating back across the Atlantic, a voyage I'd been far too young to remember. The only time I'd ever crossed the ocean. Back to Boston, where I was born. I knew Grandfather, Mama, and Tia had come there from a tiny corner of Brazil, so I imagined the route to the south. When I began to waver over the Caribbean, I told myself to remember the albatross. The bakery. How I had found my way back. I didn't have to know. Only follow. Only see.

His path broke open before me. Before Brazil, Boston. Before Boston, England. A wild journey unspooled: A patch of islands in the north, Scotland and Holland, Cairo and Cádiz, Singapore and Sri Lanka, rushing back in time and around the globe. Okinawa, the Aleutians, Fiji, New Plymouth, a dozen ports and islands in between. A long delay in Lima, reached from Valparaíso, the Falklands, Buenos Aires, Barbados. Back to Boston, Amherst, and Northampton, until

Grandfather's path blinked out at his birth. I opened my eyes and gazed straight into his.

"I saw it. I saw it all."

"I knew you would."

He looked at me as if I were diamonds or rubies, had he been a man who adored such things. As if I were a being of pure light.

"I searched nearly fourteen years for your mother. I would have searched a thousand years more." His words came quickly, breathlessly. "But I never would have found her at all if I hadn't exhausted myself, if I hadn't surrendered and gone home. Do you remember the story? There was a letter from a priest waiting for me at the address of my old office, having arrived mere months after I had left, begging whoever read it to tell whatever was left of the Sweet family that Mara lived. No one realized what a miracle the envelope held, and so it remained unopened until I returned. I never would have gone to Brazil without that letter. And why not? Look for it, Annie. You can see it."

I closed my eyes once more. Thought of his whole route again, like bright lines on the globe. Crossing oceans, seas, bays, straits, gulfs. Bouncing from port to port, island to island. The way seemed random at first, until I saw. There was some sense to it. Some pattern.

"You weren't looking for Mama just anywhere. You were following someone."

"Yes," he rasped. "Yes. You can finish the part of my journey I never could. You can fix what I have broken. Your mother thinks she can leave him in the past, as if he had nothing to do with all that happened. She made me promise to forget about him, as she has tried to. I tried to respect her wishes, but what have I to lose? I believe you can find him. You must find Ishmael."

~~~~~~~

I WISH THAT everything had been easy after that. That we'd stayed up deep into the night, plotting a path. Making a plan. That I'd learned everything he knew about Ishmael in the days to come. He would have drawn me maps, left me names, explained secret histories. He would have unveiled all my mother's lies, and all his own. But instead he gathered me to his chest with trembling arms and whispered that he was tired. I let him sleep. In the morning I found he was gone.

Chapter 18

MAMA LIT CANDLES for Grandfather at Santa Croce after we buried him. Tia shut herself in their room to write words she refused to share. I hated them for it. I hated how they could do something, when all I felt was emptiness. The unfilled spot at the table. The quiet in his study. The stillness where he had brought so much motion. I didn't cry or rage or think of him wistfully. I just felt nothing.

I lay in my bed in my clothes all afternoon. All night, wide awake. Thinking about what I should do with all that had happened the day he died. Grandfather's excitement, his strangeness, couldn't have been for nothing. I had to come up with some sort of plan. I had to fulfill the mission he'd left. I knew he wanted me to find someone named Ishmael, someone associated with my mother's terrible shipwreck as a baby. And I knew, as he had shown me, that my sense of where I'd been in the world was bigger and stranger than I'd ever understood. But how were those things supposed to fix something about my family I didn't even know was wrong? He'd handed me two keys and no lock. No clue even as to what the lock might look like or where it might be.

Sometime after midnight, when my mind was still numb and my body was starting to feel too heavy to ever get out of bed, I remembered. The paper he'd been writing on when I walked into his study, just before he'd asked me to track his journey and told me about Ishmael. *Mara has spent her life running from every memory of her mother.* That line made the few details I knew stack themselves into sense. Mama had been with her mother, my grandmother, on that ship in the storm. She didn't like to talk about it, but I knew that much of the story. And if Grandfather thought chasing Ishmael would lead him to his family, that meant my grandmother had been chasing Ishmael, too.

I felt pity for Mama. I thought of her as a little girl in a bonnet, curled in the corner of a bunk in a ship, being dragged away from Grandfather to search for someone she'd probably never known or heard of. Or had she? Grandfather didn't say who Ishmael was. He didn't tell me nearly enough. And if Mama hated Ishmael so much she didn't want Grandfather to talk about him, how on earth was finding him supposed to fix something? I felt a bolt of anger at Grandfather for acting as if I could solve problems he couldn't. A wave of guilt followed. I couldn't be angry with him, alive or dead.

And then I thought again of the letter he'd been writing. Of course. He hadn't left me with nothing. It had to contain some sort of explanation, some sort of instruction. I jumped up and sped through the dark apartment, my bones buzzing with fresh energy.

The letter was not in the middle of his desk, where I'd seen him place it the night before. I scoured the surface. When I didn't find anything, I searched the shelves and drawers. Everything looked in its place. Anyone else would never have guessed Grandfather's belongings had any order to them at all. The desk was cluttered with pens and pencils, blotted with ink, and dotted with scraps of paper. He'd refused to get a typewriter, though he'd worked with people who raved about them. Plenty of things in his desk had nothing to do with work. A collection of smooth stones we'd picked up on walks in the woods. An empty tobacco tin full of keys to places we'd lived over the years. The dried husk of an orange. But among them, no letter. My hope gushed out as quickly as it had flowed in, leaving me empty again.

I curled into Grandfather's chair and wished I were tall enough to tilt my head against its top wing, as he had. Instead I leaned into the creases, smelling the remnants of his pipe smoke and pencil shavings. I closed my eyes and imagined that he was there. He was always trying to get me to see patterns in things. The arc of a harrier skimming the top of a distant wheat field. The perfect angles and symmetry inside a cathedral. The rhyme scheme of a poem.

A realization lodged in my throat. Mama didn't want to remember her mother, so she didn't want to remember Ishmael. So much so that she forbade me to learn about him. So much so that she must have stolen Grandfather's letter so I couldn't find out any more.

Or maybe I'd just missed it. I hopped back up and opened a drawer I'd already searched.

"Looking for something?"

I choked on my own breath at the sound of Tia's voice. I hadn't heard her sit down behind me. The way she asked the question, I knew she already knew what I was looking for. Which meant I was right about Mama stealing the letter.

My gut told me to shout at her, to holler until Mama woke up, to gather up all my emptiness and disappointment into rage and let it all out on them. But something stopped me. A little whisper to slow down. Find the path. Tia and Mama shared everything, but sometimes they disagreed. Sometimes I'd overhear her telling Mama not to hold so much back. Not to worry so much. Maybe I could get her to see that I was old enough to handle whatever it was Grandfather had written in that letter. Old enough to carry out the mission he'd given me.

"I am looking for Grandfather's letter he left for me," I said.

I pulled myself up to my full height, attempting to imitate Mama's regal way of lifting her chin and squaring her shoulders. The way she always talked to employers and landlords.

"I'm sorry, Antonia," Tia said. It was already too late. She'd come into the study to say these exact words. "It's not here."

I lost all my bearing and slumped into the hard wooden desk chair.

"Could I tell you a story?" she asked.

I laughed as sharply as I knew how, imitating the way Tia sounded when she couldn't believe something. I loved her stories, but they were always silly and bizarre and never had much of a point. She said she used to tell stories that meant something but had grown tired of trying so hard. Lately her plays, at least what she was willing to let me read, were full of talking trees and interplanetary visitors and women who could fly and control the weather and turn into fish, and without any apparent plot.

"It wouldn't be the story I wanted," I said.

"Of course not. No story ever is, precisely. Not for you, not for anyone."

Her voice was gentle. When I looked over at her I saw she was sitting with her hands spread open, warm and soft. I was too big to climb into her lap. Growing like a wild vine, she liked to say. But still I wanted to. I wanted to beg her to tell me everything she could about Ishmael, to explain why Mama kept that story secret, to convince Mama to let me know everything. At least to give me the letter back. To let me have something, so I wouldn't go back to feeling nothing. Instead I curled into my chest, trying to fit my whole body into the desk chair.

As I pressed my forehead against my legs, I felt her surround me. Her hands stroked my hair. Her breath filled my ears.

"Some stories should never be told. But most simply aren't," she whispered into my shoulder. "In this case, I'm not the one who gets to choose. For something closer to the story you want, I suggest you ask your mother."

I stiffened. I wouldn't. I couldn't. Mama would probably try to forbid me from speaking of Ishmael ever again, for the rest of my life. And how could I possibly respond if she did?

Tia stepped backward, sliding her hands to my shoulders. "I know I can't force you to do anything," she said. "You're as much my child as

hers in that way. Consider the idea at least. I can't promise you it will
be the easiest route, but it will be the best. Talk to her."

I felt the urge to nod. Try to pretend I might take her advice. But
I knew better. She'd see right through me. I dropped my face back to
my kneecaps and listened as her footsteps crossed to the door. I heard
the squeak of the doorknob, but not the rush of the opening door.

"If you're interested in cleaning up his desk," she said, her voice
light again, "don't forget those little drawers in the upper portion.
They're so easy to miss."

I could barely hold myself in the chair as I heard the door
swing shut.

~~~~~~~

I FOUND AN object wrapped in black velvet in the very back of a
narrow upper drawer. I'd never really explored the drawers before, as
Tia had hinted. After watching Grandfather stuff receipts and half-
finished lists into them for years, I didn't realize they were worth
it. But I knew I'd unearthed a treasure when I pulled out the scrap
of fabric shrouding something cool and solid. I couldn't risk opening it where Mama might sneak in and see me. Especially when Tia
had practically told me where to find it. I shoved it up my sleeve and
hustled to my room,

I yanked the velvet back and let what was inside tumble onto
my quilt. It was a tooth. I could tell that much right away. I'd never
seen a tooth so big, and at first I couldn't fathom what animal it had
come from. It was an ivory spike, widest at its middle, tapering to a
rounded end. I picked it up and felt the scrape of something on the
bottom side. When I turned it over, a whale stared out at me, engraved
in thin, dark gray lines. Simple, but not crude. A few delicate strokes
suggested muscle, blubber, and bone. An arch and circle formed an
eye, staring out at me.

I thought of reading Grandfather's path around the world, of navigating across Florence, of finding my way back from the albatross.

I imagined the moment I'd drawn the tooth from the desk drawer. Imagined it sitting there in the dark. Rattling around in a box of Grandfather's writing supplies as we moved from city to city. I felt it cross the ocean with us. I followed it back and back. Grandfather had carried it through every mile of his journey around the world, but their paths diverged in Boston. The tooth skittered around Massachusetts, with a few pauses. It crossed seas, rarely stopped on land for long. It paused again on an island, tiny and remote, where the tooth had become art. Near where, in a swell out of sight of shore, the tooth had been separated from its whale. I couldn't know anything about the creature, but I followed its loops and whorls. Its determined drives and languid rests. Thousands and thousands of miles, through wild and distant seas. I slowed as the path drifted to the heart of the Atlantic. To the warm, turquoise water where the whale was born.

The waves faded. I was back in my slope-ceilinged room, surrounded by the creaks and cracks of our old building and the lingering smell of fried mushrooms and my mother's perfume. I turned the tooth over again in my hands. Tia couldn't possibly have known what, exactly, she was pointing me toward. The tooth was a perfect map of Grandfather's travels, in his absence. And I'd already figured out how it would help me find Ishmael.

I sank into the tooth's path again and again, until I was sure. Grandfather said he'd gone back to Boston after giving up on chasing Ishmael. The last leg of his journey before returning across the Atlantic was a loop. He had spent some time in London before crossing the North Sea to a jagged clump of islands, which I knew only by the tidy script on Mama's globe: *Faroe I.* A brief stop on a scrap of land between two long inlets. Then back to London and, within days, to Boston. It wasn't difficult to construct a plausible story. If Grandfather spent months in London, he must have followed some trail of clues about Ishmael while he was there. Those clues led him to the Faroe Islands. But Ishmael was gone again when Grandfather arrived.

If I could get myself to London, I could follow Grandfather's tracks. The realization that I could see and make sense of paths was so new, but I was confident I could do whatever I needed to. I had no idea of the multitude of stumbling blocks the world could drop in my way, or of all the ways I could knock myself off the trail. I was certain I could use the tooth to go everywhere Grandfather went. It wasn't that long ago he'd been there. Not much more than thirteen years. People would remember him. Since he'd carried it so diligently with him, the tooth could even be proof of who I was and what I was looking for.

I fell asleep with the tooth resting on my chest. I dreamed I remembered what it was like to cross the ocean, to float like a feather on endless water.

~~~~~~

IN THE WEEKS and months after Grandfather's death, we started to fill the spaces he'd left. We spread out without meaning to, finding new ways to occupy furniture and rooms so it wasn't so obvious that someone was missing. On warm days we opened the windows and let the smell of him float away. I helped Tia and Mama sort through the rest of his desk, never saying a word about the tooth or the stolen pages. But what filled up the emptiness most was the knowledge that I could carry out his final wish. I had a plan.

I went to the Santa Maria Novella train station and spun a tale for a man at the booth about a rich grandmother in London and a mother too sick to travel to ask for help. The ticket was more than I had money for at first, but I started saving every coin I could find. I even took a few from Mama's pockets. I figured she deserved it for stealing from me.

I practiced following paths, too. I'd begun to think of the ability Grandfather helped me uncover as a sense. I didn't share Mama's skill for languages, but I remembered how she'd pointed out that the Italian verb *sentire*, born from Latin, could mean *smell* and *hear* and *feel*. Once I accepted my ability as part of my body, it was almost as effortless as using my eyes or ears. Without Grandfather to accompany me on errands, Mama and Tia let me venture out into Florence alone more often, with strict orders not to go too far. I didn't listen. I often wandered with my eyes closed, dodging carriages and grumbling pedestrians, until I was thoroughly lost. It was never difficult to find my way back to where I wanted to be.

I tested my sense on objects, pressing my hands against the stone of statues and churches and tracing them to their origins deep within the earth. When I decided to attempt an animal, the pigeon I grabbed pecked me so hard I dropped it before I could sense anything. But I wrapped my bleeding thumb in my skirt and focused on the fleeing bird. For a split second I could see the path it had followed that morning, chasing insects across the cobblestones. I kept practicing on the whole flock, scattering pigeons across the piazza. Reaching out to feel the countless spirals and jags of their lives.

I stretched my sense until it felt strong. I could understand the path of anything I touched in moments, of anything near me if I slowed down and tried, like focusing on a spire in the distance. Soon I'd learned the routes and habits of everyone in our neighborhood: booksellers and milkmen, butchers and artists, fancy ladies and grubby children, the rats that scurried into the crypts and the priests that stood above them. I knew each bridge and stairwell and alleyway of Florence as well as I knew the globe in our house. Soon, I was sure, I would know London just as well.

But Mama had plans of her own. One night after dinner, she brought out a box of cookies and didn't blink when I filled my plate. The almond and anise distracted me from her expectant look. When my mouth was full, she reached across the table and took Tia's hand.

"We have decided it is time for us to move on from Florence," she said.

I stopped crunching.

"I have begun searching for employment elsewhere."

I swallowed too soon, a lump of dry cookie scraping my throat. "You have? Where?"

"We haven't decided on any one place yet," Tia jumped in. "But we have plenty of options."

She raised her eyebrows at me, which I knew was meant to be a message to go along, be happy. But I couldn't let Mama ruin my plans. I wouldn't let her take away my mission from Grandfather. The only thing I had of my own. I wouldn't just follow.

"I suppose I don't get any say in those options. Are you even going to tell me what they are?"

I spit the words at them, dipping into my well of anger. Mama jutted out her chin but didn't try to cut me off.

"Of course you won't. Because what would it matter where I want to go? Let's go to Norway, Antonia will be fine! We haven't lived in Turkey yet! How about Cairo? Iceland? What does it matter? All I'll get to do anywhere we go is finish my lessons and run little errands and be good and quiet while you get to make choices and I don't."

Tia looked exhausted. I could see Mama working to keep her face steady, her eyes jumping between confused and furious.

"Where on earth is this coming from, Antonia?" Mama said.

"Seven countries! Eleven cities!" I shouted. I suddenly hated all those cities. Every block I walked and never went back to. Every beautiful building I barely got to know. "Did you ever ask me about any of them? No. So why would you start now? You don't care what I want. You don't care about me."

Mama's face froze, no longer conflicted. "That is enough. Enough. We have given you the world. And I care more about you than anything in it."

I heard the words, but they felt walled up behind cold, hard stone.

"If you cared about me, you wouldn't take my things without asking. And you wouldn't drag me places I don't want to go."

"You do not understand what you are talking about," Mama said. Flat and firm.

I saw Tia squeeze her hand. "We were going to include you in the decision, as you so rudely assumed we would not, but you have proven you are still a child. I will tell you where we are going, and you will come with me."

She slipped her palm from Tia's grasp, stood, and soundlessly swept into the kitchen. I hated her for being graceful even when storming out of a room. I hated how she could cut off any conversation, no matter what anyone else wanted to say.

Tia stood to go after her. She paused to toss an exasperated look at me. "Good Lord, the both of you," she muttered.

I sat and let all my emotions boil in my head. Why shouldn't I just gather my money and go to London right there and then? Even though I was short on funds, I might be able to persuade the ticket seller with a few desperate tears. But I'd memorized his schedule, and he wasn't working that evening. At least the night would give me time to pack. I shoved as much of my clothing as I could into a carpetbag from Grandfather's room I'd stashed away. The only object I was careful with was the whale's tooth. I wrapped it back in its velvet and tucked it into my coat pocket, where I could sense it anytime I wanted. Everything else I would figure out in London.

I forced myself to pause and breathe, to settle my thumping heart so I wouldn't give myself away with a slammed door or stomp on a loose floorboard. Mama's dismissal echoed in my brain. *You have proven you are still a child.* A whisper of my own doubt chased it. I was nearly fourteen, yet I could still be distracted by a box of cookies. I could return to any place I'd been and trace the paths of people and animals and things, but that was different from forging ahead into unknown waters.

But Grandfather had done exactly that to find Mama. And my grandmother had done the same to chase after Ishmael, whoever he was. Why shouldn't I?

Just after sunrise I slipped down the stairwell in my stockings and slid into my shoes in the foyer. Shut the building door so silently, someone passing in the street wouldn't have heard the click. I ran the whole way to the station with my eyes closed. Each cobblestone under my feet felt familiar. I knew my path.

The ticket seller ate up my whimpering. I wore my rattiest dress and stacked each coin on the counter as if it were precious. "Please, sir, my mother is dying." It helped that I still spoke Italian like a younger child. "You must let me go."

I felt triumph like a lightning bolt when he pulled a coin from his own pocket. He pointed me to the platform, though of course I already knew where it was. I had given myself only a few minutes to spare before the train departed. I hugged my bag to my chest and ran up the steps. In my seat, I shut my eyes tight and ran through my route across the continent. I let my mind spin away, imagining the room I would plead my way into when I arrived. The way I'd march through the streets pulling aside old sailors with my demanding questions, sensing their paths as they talked. Revealing the whale's tooth to gasps of awe and recognition.

And then I felt someone step into the row in front of me. Hovering without sitting. My mother's hand rested on my cheek and my eyes flew open. She stared straight into them, breathing sharply through her nose. For a moment, neither of us moved.

"London," she said. She pulled her hand away. "That explains your outburst. I suppose your poor grandfather never had the chance to tell you he was swindled there. He chased an illusion, and when he finally realized it, he went home. I refuse to lose you to the same foolishness."

I clutched my bag tighter and pretended to look out the window. She had to be lying. She couldn't possibly mean to say Ishmael wasn't even real.

"I do not wish to ride this train halfway across the continent and carry you home from there, but I will do so if I must."

I bit down on my lip to keep myself from snapping back at her.

"I do not wish to treat you like a child, Antonia, but you give me no choice. Give me the tooth."

My mouth dropped open. How did she know? How long had she known? My resolve melted. All this time, my secret plan had been a sham. A pathetic lie. I dug the tooth out of my pocket and let it flop from the velvet into her waiting palm. She held my hand the whole way home. I kept my eyes wide open.

Two months later she announced she had accepted a job in Idaho. I'd never heard of the place in my entire life.

Chapter 19

OF COURSE MAMA didn't let us leave through London. Of course she didn't say she refused to. She hauled me with her as, in flawless French, she arranged our trains to Le Havre and passage to New York with the Compagnie Générale Transatlantique. When I saw how much it cost, I understood how absurd it was to think I could get to London, stay in London, on my own with nothing but a pocketful of coins. I was powerless. A child, like my mother said. All I could do was protest by being surly and mostly silent. The salesman cheerfully inquired whether I was excited to travel on such a fine steamship. I said no.

We lived like monks for months to save up money for the trip. Mama and Tia started selling off our furniture and clothes. Mama'd never struggled to give things up when it was time to move on. And she said her new employer had assured her we'd be able to get everything we needed out in Idaho. I still refused to look the place up on a map. Even beyond our travel preparations, I felt like I was doing penance. Mama didn't let me go out on my own anymore. She hardly ever left me alone at all. When she had to leave the apartment, she left Tia as her proxy. I thought I might gain sympathy from Tia with deep sighs and penetrating stares. All she ever gave me in return were calm

smiles and suggestions of good books to read before we sold them. I
spent most of my time looking at the patterns in the floorboards and
wallpaper. Willing some grand idea for escape to appear.

The morning after Mama sold our globe to a fat old man, I tried
to walk right out the door without a word. Tia slipped between me
and the doorway.

"Do you think she sold it to hurt you?"

Glaring down at her, I realized I was finally taller than her. Tall
enough that I could push right past her, if I wanted to. But she shoved
her arms out to block the doorframe.

"Do you really?"

"She didn't even ask me."

"So you wanted to cart that thing across the Atlantic?"

"I wanted . . . I wanted her to ask me if I wanted to."

I squared my shoulders and took a step forward. Tia's nose almost
rested on my chin, but she didn't waver.

"I'm not a telegram boy," she said. "I'm tired of being the only
person in this family who will even attempt to have a simple conversation. But listen to me: I don't care how angry you are. You will get
on that train, and you will get on that ship, and you will go where
your mother goes, because it will destroy her if you do otherwise. Do
you understand?"

She said it with such conviction, I wanted to blurt out yes. Promise anything I needed to. I tensed my muscles and held my breath, trying to keep it in. Trying to prove to her that I wasn't so easy to topple.
But I could see how she remained so still, so steady, and I knew who
would win if I continued the battle of wills. I could barely handle having Mama lead me around like a disobedient dog. I wasn't willing to
become a prisoner to Tia, too. Whatever tense peace we had was better than that. I went back to staring at the floorboards, which decades
before had been carted to Florence from a single grove of trees on a
distant mountain. What good was it to know that? I was worse than
powerless. I had power, but it was useless.

~~~~~

I COULDN'T REMEMBER the first time we'd crossed the Atlantic, so I expected the sea to shape the whole of Le Havre. To take over the horizon, dwarfing buildings and cathedrals. To rival the sky. But I couldn't see it at all as the train rolled into the city. Le Havre seemed no different from any other place I'd been. The train station was like any other. Dusty and crowded and loud. I couldn't even tell which direction the ocean was when we gathered our luggage and made our way to our hotel. Mama claimed a headache and retired to the bedroom, leaving Tia and me to stare at each other in the tiny sitting room. The wallpaper was patterned with ruffled leaves.

I assumed Tia would use the opportunity to lecture me again about talking to Mama. But instead she said, "I'd like to walk to the harbor and see the ship." Like setting a slice of cake on the table to see if I'd take a bite. I said yes. I was too tired to fight. And I didn't want to sit there in silence all alone, no company but Mama's snores from the next room and my own disappointment.

The water of the port shimmered in the evening light. The SS *La Loire* was docked, bustling with workers preparing for the next day's departure. I could sense it was still fresh from the shipyards, having only made the voyage to New York and back once. The hull gleamed black as gulls swooped past. Two funnels, two masts, ready to sweep us across the Atlantic. I felt a stir of excitement, but squashed it. Tia kept trying to talk to me about what it was like on a ship, about all the new luxuries on the big ocean liners she'd read about. But I wasn't having it.

"What do you think?" Tia said. Another nudge of the cake and fork.

"It looks . . . serviceable."

She squawked at that, gripping her hat as she laughed. "Serviceable. I see. I suppose you'll be equally unimpressed if we walk to the beach, so we might as well get it over with."

We wound back through the city. I kept expecting to be hit with the scent of salt and fish, a sudden boom of surf. But the ocean snuck up on me. We crossed a busy street, and there it was. A strip of blue-green against the graying sky. It rose as we crunched across the stones, gaining whitecaps and the gentle shush of waves. It never got as big as I expected. My sight followed the misty line where water met uninterrupted sky. Even if I couldn't see it, I could tell the sea went on and on and on.

Tia sat, spreading her skirt out on the rocks, and pried off her boots. I'd seen her run around in bare feet in vineyards and meadows, but it was a shock to see her parade across the rocky shore. Right there in sight of the city.

"When I was a girl, I never went long without my feet in salt water."

My toes curled in my own boots as I watched her lift her hem and step into the surf.

"Your mother never liked the ocean, so I usually went when I needed to be alone. Or when she wanted me to leave her alone."

She grinned and turned to look out at the horizon. I stayed back. Watching her. Mama never wanted Tia to leave her alone anymore, from what I could tell. They were a pair, and wherever Mama dragged us, Tia was happy to follow. She never hesitated to dive into a new place. She was probably even looking forward to Idaho. I'd been just like her for most of my childhood, blindly eager to explore each new city. But the moment I wanted to do something other than follow, Mama treated me like a traitor. I didn't understand how she could ever have expected my desires to line up with hers forever.

Tia drew her fingers out of the water and waved at me. I didn't wave back. She turned and continued searching through the sand, slipping seashells into her pockets. She didn't care what I wanted, either. If she did, she wouldn't be trying to ply me into the water. Excite me about the ship. She would be fighting Mama to take me to London. She would give me the tooth back. She would never have let Mama take Grandfather's letter. She thought Mama would die if I ran away. What about what would happen to me if I was forced to come?

I spotted the body of a crab amid the sediment at my feet, its meat sucked out by birds. I imagined myself like it. Just a shell. I anchored myself in that feeling as we walked back to the hotel and readied ourselves for bed and the voyage to come.

Mama rose early, waking Tia and me by rummaging through her trunk and repeatedly changing her hat. Her headache seemed gone, but her mood hadn't improved a bit. She grumbled through the morning. Insisted Tia check the time on our tickets again, even though we all knew exactly when we needed to return to the port.

She'd reserved a second-class stateroom at midship. The best we could afford, where she was least likely to feel the sway of the ocean. I'd attempted to avoid all talk of the voyage, but it was impossible to miss how much she dreaded it. I always knew Mama preferred trains to boats and didn't want to have holidays at the seaside. I didn't realize that the water made her lose all sense of balance and direction. Tia comforted her loudly all morning as we dressed and packed. Assured her the larger ship would keep her from becoming as miserably ill as she had apparently been on our last crossing. Once I caught Tia staring right at me as she said it. As if I would pity Mama.

While the other travelers crowded onto the deck, we retreated below. Tia disappeared into the maze of the ship to ensure that a butler knew Mama would be taking limited meals in our room. Mama and I stayed behind. Once again I was staring silently into an unfamiliar space. I couldn't argue that Mama and Tia's investment was worth it. The stateroom was simple, but more luxurious than most hotels I'd stayed in. Two narrow beds with embroidered pillows and soft duvets. Brass lamps, molded ceilings, a polished oval mirror. A set of plush chairs around a round table. Mama took off her dress as soon as the door slid shut. She buried herself in bedding and rolled over to face the wall.

I lay down on the opposite bed. I didn't feel bad for her. I felt smug, thinking how she was willing to put herself through all this just to get to the next place on her list. London would have been a much shorter voyage.

Tia burst through the door, interrupting my thoughts before I could wallow in my arrogance much longer.

"Get out your best dress. The white lace."

"Mama sold it."

"She did no such thing. I put it in your trunk myself."

She pulled her own cabin trunk from beneath the bed where Mama lay. She rummaged through, popping up with a dress I'd never seen her wear before. Plum purple satin with gold trim.

"Don't lie there like a dead fish. We have to look presentable for dinner."

A wrench in my gut reminded me how long it had been since we had eaten that morning. The ship skipped luncheon during boarding, hosting an early dinner. No one had told me it would be so formal. I found the dress, struggling into the scratchy fabric while Tia pinned on her hat.

She waved me to the tiny dressing table. "Your turn. I've been practicing."

I shuffled over, picking at my braid. I supposed letting Tia twist knots into my hair was better than nothing. It was just that she never was much good at anything but my usual two long plaits.

"I did this style on your mother last week," she said.

I hadn't seen it. Whether because I was avoiding Mama or because she combed it right back out, I wasn't sure.

I flinched and winced through her work. The resulting pouf of hair on my head was slightly lopsided, but it almost seemed deliberate with my unruly mass of dark brown hair. I turned my head in the mirror. Wondered if people in the dining room might think I was a grown woman.

Mama didn't move when we left. My stomach fluttered as we ascended the grand staircase to the first-class dining room. I was sure we'd be turned away, but the tuxedoed man at the door winked as Tia swept past. The smugness I'd felt in the stateroom rushed back when I saw what Mama was missing. A domed stained-glass ceiling scat-ered diamonds of light across the deep violet carpet. Fresh flowers decorated every table. And the food! Mama had forced us to live on bread and beans for months. The menu listed consommé royale, pom-mes parisiennes, croquettes de homard, petits pois au beurre, asperges mousseline, filet de boeuf, and a dozen dishes more. Even with my terrible French, it was mouthwatering. The dessert list nearly out-paced the rest of the meal. Charlotte à la russe, bavarois au kirsch, tartelette au citron, mousse au chocolat, fromages, fruits, pralines. I always remembered the words for sweets. And there was something in English, an apple hedgehog, which turned out to be a stack of fruit and jelly wrapped in meringue and decorated with thinly sliced almond spikes.

I tucked into every dish like I really had been imprisoned. Each bite tasted all the better knowing that Mama couldn't enjoy it. Between my first and second glasses of mousse, I decided I would indulge in everything the SS *La Loire* had to offer. Make it my last hurrah. Forget Ishmael, forget London. Forget Mama, forget Idaho. Forget being a useless shell. I could pretend to be a rich girl on a glori-ous ship, living a life of pleasure, if only for a week.

"You seem to be feeling brighter," Tia said as she scraped meringue off her plate with her fork.

"I am," I said. I set my own fork down and leaned back in my chair.

A sudden lurch forced me up again. "I suppose the wind is pick-ing up."

Tia raised an eyebrow. "The wind?"

A lurch again. The room seemed to tilt. I grabbed my glass, expecting it to slide across the table. But it didn't move. The tilting turned to spinning. I tried to stand and clattered back down. China and silver skittered across the rich carpet.

I awoke to a flurry of concerned waitstaff. Tia frowned above me.

"Nothing to fret over. Only a touch of seasickness," she announced, then leaned in to mop my forehead with a damp napkin. "Yet another trait that runs in the family."

~~~~~~

IN THOSE MISERABLE days on the ship, I had no choice but to spend time with Mama. We'd been together almost constantly in the months since my attempt to go to London, but it had been far from companionable. Mama commanded, I pouted. In those long, nauseating hours on the SS *La Loire*, we couldn't do much but lie beside each other. We nibbled ginger biscuits and sipped water and covered our faces with cool cloths. Tia tried not to say much about her forays out of the room. When she was with us, she mostly scribbled in a notebook or read aloud to us. But I could smell gin and sugar and cigar smoke on her, and sense her path all over the ship. I knew she was managing to have a little fun on her own.

I lost track of time almost immediately. Our room had no windows, and Tia's coming and going had no pattern I could discern. I was too sick to try very hard. I woke up one morning or evening, wondering how far we'd gone, and realized I could sense it. Feel the ship's path like the tail of a comet. We were a little less than halfway across the Atlantic. Surrounded by nothing but water, as I'd dreamed of seeing. But the thought of climbing staircases and crossing decks, even standing up for more than a few minutes, felt terrible. I glanced over at Mama. Her eyes were closed, but she breathed like she was awake.

I asked the question before I could remember I wasn't speaking to her. "How come you went across in the first place, if you get so sick?"

She half opened an eye and cleared her throat. Her voice still came out a croak. "Went across?"

"The ocean. When I was a baby. You could have stayed in Boston. Or somewhere else that didn't require a ship."

"I wanted to go. As I do now."

The path I knew so well popped into my mind. Before all the

places we'd lived in Europe, she'd been across the sea twice before. But not because she wanted to.

"Was the sickness so awful when you were on your way to Brazil? And when Grandfather brought you back home?"

She glazed over, slipping into her mind. She was quiet for so long, I thought she wouldn't answer. I felt a surge of nausea. Then she spoke.

"When I was a girl, no. After your grandfather found us, yes. And even more so after you were born. The moment we left the harbor on our way to France, I vomited over the side of the boat."

I groaned. "Don't say it."

She wheezed out a little laugh. I was too weak not to smile in response. It was the kindest look I'd given her in months.

"I had so looked forward to France," she said. "I had a friend—do you remember our stories about Rosi?—she always talked about eating a French pastry, and how it was the most delicious thing in the world. Tia and I always wanted to go to France for pastry alone, when we were very small. When we were older, we read the tales of the kings and queens, and of the saints, Joan of Arc and Martin of Tours and Saint Radegund the princess. Otávia always liked Denis of Paris, carting around his own severed head."

We both laughed at that. Stronger this time. The throbbing in my temples that had plagued me since my ill-fated dinner faded. I had tuned her out for so long, I forgot how my mother's voice could soothe me.

"I was distraught when I became sick on the ship. I had thought love was enough to overcome my fear. Otávia and I had envisioned sailing the world, but the body knows what the mind resists."

She paused to yawn, but continued. "Paris made me forget my fears, for a while. When the boys I tutored went away to school in Switzerland, we planned to return to the United States—to Philadelphia, where your grandfather was offered an editorship at a newspaper. I tried not to reveal my panic to him or Otávia, but they both saw through me. So we stayed. And it turned out there was so much more for us all to see in Europe."

She smiled at me again, but closed her eyes. "I am afraid sleep remains my best remedy. I will tell you more later, if you would like."

I said I would. She drifted off. I stared at the cornices along the ceiling, thinking. Arguing with myself. I had formed so many of my beliefs around the idea that Mama dragged me around. Followed some whim wherever she wanted to go. But my wretched state had softened me enough to consider our path from her point of view. Hearing how she spoke of it, I realized how her own body had limited her choices. And how she'd had no choice at all in the first journey of her life, the crossing with her mother to Brazil. The crossing that stole her away from her father for her entire childhood, and separated her from her mother forever. There was more for us all to see, she'd said. Maybe she wasn't trying to force me to follow. Maybe she thought I was along for the adventure.

But she stole Grandfather's letter, a piece of me whispered. *She forbade him to tell you about Ishmael. She didn't want you to go to London to find him. She doesn't let you choose where you go at all.* I couldn't muster the energy I needed to be angry as I fell asleep. But I couldn't quite drown out that voice.

~~~~~

I TRIED TO hang on to my softness toward Mama. To enjoy our time in the stateroom like an oasis. When she felt well enough, I asked to tell me stories about our adventures in Europe when I was a b her memories of her own childhood with Tia in Brazil. All famili and comforting. If I didn't think about all she left out. And I managed not to, mostly, if only to cling to whatever good feelings broke through the constant swishing dizziness I felt on the ship. If only because I couldn't imagine how I'd turn back. Where I'd even go, if London was a false trail. If Ishmael might not even be real.

Some of our best conversations were about our destination. For the first time, I felt some eagerness to arrive. Mama said she hadn't thought of Idaho when she began looking for somewhere new to go. She'd hardly been thinking of the United States, but she kept encountering a multitude of positions at American schools and colleges, which had sprung up like daisies across the country in our absence. The University of Idaho had only been established a little more than ten years earlier, but the professor who hired her told her that students and faculty were coursing in. The city of Moscow, Idaho, was growing, too. Booming even. *"Moscow is a veritable citadel of education amongst the beauty and abundance of the West,"* Mama read to me from one of his letters. I pictured brick buildings and church spires against a clear blue sky. Snowy mountains in the distance. Something like Zurich, but with jolly American students strolling busy streets lined with tall, leafy trees. The sweet feel of solid ground under my feet.

I didn't see the ocean again until we reached New York Harbor. Only a glimpse as we hurried off the ship. I felt a fleeting sorrow for the sea, and all it turned out not to be. But mostly I was happy to be leaving the shore. From then on it was trains, blissfully boring. No wonder Mama preferred them. Without the nausea, I felt well enough to read the copy of *The Wonderful Wizard of Oz* Tia had bought me at the station. Mama and I held on to the unspoken peace we'd made on the ship, though her attention turned to discussing our plans with Tia. We had some money left after the stateroom and train tickets, and Mama would start teaching summer classes right after we arrived. We'd rented rooms but would buy additional furniture. Maybe a few extra comforts. I would need a mathematics tutor. Tia would teach me literature and history, but Mama would oo busy to instruct me in anything other than Latin. Maybe we vould hire someone to improve my French or Italian, too. Mama nd Tia would find friends among writers and artists, and perhaps I was old enough now to be brought along to evening events. We ld attend the theater and opera and dinner parties. Tia might nsider staging one of her plays. I stayed buoyed by their optimism as I watched endless miles of prairie rush by. As flat and wide as I'd imagined the sea.

I was relieved to be done with seasickness. But a new unsettling feeling seeped into me as our train entered Denver. I'd heard of Denver in magazines and from fellow travelers. While the snow-tipped Rockies were almost as impressive as the Alps and the land felt infinitely old, when I stretched my sense into the buildings outside the train window, every structure felt so young. Like someone had barged in and tossed the bricks together just moments before. The city was an infant compared to Florence, and it seemed so small. I hadn't realized there was much of anything west of it other than California.

I tried to dredge up a scrap of hope at our next-to-last stop. Idaho was so empty we had to pass right through its skinny panhandle, over to Spokane, Washington, to catch the train to Moscow. Spokane was smaller than Denver. Even newer on the surface. But I noticed well-dressed ladies streaming from a theater with electric lights. Gentlemen in suits tipping their hats from the seats of their carriages. Cream-bellied hawks skimming above rocky falls in the river that flowed through the city, a hint of the western beauty the professor had boasted about. There were men camped out near the river, but Tia had told me the area was full of miners and loggers and trappers, so I figured they liked to be outdoors. I had a shock when I looked out the window as we pulled away from the station and one of them grabbed onto the side. His head lurched in front of my window and his eyes locked on mine for a second. It wasn't that I'd never seen a man hop a train before. It was that in the brief glimpse I got of his life, I saw an endless circle, never settling. Never going farther than the reach of that one little train.

In my anger at Mama in Florence, I'd refused to learn where, on a map, we were going. On the ship, I'd been lulled enough by the dream of the place, and I hadn't asked. But I'd assumed Moscow would have most things in common with the other places we'd lived. The professor's letters Mama read me sure made it sound like it. I was certain it would be another big, old city. A cosmopolitan place, full of people. Probably along a river, almost certainly far from the sea. In America, in the West, but not so different from the places I'd had at least a little chance to love.

For the first time, I closed my eyes and envisioned where the land we were traveling through would be on my globe. So far from Florence. From Europe as a whole. I imagined the whole path of my life, and Idaho was so far from every stop. Just about as far as you could get from Boston and stay on the same continent, even. I thought back to the path of the whale's tooth, which I'd had time to memorize before Mama took it from me. The path Grandfather told me followed Ishmael. The path I'd attempted to follow when I ran away to the train, trying to flee to London. The path my mother had called foolish.

I saw it all. My mother had lied to me. This city was not some lucky spot plucked from a thousand choices. It was not some pleasant surprise she hadn't meant to look for. It was her only choice. I had tried to find Ishmael. Mama claimed he was an illusion, but she acted as if he were very real. Moscow, Idaho, was proof enough. My mother had tracked down a place on earth as far from anywhere Ishmael had ever been as she could find.

I squeezed my eyes shut harder to push back tears as the train lumbered over a hill. Sickly sweet saliva flooded my mouth. Tia's gasp captured all my feelings.

"Oh, Maré. Where have you brought us?"

Chapter 20

WE GAWKED OUT the train windows as we rolled past sparse houses and buildings, none older than Mama and Tia. The University of Idaho was a handful of structures up a muddy hill from the town. A single, cathedral-like central building stuck out as if it had fallen from the sky. Everything else was dusty timber and red brick. The whole city of Moscow, I thought, would probably fit inside Florence a thousand times. I didn't dare say so out loud. I looked for a river and found nothing but a spindly creek that followed the train tracks. Instead of mountains like the ones we had seen in Denver, I saw only a few pine-covered lumps among the grassy hills that dipped and rose like waves. I reached out to the land and sensed dirt laid down by wind, layer upon layer. And layers of people had surely settled and moved through here, but I could guess this little nowhere city was built by the newcomers. A rough veneer on top of something ancient.

Our landlady was as much a surprise as the landscape, though less dismal. She met us at the train station wearing an enormous bear-skin coat that was twice as old as she was. Mrs. Alfred Aster, as she introduced herself, couldn't have been more than five feet tall. Even Tia towered over her. But she strolled up like a giant. I caught a faint stink that must have been from the coat's thick, thatchy brown fur, shining in the sun. She tugged it around her shoulders even though there wasn't a bit of shade on the gritty platform. Silver hair poked out from under her peacock-blue hat.

"Judging by the looks of absolute bewilderment, I take it you are Margaret Sweet and family," she said. "Welcome to Moscow, on the glorious Palouse prairie." She pronounced Moscow with a long *o* instead of a rhyme with *now*, like Mama had been saying on the ship.

Mrs. Aster held out a hand, her glove the same color as the hat. Tia shook it. Mama just stood there and scowled.

"I would have sent a letter if I thought it had any chance of reaching you in time," Mrs. Aster said, sauntering over and giving my hand a firm press. She turned to face Mama. Tipped her head back to talk right at her. "If I'd realized Dr. Brighton was the man who hired you, I would have warned you right from the start. Bit of an exaggerator, that one. And long gone now, too."

"Long . . . gone?" Mama's voice drifted out dreamily, despite her stony face.

"Bound for San Francisco two weeks ago on the nose. I'd say he would have told you if he had a way to reach you, but he wouldn't have even if he had."

She grabbed my carpetbag. I expected her to bend under the weight, but she strode to her waiting wagon, shouting at the boy driving to go gather our trunks. We'd left them stacked on the platform where the porters had dropped them. Let the crowd waiting to board shuffle around us. The noise of the lumber mill flanking the station pounded into our skulls.

"Onward through the Cambridge of the West," Mrs. Aster announced once we'd all climbed into the wagon.

When no one laughed, she did so for us.

We rattled down Main Street, which as far as I could tell was the only street of significance in the whole town. And that was a stretch. Mrs. Aster's wagon climbed a hill that might have reminded me of Florence, if much of anything had been on it. A few spruces and aspens poked up. Otherwise the ground was covered in dry grass with spatters of mud from the road. I heard Mama let out a breath when we stopped in front of one of the bigger houses. It had a long, railed porch and tall windows. A white picket fence matching the bright white siding. Green trim to match the scrawny maples that lined the street. A runty, fluffy, black-and-white dog skipped around the side.

"Greet our guests, Magpie," Mrs. Aster said.

The dog sat and watched as we slumped in under the weight of our luggage. Her tongue lolled out like she was laughing at us.

"Your rooms are upstairs," Mrs. Aster said in the foyer. "The bathroom is through the kitchen. You'll be pleased to know I've invested in a flushing toilet."

"Thank you, Mrs. Aster," Tia said. I glared at her.

"I prefer quiet in the evenings. If you are up early, please let Magpie into the yard. I read the paper first thing in the morning, but after that you may have it until I need it for the fire. I own a good number of books, and you are welcome to them all." I'd already spotted the shelves stacked with well-worn volumes. "I imagine Dr. Brighton failed to mention we do not yet have a full-sized municipal library."

Mama looked like she was going to be sick again.

Mrs. Aster shrugged off the coat. The boy who'd been driving the wagon hung it on a rack in the corner of the parlor between two pink velvet couches. Mama, Tia, and I huddled just the same as we had on the train platform.

"It's not that bad around here," Mrs. Aster said. "Not as good as Dr. Brighton liked to sell it, but a decent place to be, even if you've got other choices. You've got work and a warm bed, and it's rhubarb season, if you like pie. Coming as far as you did, can't hurt to settle in and stay a while."

I heard a clunk. Mama had picked up her cabin trunk and was marching toward the stairs. She paused at the bottom.

"She's absolutely right," she said. "We meant to come here, and we are staying."

She couldn't possibly mean it. She'd been as fooled by the professor's letters as I was. Hadn't she? Even though I was certain she'd chosen a place far from Ishmael's path on purpose, she couldn't possibly be so dedicated to that notion as to actually make us live in this empty place. Couldn't it serve as a warning not to run away again? I would listen. Lesson learned forever, if only we could turn around.

I looked to Tia, praying she'd contradict Mama. Hoping she'd pivot and walk the other way. Take us right back to that train. Right back home, to any other home we'd had. But she shook her head and picked up her trunk. Followed Mama right up those stairs, sentencing us all to Moscow, Idaho. Mama's perfectly picked middle of nowhere.

~~~~~

MRS. ASTER'S BACKYARD was as wild as her coat. The front yard had rows of roses and trimmed grass, but the back seemed overgrown on purpose. Like she'd let the prairie keep a bit of the town. I'd never lived in a place with a yard before. I stepped into that tangled mess and knew I'd found the one place I might be alone in our new home. A good place to hide from Mama. Thistles weaved through the fence slats. Songbirds I couldn't see tittered inside a shrub with clusters of white flowers. They scattered when Magpie appeared, following me as I explored. I found a spot as far as I could get from anyone watching out a window. In a gap behind a mass of wild roses, I tucked myself into the corner of the fence. A thorn scratched beads of blood up my arm, and Magpie licked my elbow. I scooted my knees to my chin. Wondered whether I should cry.

"You're going to ruin that dress," a voice said.

"I don't think she cares," said another.

"But her mother might."

Forgetting for a moment that I'd been looking to be alone, I said, "I don't care what my mother thinks."

This was answered with one sigh and one giggle. I hauled myself up to my knees and peered through the tangle of flowers and thistles. Another yard met Mrs. Aster's, tidy and bordered with a wrought-iron fence. A girl in a cream-colored dress sat in a wicker chair. Wearing a hat and gloves in her own yard. She waved.

"The real question is whether your mother cares, no matter what you think," she said, glancing toward her house before adding, "My mother cares about *everything* I do."

She pressed a hand to her porcelain-doll face. "Look at me, forgetting my manners. That's exactly the type of thing Mother would be upset about. My name is Patience Fisher. I'm pleased to make your acquaintance."

I'd seen plenty of people my own age before, but rarely officially met one. Never while hiding out among brambles. At least I'd picked up a handful of manners while I was being lugged around by my family.

"Pleased to meet you, as well. I'm—" I stopped myself before I could say *Antonia*. Mama had a habit of correcting Grandfather when he shortened my name. And since there was no chance I was being friendly with Mama anymore, it felt right. "Annie Sweet."

"What brings you outside on this lovely day, Annie?"

"Pardon me, Miss Fisher, but aren't you forgetting to make proper introductions?"

I'd almost forgotten about the second voice. It was raspier than Patience's. Louder. I couldn't see anyone else in her yard. But Patience cast her gaze to the sky and pointed a dainty finger at the weeping willow tree in what I'd thought was an empty field beside the two houses. A girl stuck her head out between two twisting branches. Her yellow braids blended into the leaves.

Patience let out another enormous sigh. "Forgive me again for my failings. Miss Annie Sweet, may I introduce Miss Polly Bloomquist?"

With a swish, Polly bounded out of the tree. She sat down on the outside edge of where the Fishers' fence met Mrs. Aster's. No regard to the placement of her too-small skirt.

"You must be the new boarder."

"I was just asking her about that," Patience said.

"You ought to be a little more direct," Polly said. "So, where're you from?"

Part of me wanted to tell these girls about my whole life. Everywhere I'd lived, everything I'd seen. Everything I thought about Mama forcing me to move to this little town. Everything I thought about Mama in general. But even as I wanted to resist her ways, I could see why Mama kept some topics quiet. That didn't mean I had to play by her rules. I could do things other than lie.

"How about I tell you where you're from?" I said.

Patience folded her hands, but Polly popped her freckled face above the fence. "What's that supposed to mean?"

I let my sense of her wash over me. She was fourteen, like me. Patience was a little older. The thrilled feeling in the pit of my stomach reminded me of seasickness as I started talking.

"I mean, how you were born halfway across the country. Two days' journey or so on a train from here. But you've been in this area since you were a little girl. Not always right here. Out of town a little more, before. You've lived here, maybe . . . eight years."

Her jaw dropped. "That's some gol-damn magic!"

"Polly!" Patience scolded.

"Oh, calm down." Polly scrabbled over the fence and sat down next to me, ignoring the wild rose branches picking at her hem. "Do Patience now."

I squinted and pretended I needed immense focus, even though I'd already seen all I needed to.

"You were born a few miles east of here. But you moved into that big house when you were too young to remember. Your room's upstairs, in the little tower. You like to sit by the window."

Patience stood up so fast she had to keep her chair from falling. She gripped her skirt and ran to the fence. "Don't let my mother hear you doing such tricks!"

"Your mother can't hear a thing from her room in there," Polly said. "But she might look out and see you running."

Patience froze.

"Come on, Pay. Have a little fun."

Patience crossed her arms after one last glance over her shoulder. I could see her fighting a smile. "I will if you keep your big mouth shut about it around my mother."

"Good," Polly said. "Now, Annie, I've got a question for you. Patience and I have been dreaming up ways to buy ourselves some independence."

"Just Polly," Patience said.

Polly ignored her. "And that trick of yours has got me thinking. How would you feel about making a little money?"

As soon as she said it, I envisioned a pocketful of coins. I looked up and saw Polly and Patience waiting for my answer, their faces shining. It felt good to think about making money. About new possibilities for escaping the trap my mother had set for me. But it felt good to think about having friends, too.

~~~~~

MAMA TRIED TO keep me home for a while, but before long she gave up. She and Tia were busy settling in, and everyone sensed that Mrs. Aster was not about to babysit me. Besides, Mama's plot was working nicely. I couldn't exactly run off to London from Idaho. Moscow might as well have been a desert island in a sea of prairie. I couldn't run off to anywhere at all, though my brain never stopped searching for a way to.

Once Patience, Polly, and I had time to ourselves, we set up the office of "the Astonishing Annie" in a tumbledown shed on the far side of the Bloomquist family apple orchard. Polly was the youngest of six. All brothers above her, all working in town or the orchard. Her parents didn't pay much attention to what she got up to all summer. As long as she did her chores, helped with supper, and didn't break anything important. Patience provided my crystal goblet and gauzy yellow shawl, though only after Mama, Tia, and I had tea with her mother. I did my best to show Mrs. Fisher I was a proper young lady. Patience clapped like a little girl when her mother granted permission for her to go on outings with me. Her family was like Polly's, but in reverse. She was the oldest, the treasured and guarded only girl. Five younger brothers, which should have given some advantage to fussed-over Patience. For all the edicts she handed down, Mrs. Fisher couldn't exactly enforce them. But Patience hovered on her behalf.

"This won't be like summoning spirits or anything," Patience said, mostly to herself. We draped an old bedsheet over a pile of scrap wood. "Mother would be very concerned about that. This is just going to be a game that takes advantage of your . . . what was it again?"

"Remarkable perception," I said, borrowing Grandfather's term for my sense. "I'm just good at figuring out where people have been. Seeing paths."

I did my best not to think about my own mother, even while Patience fretted over hers. Mama had started teaching summer courses in Latin and Greek, as expected. Never mentioned Dr. Brighton or his lies again. She and Tia swiftly adapted their plans, ordering a bureau, a bed, and a new writing desk for Tia from the Sears catalog and dishes from the department store downtown. Tia made quick friends with the local theater proprietor and started musing on ideas for a play she might actually let people perform. Mama had gotten involved with the women raising funds for Moscow's first permanent library. Rather than hunt down tutors among the farms and fields, they enrolled me in the public high school for the fall. I didn't argue. In part because that's where Polly and Patience went. In part because I said as little to Mama as I could get away with. She'd tried to restart our stateroom conversations in our first days in Moscow. After a few days of my chilly responses, she stopped trying. I read every overture as another attempt to control me. She demanded to know where I was going. Commanded me to sit down and tell her about my new friends. Insisted I answer when I ignored her. I kept my responses short and spiked. Tia wasn't any help, avoiding my attempts to draw her allegiance toward me. Repeating, when I tried, "Just talk to her."

Of course I didn't mention the Astonishing Annie. I just said I was out with Patience and Polly. Mama didn't deserve to know about all the things I did without her. All the things I could do. I was determined to never be an empty shell again, or fill myself up with mindless things. I'd lay my own path.

Polly spread the word to all the girls in the Swedish Lutheran church, who told all the girls in the Norwegian Lutheran church. Patience told the Methodists, the junior sewing circle, and the other girls in her etiquette class. I was careful to be sure they billed me as clairvoyant rather than as a fortune-teller. I didn't want anyone getting upset when I couldn't tell them who they'd marry or whether they'd grow up to be rich. I just needed to impress them enough to get them to tell all their friends to hand over their own nickels.

Polly and I huddled in the shed on opening day, while Patience stood guard outside. We let the crowd wait long enough for me to get a good sense of our first customer. Her name was Agnes, Polly said as we peered through a crack in the wall. A freckly, bosomy girl about to start her senior year at the high school. I saw her path right away. A few theatrics would buy me time to sort out the story behind it.

Polly rapped twice on the inside of the shed door to let Patience know we were ready. The crowd went quiet.

"Who awaits the wonders offered by the Astonishing Annie?" For all her jitters about divination, Patience had a talent for drama.

I heard giggles, and Agnes's name. When Patience guided her in, I was veiled in shadow in the back corner of the shed. I emerged, flinging back my arms and letting the shawl flutter around me, as I'd practiced several times in the days before. A hat with an entire stuffed dove on it, coaxed from the collection of Mrs. Aster, perched on my head.

Polly poured a splash of sour apple juice into the goblet on a wobbly table. "Behold, the draught of truth."

I took a sip, checking Agnes's path once more before I spoke. Born in Moscow, lived in the same house her whole life. Not much to see, except for a recent spate of evening walks. I'd spent a few days wandering around town with Polly, taking note of landmarks and shops. Trying to memorize the town made Moscow seem a little bigger, though there still wasn't much to it. I could see perfectly well where Agnes liked to take her walks.

"You spend a lot of time on the west side of town, even though you live two blocks east of here," I said to Agnes, keeping my voice just above a whisper. "I sense . . . a beau? Perhaps one your parents don't know about? Dare I say . . . a college boy?"

She blanched. I knew we'd have a line twice as long the next day.

~~~~~

I USED ONE of my nickels from our first week in business to invest in a green paperboard notebook from the drugstore downtown. I'd never tried to draw a map before. Turns out I wasn't too bad at it. Soon I had pages filled with detailed sketches of Moscow's streets. The names of stores and parks. Who lived in which house and owned which field, as far as I could tell. Polly came up with the idea to allow customers only twice a week, and only the first dozen girls who showed up. No repeats until a whole week had passed. We had to keep the Astonishing Annie sufficiently astonishing, she said. Patience got antsy if I started talking about the nature of my sense. But Polly ate up every detail I could give her, and she knew I needed time to think and study. Even though I was getting lightning-quick at seeing paths, I had to put them into a story—make them mean something—if I was going to impress anyone.

Patience and Polly got excited when they saw the notebook, helping me fill in blanks and marveling at the detail I hadn't realized I could capture.

"Mother made me take two whole years of drawing classes, and I still can't draw a straight line," Patience said. "And look at that! I'd know that was Mr. Ryrie's house even if you didn't label it. You've got every little window and gable exactly as it should be."

Polly elbowed in and pointed to one of the sketches of downtown storefronts.

"Minnie Olsson's sweet on the kid who started working at the candy shop in the afternoons," she said. "If we go tomorrow, I bet you can dig up something good on him. And they've got Hershey bars now."

My mouth watered thinking of chocolate. "I don't really like them," I lied. "But we can go in."

I couldn't spend all my money. That seemed to be Polly and Patience's plan, though. Patience's mother bought her whatever she wanted—as long as it was on her list of acceptable feminine interests. Hats or hair ribbons or pretty trinkets for her room. Polly said her folks considered it a stretch to feed her. The two of them bought piles of treats. Soda floats, pastries, candies, ice cream. Patience wanted to get her portrait taken downtown. Polly wanted a pair of good boots that hadn't belonged to one of her brothers. They talked about saving up for train tickets, but just to go up to Spokane and see a vaudeville show. I hadn't told them I was getting out of Idaho as soon as I could. How could I explain why I was running, who I was looking for? At best they'd tell me my new plan was impossible. At worst they'd tell Mama. Part of me worried that if I told them, I'd curse myself. I'd wind up stuck forever.

By the time fall arrived, I'd met every girl in town, and every girl had met the Astonishing Annie. I didn't need to feel nervous about my first day of real school. Mama made pancakes before leaving for work. I said I wasn't hungry, even though they made the whole house smell like butter. She declared she had to go in early to organize her desk and left, slamming the door.

Tia did my hair while I fed pancake scraps to Magpie. She'd gotten better at the Gibson Girl style, though my waves still resisted too much order.

"I would give you advice, but it wouldn't be much use, considering how I was educated by a nun who didn't make me stay at my desk," she said as she wrestled in a few extra pins. "And my only classmate was a bit of a show-off."

That got a smile out of me. I wasn't so mad at Tia anymore for not trying to find us a way out of Moscow. I knew even she couldn't reason with my mother. But ignoring Mama, and running around with Polly and Patience, naturally led to less time with her.

"If you figured out how to read two languages and do sums in the Brazilian forest, I think I'll figure out how to do geometry and read Shakespeare on the Palouse prairie."

"There's more to school than education, you know." She patted my dome of hair, testing whether it would hold up to the wind. I could feel her pause, her hands tense. "For example, friends. Boys."

I gritted my teeth. Mama and Tia had always been plain about what people did behind closed doors. That didn't mean I wanted to talk about it any more than I had to. The only boys I'd met in Moscow so far were Polly's shy, sturdy brothers, who seemed to talk less among the five of them together than she did by herself. Patience was desperately in love with the youngest, Kristian, the boy who drove the wagon for Mrs. Aster. Her mooning was enough to scare me off any ideas about romance. Besides, I had more important things to focus on.

"I don't care a lick about boys," I said.

"What do you care about, then?" Tia arched her eyebrow. That always meant she knew more than she was letting on. But I wasn't going to satisfy her, knowing she'd go straight to Mama.

"My education, of course," I said.

A lie. And I was sure Tia knew it. But Polly started banging on the door, and I grabbed my book bag and fled.

I was greeted with squeals and hugs in the schoolyard. My classes were crammed with my customers. They jostled to sit next to me at lunch, but Polly and Patience shepherded them away. Polly's latest plan was to announce that I was too exhausted from my studies to use my clairvoyant powers. At least for a few weeks. I could use the time to draw information from the boys and teachers at school. The Astonishing Annie could reemerge with even more mysterious insight. And we could start charging a dime.

The higher price was my idea. After a whole summer as the Astonishing Annie, I only had a few dollars stashed in a jar in my bottom bureau drawer. I'd need a lot more than that to carry out my plan. It started as the faintest outline, driven by my need to never end up looking like a fool again. My need to prove to my mother that she couldn't stop me. I could buy my way out of Idaho. First purchase was a train ticket to New York, then a ship back across the Atlantic. Steerage if I had to, as long as they gave me a bed and a bucket. I wasn't looking forward to another sea journey, but I told myself I'd do what I must. I'd need enough to pay for a boardinghouse until I could find work. Enough to feed and clothe myself. Enough to move on to a new city, or a new country, if the trail took me there.

I was going to make it on my own, even if it took years. I'd complete the mission Grandfather gave me. Sail to London and hunt down either Ishmael or his grave. Without Grandfather's letter to tell me more of the story, I couldn't know whether London held any clues unless I looked for myself. Mama had said Grandfather was swindled there, but she could have been lying to throw me off the trail. I'd learn who Ishmael was, why he'd lured my grandmother away. Find out every facet of my family's great mystery and answer the questions that had gnawed at me since that night in Grandfather's study. Fill myself up with the pride of knowing.

Chapter 21

OUR FIRST WINTER in Idaho stretched well into what I thought should be spring, shutting down the high school when the prairie winds shoved feet of snow across every road and peeled the skin off your cheeks if you went out unprepared. I spent those days with the entire set of the ninth edition of the *Encyclopædia Britannica*. Mrs. Aster had ordered it over the years from a catalog. I'd read about anything, though tropical islands tended to rise to the top of the list. I could pretend I was dreaming of warmth while tucking away more information about ships and trade winds and whaling ports. Anything that might come in handy in my search for Ishmael. Even if the search was hard to believe in on the days the house shook from drifts slipping off the roof, and I couldn't walk across the yard, let alone sail across the world.

One day I was thumbing through the entry on London for the dozenth time, daydreaming about the route Grandfather and his whale's tooth had taken. And I remembered the short stop they'd made after London. The Faroe Islands. I got out Volume IX, FAL–FYZ, and found the listing. I fell in love as I read. *They everywhere present to the sea perpendicular cliffs. The climate is foggy, and violent storms are frequent at all seasons. The cod fishery is especially important.*

I'd sketched out my search, but this new step appeared bright and clear as a photograph of those tall, jagged cliffs. A way to wrap up the story to my satisfaction.

It wouldn't be easy. My voyage would be wretched. But if Mama cared about me at all, if she really couldn't live without me, she would have a chance to prove it. Once I'd found Ishmael, I'd sail for the Faroe Islands. I'd write and tell Mama right where to find me. She would know she hadn't been able to forbid me anything. She would know she couldn't drag me around or lie to me or trick me anymore. And because I refused to be like her, I wouldn't force her to do a thing. I'd give her a choice. If she ever wanted to see me again, she'd have to choose to come to me.

I planted the vision of the Faroe Islands deep in my gut. I watered it with resentment. Let it choke out all the compassionate thoughts I'd felt toward Mama on the ship across the Atlantic, any soft memories I had left of her. I told myself those didn't matter. I could fulfill Grandfather's mission and prove I wasn't powerless, all at once. Grandfather had seemed convinced that finding the man would help my family. Fix my mother, somehow. I wasn't so sure. She was blind to the ways she needed fixing. Blind to the desperation for control that defined her every move. Mama had controlled the story of Ishmael my whole life. Maybe I couldn't fix her. But maybe I could break her control over me for good.

I liked to imagine her pausing outside my little moss-roofed house overlooking the stormy sea. Tia behind her, a hand on her back. Mama wincing as she prepared to knock. I'd open the door before she could. Welcome her in. Tell her I knew everything.

I wasn't making short-term plans anymore. I realized I needed far more money than I could make as the Astonishing Annie. Plenty of skill, too, if I was going to make it in the harsh environment of the Faroe Islands. So I turned my attention from the encyclopedias to their owner.

Mrs. Aster had no family that I'd ever seen. She often went out to visit with friends, but the only companion she kept in the house was Magpie. She had money, but not too much, otherwise she wouldn't have bothered with boarders. Still enough that she could order fancy clothes and stuff her house with leather-bound books and gilded clocks and chairs that were for looking at, not sitting on. A whole wall of her bedroom was hung with hats. Her book collection never had a speck of dust. She was self-assured in a way I'd never seen before. The artist types Mama and Tia tended to favor always seemed to be performing. Grandfather's editors and journalists always seemed to be competing. Mrs. Aster only went about her business, and she knew more than anyone I'd ever met. She could command respect in any room. Discuss any topic from the newspaper, which she read every single word of each morning. She followed the prices of crops and the patterns of weather and business that changed them. She knew how to track down edible plants and mushrooms, even in town. She trimmed her own roses, cleaned her own toilet, hemmed her own dresses, made her own bread. I was pretty sure she could climb up on the roof and patch the shingles if she had to. I needed her to teach me everything I didn't know.

I waited for a soggy morning when it was only Mrs. Aster and me in the house. Mama and Tia were shopping, Patience was practicing her piano, and Polly was doing chores. Mrs. Aster read the newspaper on one of the pink velvet sofas, her boots swinging a few inches off the floor. Magpie sprawled beside her. I worked on a map of the university's Administration Building, that cathedral-like building on the hill, in my latest notebook. I had half a dozen by then, stacked under the bed in my room. Some still came in handy for the Saturdays I was Astonishing Annie, though the act was losing its novelty. Mostly they kept me occupied. Kept me focused. Once a week I practiced the cliffs and fjords of the Faroe Islands, pulled from the descriptions in the encyclopedia and my memory of the whale's tooth.

"Can you teach me something practical?" I asked Mrs. Aster.

"If you insist," she said, still looking at the open newspaper. "What, exactly?"

"I'm not sure. What do you think a person needs to know to get by in the world?"

"Fighting men and wrestling bears." She laughed at herself as she folded the paper and stacked it by the stove. "Or making your own food. Ever done that?"

I could boil an egg, on occasion. Put together a sandwich. "Not really."

"Perfect place to start, in that case. And what would you like to make?"

Of course I thought of desserts. All the things Polly and Patience bought at the shops that I denied myself. What, if anything, would I want to make to enjoy? What might I be able to sell, if I had to? I remembered the dinner on the SS *La Loire*.

"How about charlotte à la russe?"

She let out a whoop and started for the kitchen. "I am woefully out of Bavarian cream, so we will be making gingerbread. Then we can discuss other things."

She clattered around and came up with a pan, shaking her head. "Charlotte à la russe, for Pete's sake. Get yourself over here and measure out the flour, if you can manage."

I figured it out, with a little correction on smoothing the top. Soon I was covered in a dusting of ingredients, my hands sticky with molasses. But the pan was full of brown batter, going into the oven.

"And now we clean," Mrs. Aster said, handing me a damp rag.

She supervised, standing beside me since she was too small to look over my shoulder. Pointing out spots I'd missed. When I was hot and tired and ready to flop back on the couch, she flung open a cupboard.

"And now we set the table for supper," she said.

"Can't we wait until later?" I stretched my arms, surprised at how sore I was from stirring.

"Later has work of its own." She handed me a stack of plates. "I can help you learn that rather quickly, at least. If you want to be practical, I can help. You need money, I suppose."

I fumbled the dishes, barely managing to keep a grip on them. How had she seen so clearly what I was after?

"Kristian reports you've been running a business of sorts with his sister," she said, straightening the plate I'd just set and reaching up to pat my arm. "Not in so many words, exactly. But I know that Bloomquist girl. Always looking to make a penny. It was her convinced me to hire a wagon driver, when she wasn't more than ten. Her papa sent her brother, of course. But she's a smart one."

"It's just a game," I said.

"And plenty of things pay better than games. Though I'm not sure about charlotte à la russe."

She was never going to give up that joke. But it was a decent trade for what she offered.

"I'll learn anything you think might allow me to make a living for myself. Wherever I want to go. But please, don't tell my mother." I searched for an excuse and landed on a truth. "She says she had to work too hard as a girl."

"I assumed not telling your mother and aunt was a given. I am accustomed to keeping secrets."

She led me back to the couches, then patted the cushion beside her. "What do you know about Mr. Alfred Aster?"

The question seemed out of the blue. I hadn't thought much about her husband, beyond the fleeting idea that he must have been the source of her money.

"I suppose he worked for the railroad? Or the lumber company?"

Her smile was bright and mischievous. "There is no Mr. Alfred Aster."

"So he's . . . dead?"

Her grin stretched larger, smoothing out the fine lines of her face. "There never has been a Mr. Alfred Aster. Sounds impressive, though, don't you think?"

I realized then that I'd never looked at her closely enough. I'd been awed by the bearskin and silk and feathers. The bulletproof charm. But I'd assumed her path was simple. I focused my sense on her, chasing back through the years in the white house. And then something happened that I'd never seen before. The path stopped. Not at birth or origin. But as if I'd hit an invisible wall, and everything beyond it was somewhere distant and soft. Somewhere I couldn't follow.

She sat, smiling. As if she knew what I was doing.

"What I'm trying to tell you, Miss Sweet, is that if a woman wants a thing of her own in this world, she's got to work for it."

She sniffed the air and rose. I'd been so intent on her, I hadn't noticed how the room had filled with cloves and cinnamon.

"But she'd better be sure it's worth the work."

~~~~~

THE END OF my junior year of high school marked three years in Idaho. Mama and Tia laughed with their friends now about their shock when we rolled into town, gawking at the fields and quiet streets. They painted Dr. Brighton, the lying professor, as some kind of folk hero, his exaggerated letters unexpected gifts that drew them to a place they'd never have gone otherwise. They'd learned so swiftly to love Moscow. I'd heard Tia say it was a happy medium between the tiny village of their youth and the sprawling cities of mine. A place they could sink into, spread out roots. We learned the ebb and flow of the Palouse. The times the swallowtail butterflies emerged and the huckleberries ripened on Moscow Mountain. The tides of college students and harvests. The town grew enough to change, so we always had new people to meet. New streets and stores to add to my books of maps. Mama and Tia still talked about other places in the world, but they became places they'd visit someday. Not live. They seemed to be content, for the first time in my life.

I might've looked content. That spring, I went to school dances and garden parties, church picnics and ice cream socials. I joined the standing ovation on the opening night of *The Titaness*, Tia's play about the Greek goddess Mnemosyne reappearing in modern Europe. Patience played the title character, dazzling in her green robes. She'd grown up to be bold and hearty. Not petal-delicate like her mother wanted. Sure, Mrs. Fisher was over the moon that Patience was marrying Kristian Bloomquist, even though he wasn't a Methodist. But after the wedding, Patience and Kristian were moving all the way to San Francisco to make her a star. I liked to think my first summer in Moscow, helping her stack up nickels to get something she wanted for once, was the start of that.

In the seat next to me, Polly stuck her fingers in her mouth and whistled. She was still a farm girl in a ratty dress and braids, but she'd grown up, too. Despite her parents trying to talk her into leaving school to work, she was set to graduate in a year. She wanted to go to the normal school a few towns away, if she could earn the money for it. But her big dream was to become the librarian at the new Carnegie library being built in Moscow. She said a person could get into all sorts of trouble in a library.

I'd been telling everyone I had my heart set on becoming a college woman but was still dreaming of places to go. I could attend several excellent literature programs within a few hours' train ride. I told my teachers I liked the idea of the women's schools, especially Mount Holyoke or Smith. Right there by Grandfather's alma mater in Amherst, Massachusetts. Tia approved of such a leap, but Mama pushed for the University of Idaho, of course. She said it was convenient and affordable, but I knew she just wanted to keep me in her orbit, as always. I was amazed she was letting anyone entertain the idea of me going elsewhere at all. I'd let myself settle into an outward balance with Mama. Learned to have civil conversations, mostly about books and school. It might have looked like warmth between a mother and daughter. But while Mama had built a home on her lies, I'd been constructing plenty of my own.

My college plans were all fabricated. I had no intention of going, or even attending my last year of high school. I didn't care about studying literature. I did well in school because it was easy. An interesting enough way to pass the time. But my mind was always somewhere else. Everyone knew I was hoarding money, once I started working at the big hotel on Main Street. Mama allowed it because I said I was saving up for college. I was pretty sure Mrs. Aster knew I had other motives. She kept on teaching me things, even when I didn't ask. I'd learned to cook, sew, forage, wash, garden. Do elaborate accounting and math well beyond what they taught at school. Repair anything. The roof had sprung a leak that winter. She did not climb up to fix it, but she shouted directions from the ground as I did. I couldn't understand why she gave me so much time. I'd tried more than once to ask her more about her past, her money. Her name. But she always deflected, offering to refine a skill or instruct me in something new.

I had almost two hundred dollars socked away in that jar in my bureau drawer. When Polly and I went to Spokane to see Kristian and Patience off, I would buy my own train tickets. I'd be gone by July. Sooner, if I could swing it. From Spokane to New York to London. And someday to the Faroe Islands.

Sometimes I almost forgot the plan included finding Ishmael, too. Sometimes I wondered if it really needed to. But I still wanted to prove to Mama that not only could I run without her catching me, not only could I survive on my own, but I could handle what she couldn't. I could know things she was afraid of. And I still owed it to Grandfather to at least try to complete what he'd started, even if my reasons were entirely different.

The time to leave drew so near I felt like it was crushing me. I reminded myself that my plan was the only thing that could possibly right the long list of wrongs I'd attributed to my mother since I was thirteen years old. I refused to let myself forget that our whole life in Moscow had started with a lie. That maybe Mama loved this place because she could rest in the knowledge that Ishmael would never disrupt her life again. That she would have taken us to Moscow even if she'd known ahead of time what it was like. The thought of her deception had hardened in my brain like stones in a chicken's gizzard, grinding up anything I put into it. I could never be content.

<center>~~~~~</center>

AS THE CROWD meandered out of the auditorium after the closing show of *The Titaness*, I kept my eyes open for Mrs. Aster. She'd be easy to spot. She'd left the house in lemon satin and a hat decorated with crow feathers. Her high-heeled boots seemed to have a hundred buttons. Polly and I had escorted her to the theater, as we had for several other performances. She shooed us off to our seats up front, but I felt compelled to find her quickly after the show.

I was finally days away from the escape I'd planned for so long, and I'd managed to keep it a secret from everyone I knew. Even Mrs. Aster, who had helped me so much. Because she was so good at keeping her own secrets, I felt less guilty keeping mine from her. We both knew secrets held power. Mine had fortified me for three years. Allowed me to focus on what I wanted, no matter what else competed for my attention.

The audience was flocking to the lobby, waiting to congratulate Patience and Tia and the rest of the cast and crew. I spotted the crest of Mrs. Aster's hat as we entered. When Polly and I pushed through the crowd to reach her, she nodded swiftly in greeting.

"Polly dear, go out to the wagon and fetch the bouquets."

Polly left without a word. Mrs. Aster was the only person she ever listened to like that.

Mrs. Aster was closer than usual to my ears in her tall boots, but she still leaned up and in to speak to me over the chatter. "An impressive show. Wouldn't you agree?"

"Absolutely fantastic."

"I've never had any question about Otávia's talent, but Miss Fisher's continues to be a pleasant surprise," she said. "Watching that girl stare into the shadows in her yard for half her childhood made me worried she would grow up to be as fretful and frivolous a woman as . . . well, you know. I don't hold Mrs. Fisher in ill regard. I only like to see a little more energy in a girl."

For all her personal secrecy, Mrs. Aster was almost always willing to offer up her opinions on others. I absorbed them all. It had come in handy during the Astonishing Annie days especially.

"What impresses me most about our lovely Miss Fisher, however, is how she has chosen her path based on what she loves and desires," she continued.

I glanced over to see if Polly was on her way back. But Mrs. Aster stopped speaking until I caught her eye again. "Rather than in opposition to something. Say, for example, her mother."

My tongue grew heavy in my mouth. Maybe it was only a comment. Truly about Patience and her mother, not me and mine. But it didn't feel like it.

Polly came stumbling through the door with an enormous armload of flowers, saving me from responding. Soon Patience arrived in the lobby in a dress her mother had embroidered with tiny wisteria vines. We gushed and fawned over her. Polly even got a little teary-eyed. After Patience left to see Kristian, we switched our attention to Tia. By the time we were on our way to Mrs. Aster's wagon, I felt wrung out with emotion. No one but me knew that these congratulations were also goodbyes.

Polly drove. Mrs. Aster perched beside me. The night was the warmest we'd had yet that year. The breeze carried the scent of lilacs and apple blossoms. I closed my eyes. Felt the rumble and muck of the streets. I didn't need my sense to know exactly where we were. And I couldn't fend off the thought of how much I'd miss this little town. I'd wanted to hate it from the moment I saw it.

Now that I was leaving, I couldn't escape the ways in which it had become my home.

And I couldn't escape the ways in which the people I'd met had made it home. I'd shown up with all the charm of a hissing goose, and they'd welcomed me. Befriended me. Who would I be if I abandoned them without a word?

"I'm leaving," I said.

Mrs. Aster leaned forward and tapped Polly's elbow. "Will you park us a moment, please?" Calmly, as if she'd known what was coming this whole time.

"Go on," she said to me once we were stopped on the silent street.

"I'm leaving," I said again. Took a huge breath. "This summer. I've been saving my money to buy a train ticket to New York. I have enough, with a little to spare. I'll have to work a while in the city. But then I'm sailing for London. I have . . . business there. It's difficult to explain. But I'm not coming back."

I could barely see their faces in the moonlight. They weren't frowning or scowling. Just listening.

"I'll try to explain it. Soon. When we have a little more time. But I want you both to know I couldn't have done it without you. I don't just mean the money. I wouldn't even know how to make it on my own. How to even start."

"Aw, Annie," Polly blurted. "Not even one more year? Not even till graduation? I could—"

I knew she was going to say *come with you.* I cut her off. "I've held out as long as I can. I'm ready."

But as the sentence left my mouth, it felt less true than it had the moment before. I shifted in my seat. Wondered when my hands had started shaking.

"I suspected something of this sort," Mrs. Aster said. "And I will bid you farewell with all the love in my heart, Miss Sweet. I have only one question."

"Anything."

"Is it worth the work?"

My ribs ached. My heart seemed to pause beating. For years, I had repeated to myself so often what Mrs. Aster had said in her kitchen. *If a woman wants a thing of her own in this world, she's got to work for it.* But I'd made myself forget the second part. I didn't know how to answer her.

Chapter 22

THE HOUSE WAS quiet when I gave up trying to sleep the next morning. I heard Magpie yipping and stumbled downstairs to let her into the yard. But Mama was there already. Watching the dog snuffle through the brambles and hedges.

"It's a beautiful day," she said. Her voice reminded me of that dreamy echo I'd only ever heard once before. At the train station the day we arrived. "Would you like to sit outside and talk?"

I didn't need to guess what had happened. My revelation was too much, even for Mrs. Aster. Or she wasn't satisfied with my lack of explanation. I felt a pinch of disappointment that she had given me up, but it was eased by unexpected relief. I'd been up all night reviewing my plan. Trying to shove down the doubt that had been climbing up my throat since the wagon ride home. I'd clung to my belief that solving the mystery of Ishmael and sailing off to the Faroe Islands was the only way to chase out the anger and grief and frustration I'd felt since childhood. I'd invested so much of my thought and effort in my plan. Enough to keep me from appreciating other things. Other people. My own life. Enough to keep me believing that it was the only way to prove to my mother that she couldn't control me. And I'd refused to see how my obsession with punishing her had been controlling me, long after Mama had given up trying.

My plans had made so much sense when I explained them to myself. The moment I tried to explain them to someone I loved, they fell apart. Mama wasn't the only person responsible for breaking what we could have been. And so I followed her out into the yard.

Mama and Tia had convinced Mrs. Aster to add a set of rattan chairs to the chaos of the patio. We'd carved out a little space for them among the chokecherries and ninebark and wild roses. When Mama leaned against the arched back of her chair and looked up for a moment at the hazy sky, I saw a lump in her dress pocket. Before I could recognize it, she pulled out the swatch of black velvet.

"This was Grandfather's gift to you, and I had no right to take it."

I'd waited years to hear those words. But my first feeling was hardness, not relief. "You're right. You didn't."

"And I have to confess it is not the only thing I took from you that day."

My first thought was Grandfather's letter. But no. She'd taken that well before I tried to go to London. What was left for her to steal?

"I know that you can do things others cannot," she continued. "You can sense paths. Understand patterns."

"So Grandfather told you."

"No. I saw it myself. Not exactly as you do. It is as if . . . I should have thought how to explain this." She drew her fingers across her lips. "It is like our faces. I look into yours and see so much of mine, and yet you are wholly yourself. You can see where someone has traveled as effortlessly as you breathe. I can see deeper, though it is difficult and often painful. Related, but not the same."

My mouth went dry as I listened to her. Magpie barked at a rabbit in the garden, but the sound was muted by the ringing in my ears. I stared at my mother. She was still so young. Her hair flowed around her shoulders, undone for the morning, shining red in the sunlight. A different color, but the same loose curls as mine. Her cheeks were lighter but marked with the same faint freckles. Her eyes were like Grandfather's. Grandfather had said, once, that my eyes were like Mama's mother's. The mother she wanted to forget.

"I remember my entire life, Annie, whether I want to or not," she said. Her eyes on mine.

She paused to catch her breath and I let the revelation swirl in my mind. I'd treasured my strange little sense. My remarkable perception. But I had never told her about it. I'd been so angry with her since the day I learned it existed, hiding it had been one more way to punish her. But she knew. Because no matter how much I wanted to escape it, she was my mother and I was her daughter. We were alike.

"I cannot shake loose my memories," she said, the quiver in her voice rising. "I can, if I must, see the memories of others. That day on the train, I stole your plan to run away straight from your mind, and I stole the knowledge of your sense. I believed it was the last thing I would ever have to steal from you. When I learned of your intention to leave again, I realized I was wrong, terribly wrong. I see now how I stole from you more than I ever meant to."

She held out her hand. The whale's tooth in her palm. I took it. It felt exactly as I'd remembered it. As I'd dreamed of it. I'd forgotten how much I'd loved it, how much time I'd spent with it in those months before I tried to chase its path to London. My mother's admission was so vast, I didn't know how to wade into it.

"Why?" I asked.

A question that contained a thousand questions. But Mama seemed to know what I meant.

"When you were born, I swore I would miss nothing. I would know every moment of your every day as well as I knew my own. But it became clear, so quickly, how impossible that would be. No matter how tight I tried to hold you, you could wander away in the time it took to turn my head."

"The albatross."

Her smile was sad. "Before you tried to leave for London, I had not thought of that moment in many years. But taking it from your mind brought it fresh to mine. I remembered it all night after I brought you home from the train. I remembered my dismay at how easily I had let you be swept away by an illusion. Not long after that day at the street fair, I asked your grandfather not to tell you why my mother took me away. Who she sought."

I remembered the lone line I had caught from Grandfather's letter. *Mara has spent her life running from every memory of her mother.*

"You didn't want to risk me chasing after him, too."

I'd never seen my mother refuse to look someone in the eye, but she whispered her confession to a patch of sun on the ground by my feet.

"I was so afraid. I was terrified I would search for you but never find you. Lose you but never be able to forget you. I was protecting you, but I was protecting myself as well. When you still found out, when you tried to board that train, I was furious at myself for failing. I thought it was such a simple thing, not to tell that story. Again, I was wrong."

I remembered Grandfather's joy when he helped me learn about my sense. His certainty that it would help us. A familiar bitterness came out with my words.

"You can't blame Grandfather. He felt like I needed to know, and he deserved to tell me. You had no right to forbid him."

Grief rose out of her depths and broke across her face. In all the times I'd spoken to her with contempt, I'd never seen anything like it. She bit her lip so hard, I expected to see blood when she finally spoke.

"I know, Antonia. He tried many times to speak to me about him. About Ishmael." The name seemed to deepen her pain. "I knew well that your grandfather wished to understand more about what happened, but I would not even entertain the thought. I demanded he stop."

"You thought you could control him. Just like you thought you could control me."

Her head snapped up. "I did not. I knew I could not control either of you. I have always known I cannot control anything in this world."

A hawk screeched from somewhere in the willow tree.

"Then why did you bring us to Idaho, Mama?"

She nodded. She knew the question was coming, as sure as I knew I had to ask it.

"When you were a little girl, I wanted to show you all the things I never got to see. I wanted the world for myself, and for Otávia, but most of all for you. I believed if I offered you enough of it, you would never find a reason to leave me. When I learned I was wrong, I told myself I would offer you space instead. Space far, far away from the story of Ishmael. Space away from the loss of your grandfather. Space to learn a new way of life. When we arrived here and you were so angry, I told myself it was all for the best. I needed only to give you more space, as long as that space was never so wide that I could not see you across it."

She sighed, running her hands over her face and into the knots of her hair. "But I was lying to myself, and I was hurting you, Antonia. I am sorry."

I thought I needed to cross the world to make my mother apologize to me. I thought I needed to make her cross the world to show her apology was real. But when it came, in the yard of our home, not at all as I'd imagined it, I was surprised at how willing I was to accept it. We'd both been wrong, in so many ways. We'd both held fast to our false assumptions and stubborn beliefs. Mama had been so focused on her fear, she'd failed to see my pain. I'd been so focused on my anger, I'd failed to see hers.

It turned out Tia was right. I didn't need to prove anything to Mama or make her prove anything to me. I just needed to talk to her. And I had one more question.

"Do you still have the letter about Ishmael that Grandfather left for me?"

I TOOK THE letter to my room to read alone. The pages were folded, my name across the front. Sealed with wax, so my mother hadn't read it. She'd kept it inside the Portuguese Bible she'd carried since she was a girl. I closed my eyes and concentrated on the tear of the paper beneath my fingernail as I opened it.

My old friend,

I write, though I do not know if you are alive or dead, though I do not know if this letter will ever reach you, because I find I cannot bid farewell to the greatest joys of my life without sharing them with you. They are part of you, in some way, after all. I envisioned for many years that I would find you with your daughter, and with mine. I know now that you never knew them. I confess the fault is mine.

Perhaps it is a revelation that you have a daughter. Her name was Rachel. I met her when she came to Boston, when she arrived at the office of my newspaper from her home on the Cape, seeking a man she called Ishmael. Seeking you. She knew so little of you, but she was filled with hope at the possibility of you, revealed in the stories you had sent to the Spyglass. I understood her desire to meet you, having read the wonders that sprang from your mind, but I was more impressed with her mind. I had never met a woman more determined and intelligent. I loved how she would not let the limits of her knowledge frustrate her ambition. I could not stand in her way as she sought and learned. I wanted to consume the entire world with her. We were young and poor, so we studied the world in books and in our work. We dreamed of the day we could explore it all.

And then a letter from you arrived, after months of silence. I knew that if she saw it, she would want us to chase you. I found I did not want the world anymore. I hid the letter, and those that came after. I tried to replace her dream of you with my own offering. I tried to give her a corner of the world to call her own, and I thought that would be enough. When our daughter was born, it was enough for me. I had all I could ever want, but Rachel did not.

It pains me to admit that I was so ignorant of the woman I claimed to love. It pains me to tell you she is gone. I did not succeed in hiding your letters forever, and when she found them, she understood what I had done, and she left without me. She took our daughter, Margaret. Mara.

I followed your letters to Peru, and when I did not find you, I chased your legend across the globe. I am too near to death to lie anymore, and so I must confess that, at times, I loved those years of searching. I saw the world, after all. Most of the time, I believed I would find Rachel and Mara in it, with you. Sometimes, I believed I would find you, alone. I confess I would have felt some satisfaction even in that. In my journey, I began to understand Rachel's single-mindedness, how one desire can overtake all others and become the only answer to all questions. Having read your stories, I know you understand this, and I know you understand the terrible cost of such certainty.

I searched for you until, in the most desolate of places, I was forced to accept that I had lost you. I had been following a false trail for months, perhaps years. If I could have given you up sooner, if I had only returned home immediately when I did not find you in Peru, I would have known the truth. I would have known Rachel was dead, and I would have found Mara. I could have spared her the pain of abandonment, the loss of both her parents, the loss of her childhood. Mara has spent her life running from every memory of her mother, and every thought of you. She blames you, but I am at fault. She has given me nothing but forgiveness, and she has brought me along on the grand adventures of her best years, making up for all I missed. I want her to have the chance to forgive you, as well.

In my last days, I have come to understand how my search for you was not in vain. Rachel longed to know you, and I long for you to know about her. I want you to know my daughter, your granddaughter. I hope this letter will be carried to you by your great-granddaughter. Antonia is a remarkable girl, in more ways than I can describe, as is her mother, as was Rachel.

My joy has been in knowing them. I do not regret my lies, because I cannot regret my life. But I am sorry my lies kept Rachel and Mara from you, and you from them. I am sorry to see how my choices left Mara with a loss so large, she cannot face it. I will not force Antonia to find you, but I hope that she will choose to. I hope I can give you each other, and in doing so, fix what I have broken.

While I could not find you, I believe my Annie possesses a gift that will allow her to. I will give her a small gift of my own to aid her. But I will not root all my hope or hers in finding you, alone. Even if you elude her, or if she learns you have died, I rest in the assurance that she will be transformed by the journey, as I was. I write this letter for her as much as you, for she may be the only one to ever read it.

Goodbye, my dear old friend. I give you my very best.

Most Sincerely,

Nathaniel Norcross Sweet

~~~~~

I HEARD GRANDFATHER'S voice in my head as I read the words. I remembered him in his armchair. The lamplight reflecting in his eyeglasses. I could imagine how he would have sped up with excitement in some passages. How his voice would have dropped under the burden of his confessions. I felt all his love, and how much I'd loved him. I finally understood what he meant about fixing what he had broken. It had nothing to do with my mother's stubbornness or restlessness. It had nothing to do with fault or blame. I had misunderstood his mission for me. Twisted it into my own bitter vision.

I wanted to try again. Grandfather thought my sense would help, but it had done nothing but taken me farther and farther from the truth. I'd done nothing but pull apart what Grandfather hoped to push back together.

I took the letter downstairs. Mama and Tia waited, holding hands. Mrs. Aster had gone out, but the room was filled with the smell of an apple pie she left baking. Sweet and tart and fragrant.

When I first tried to speak, my voice was strangled by the threat of tears. I took a deep breath.

"So, Ishmael is my great-grandfather?"

Tia looked at Mama. Mama took a breath that matched mine. "You didn't know?"

"Grandfather never said."

"Yes. I suppose he would be."

I nodded. I wanted to tell them Grandfather's letter had revealed everything, solved everything. I wanted to believe it had, but I knew it hadn't. I bit my fingernail, trying to figure out how to tell them what I still didn't know.

"What's wrong?" Tia asked.

"I don't understand," I said. "I don't know what I expected. It's a wonderful letter. I see now why he wanted me to find Ishmael. But I don't understand how I'm supposed to."

Tia reached out. "May I?"

I let her read it. Mama tried to decline when Tia offered it to her, but Tia whispered to her until she took the pages, too. Mama dabbed her face with the sleeve of her blouse as she read, trying to hide her tears. I was glad to see her crying. Not because I wanted to see her hurt. But because I realized how much she'd held back. How much she'd refused to think about, or feel. And now she was seeing another side to the story. We both were.

"He said he was going to give me a gift. He must have meant the tooth," I said. "I thought it led me to London. But it wouldn't have done any good if I'd made it. I thought you were lying when you said he was swindled there, Mama. But I was wrong. It would have been the same dried-up trail."

Mama shifted the paper in her hands, reading and rereading. I couldn't tell if she was looking for something for me, or for herself.

"Do we have any of Ishmael's letters? Anything else?" I asked.

Mama shook her head. "Your grandfather took them on his journey. When we returned from Brazil, I—" She swallowed the words. Deciding what she was willing to say. "I asked him to destroy them, or at least hide them away. I do not know which he chose."

"It's all right," I said. I realized I hadn't tried to comfort her, for any reason, since we'd sailed across the Atlantic. But I could remember how it felt to try to ease her pain. "I see why."

Tia stood suddenly and paced across the room. Paced back. She chewed her index finger, like I'd seen her do when she was trying to puzzle through a plot problem in one of her scripts. When she was coaching actors onstage and couldn't get a reaction she wanted. When a thought was rattling around in her brain and she couldn't let it go until she made some sense of it.

"I didn't know about your gift when I pointed you toward finding the tooth," she said.

Mama's chin snapped up, her brow furrowed. Tia must have kept a few secrets of her own, after all.

"Not exactly. But he and I talked about this matter sometimes." She glanced at Mama. "All those late nights telling stories with him and Clary in the Boston years."

"Do you remember anything that might help me know where to start?" I asked.

She kept pacing. Burrowing a track into Mrs. Aster's plush carpet from the couch to the stove. "I don't know. I'm thinking."

"You could go to the library," Mama said. "The Boston Public Library would have old copies of the *Spyglass*. We know the era of Ishmael's stories. Perhaps if you read them, some connection would reveal itself."

Almost hope. Not quite. I liked the idea of a first destination at least. "Maybe."

"No," Tia said. She stopped her pacing and stood between us. Crossed her arms tight against her chest. "If he wanted you to read the stories, he would have told you to read the stories. He was going to give you the tooth."

"We can't know for sure the tooth was even meant to be the gift, Otávia," Mama said, in her teacher's voice. "Research will—"

"Oh, Maré," Tia said, rolling her eyes. She grabbed Mama's hand and pressed it to her cheek.

Mama's expression wavered between grief and awe. "He told you?"

"Not everything, but enough. He wanted some assurance that his heart was pointing him in the right direction, and I believe it was. Are you ready to know about Ishmael?"

Mama lifted her hand and held it over Tia's. "I hope so."

Anticipation churned in my stomach, becoming urgency. I had no question anymore. If only I could figure out where to go, I would go there. I'd go wherever it took. The day's revelations had already released so much, I could see the cascade waiting for us in the future. The journey waiting for me.

"But why would he leave it such a puzzle? Why not just tell me where to start?"

As I said it, I realized the tooth was the only map he could give. All he had was faith I could read it right. He was sure I could find what he couldn't, if I let myself.

I'd been guarding the tooth ever since Mama gave it back to me. When I was in my room I'd changed into a dress with deep pockets I'd added when Mrs. Aster taught me to sew. I'd reached in and felt the tooth, tucked in safely. I'd felt the thrum of years in it. The depth and breadth of its roving life. Beyond Grandfather's. Beyond Ishmael's.

An idea burst into my mind. "I'll be right back."

I ran upstairs to my room. To the stack of sea-green notebooks. I dug through them, scattering them across the floor until I found the one I wanted. The first notebook I bought, full of Moscow streets and buildings.

I flew back down the stairs and leapt onto the couch next to Mama. Pulled Tia over to sit beside me. I opened the notebook, turned to the last two pages. Traced over the shaky lines that shaped the continents. Adjusted borders I hadn't yet mastered when I'd drawn them the first time. The globe stretched out across two ovals.

"I drew this when we first came here. This was the tooth's path as I remembered it."

I tracked my pencil across the looping, jagged, seemingly random line I'd drawn. The route of Grandfather chasing Ishmael. So many familiar places. Boston and Brazil and London. The islands where he hopscotched across the Pacific. The cities tucked into the throats of bays where he'd searched and waited. The cold end of his journey, in the Faroe Islands.

"But this isn't all I see."

I gripped the tooth in my free hand. Rested the tip of the pencil in Boston, where Grandfather's journey and the path I'd drawn started. I closed my eyes. Guided my hand with my mind to tiny places, invisible on the map. The knotted rope of sea voyages. And the longest path of all, the life of the whale. I opened my eyes. My hand hovered above the open ocean.

"The tooth didn't always belong to Ishmael. Somewhere in here, he got ahold of it. And somewhere in here, he left it, and Rachel found it. I had to go back to the beginning, like Grandfather said."

I asked to have the letter back. My eyes darted across the words so fast, I barely spotted what I was looking for. I flipped the notebook over to its paperboard back cover. Sketched a rough, glacier-carved coastline.

"Massachusetts," Mama said.

"Yes. And see?" I started in Boston. "Rachel came to the city from her home on the Cape, Grandfather wrote." I drew a line that paralleled the coast, the path of the railroad to the curve-toed peninsula. "And she did come from there. But—" I squeezed the tooth tighter. Running over the path again and again in my mind. "The tooth was on the Cape almost no time at all. Maybe only a few days. So she found it right before she came to Boston, or she lied about where she'd been. Either way, we can guess where Ishmael left the tooth. It stayed in one place in that time more than any other." I drew a line out into the Atlantic. Sketched a curving coastline far offshore, like the mouth of a gull gaping toward the mainland. "Here. This little island. I don't know what it's called."

Mama took the pencil from my fingers. Added her swooping, even script to the map. *Nantucket.*

Chapter 23

I KEPT MY eyes fixed on the horizon. Mrs. Aster said it would help with the seasickness. I wasn't sure how she knew, but she was right. I inhaled the cool ocean air as I leaned over the rail along the deck of the steam ferry. The day was clear, the sun's halo directly above me. The bold blue of the sky faded as it reached for the blue of the water. Nantucket was thirty miles offshore, but still I swore I could see the faint shape of a sandy bar in the distance. I gripped the rail and turned my head just enough to see the outline of Cape Cod disappearing. A burble from my stomach got me looking at the horizon again. It was wider than I'd ever imagined it. The sea spread out like delicate fabric. The ripples from the wind like tiny wrinkles.

The other people on the ferry were a type I recognized. The rich American version of the artsy folks Mama and Tia had always drifted toward in Europe. A mustached man down the deck from me dabbed oil paints onto a canvas, occasionally bracing himself when we hit a swell. Three women in expensive dresses whispered in a corner. A couple sat with their hips touching, glancing at each other and blushing. I could see they hadn't known each other long at all. If any of them noticed me, I couldn't tell. I figured I stuck out at least a little.

As if people could sense the Idaho on me, with my simple dress and mussed hair. I'd outgrown the white lace gown I'd worn on the SS *La Loire* and hadn't had much patience for nice dresses in Moscow. Mama and Tia gave me a new one with a ruffled collar before I left. They'd planned to give it to me for my first day of college. But I didn't wear it on the ferry, because I figured I should save it for that occasion, if it happened. I still didn't know whether it would. How could I guess what would come in the future when everything I'd planned had already changed?

I loved waving out the train window to my friends and family as I left Moscow. It felt better than the furtive goodbye I'd first planned. But as I rattled away, I got more and more uneasy. For years I'd been cocooned in the comfort of certainty. I had a plan. I had a path. New York, London, Ishmael, the Faroe Islands. I'd done the work to make it possible, as well as I knew how. And I suppose that's why I'd gripped my plan so tightly for so long. Even when some part of me started to doubt it was worth it. It felt good to *know*. I'd learned young how easy it was to pick up and leave a place. How simple it was to carry a secret. How swiftly that sparrow of death could land. When the world seemed like a rough and bottomless sea, it felt good to think I was sailing for land.

Now I was off into the unknown. The trip to Nantucket might lead me to a trail, or it might not. I might find Ishmael, or I might not find a single soul who knew his name. If I did find him, what came next? Would he come back to Idaho with me, would I send for Mama and Tia? And what then? Grandfather had hoped we would meet, but hadn't laid out any sort of plan for what life would look like after that. I was heading into unknown waters.

I did make a promise to Polly before I got on the train. Even after she'd confessed it had been her who told Mama I was planning to run away, not Mrs. Aster. She stumbled through her explanation, more at a loss for words than I'd ever seen before. But it came down not to jealousy that I was leaving or an unwillingness to see me go. Polly was always looking for the possible. She could see the way my mother cared about me, even when I couldn't. I forgave her. Thanked her. And promised to bring her back a real whaling harpoon, if I could get my hands on one. If I ever found myself back in Moscow. She thought it would make an unexpected coatrack for the library.

The ferry sailed into the gull's mouth of Nantucket, and land started to replace the sky. A few boats were scattered across the water. Sunlight reflected off the gray roofs of the town as we curved past a stout lighthouse and into the harbor. The beaches were empty. I spotted a lone figure carrying a parasol down the wharf. A handful of men unloaded crates from a smaller ship. But otherwise, Nantucket was quiet.

Onshore, I left the wharf and crossed a cobblestone street, gritty with sand. My head felt fizzy with the thrill of being close, finally, to answering questions I'd thought about for so long. I reminded myself that I still might find nothing at all. One of the most likely outcomes, as Grandfather wrote, was learning Ishmael was dead. But actually looking for him, instead of just thinking about it, felt like a huge leap. I pulled the whale's tooth out of my pocket. I'd never been to Nantucket before, but it had. I could feel where it had rested during its time on the island. I let it pull me through streets and alleys, past crumbling buildings and large, elegant homes. It stopped me outside a gray-shingled house that matched all the ones surrounding it, except for an ornate glass lantern hanging from a hook by the door. I rang the bell.

A woman in a white apron, her tight curls shaped into a pompadour, answered. "May I help you?"

Her accent was unfamiliar. I let my sense brush briefly across her and saw she'd come to the island less than a year before, from another island thousands of miles away. But maybe she knew of some documents remaining in the house. Or of a previous owner.

"I'm so sorry to bother you, ma'am. I'll only take a moment of your time."

She crossed her arms. Probably thought I was trying to sell something or preach.

"My name is Antonia Sweet. I'm hoping to find information about a man who might have lived here once. Many years ago. Do you know much about the history of the house?"

"I am afraid I cannot help you much with that, Miss Sweet." She held out her hand to shake mine and introduced herself as Mrs. Lopes. "If you are looking for a room to rent, I can be more helpful."

I'd planned to stay at a seaside hotel I'd requested a booklet for by mail. But I couldn't pass up what was right in front of me. "I am looking for a room, actually," I said.

Mrs. Lopes opened the door wide and swept out her arm to welcome me in. I could smell cookies baking somewhere. Through a doorway I could see tables stacked with dishes from a lunch that had recently ended. A narrow staircase led from the entryway to what I figured were the boarders' rooms.

"The house was abandoned when we moved in. Not a scrap in it," she said as she guided me to a desk stacked with a register and other papers. My heart sank. "I do not think you will find anything, though you are welcome to look anywhere in the main part of the house. We're not so busy with guests. Nantucket has not been an important destination for many years, but my husband's aunt assured us visitors were coming more and more. The artists and tycoons, she said." She handed me a brass key with a tag engraved *201*. "I'm guessing you are not either of those. But I am glad you found your way here."

~~~~~

THE ROOM WAS warm and humid. If I concentrated, I thought I could hear waves, even though the wind was gentle. I hung up my clothes and got out the first of several notebooks I'd packed to document my travels. It was hard not to feel discouraged as I drew my path through Nantucket's streets to Mrs. Lopes's house. I was tempted to write *dead end*. Finding evidence of Ishmael connected to the place where the tooth had stayed was my first and best hope. But just because I didn't find anything immediately didn't mean nothing existed. I was too tired from travel to look elsewhere just yet. I wrapped myself tight in the pink-and-yellow quilt on the bed. Stared at the shadows on the ceiling.

Even though I was used to sleeping on trains, I always left them feeling worn out and soupy. And I had gotten hardly any sleep the night before I left Moscow. I'd been up all hours, thinking of what I'd say to Mama. She and Tia had assured me they didn't expect anything to come of my journey. They would be happy to know any story I found, any way I wanted to share it. But I could see how hard it was for Mama not to beg me to come back as soon as I could. To tell her everything. It was hard for me not to give in and swear I'd come home and never leave. I needed to assure her that whatever happened, whatever I found, wherever I went, I'd see her again someday. We were still figuring out how to trust each other's words. I needed to give her more than that.

After I hugged Tia on the train platform, I turned to Mama. I lifted her hand to my face. I closed my eyes and poured all my thoughts into remembering the day I'd chased the albatross. I remembered the pull I'd felt toward it as I saw its feathers ruffled by the wind. I remembered how I'd seen nothing but the bird as I wound through the crowd. I remembered turning back around. Following the path I knew without knowing. Finding my family at the end.

I didn't have to say anything else to Mama at all.

I drifted off with that memory fresh in my mind. When I woke up not long after, I felt the spark I needed to keep going. I wanted to find Ishmael, or learn more about him at least. I had faith it would mean something to my family if I did. So my first attempt failed. That shouldn't have been a surprise.

Even with the remarkable things I could see, I knew so little about Ishmael. I had no way of knowing whether he'd brought the tooth to Nantucket when it first arrived on the island, more than fifty

years before. Or if he'd come into possession of it closer to the time
it left the island nearly twenty years later. He couldn't have stayed
the whole time. I didn't know for sure that he'd even stayed in Mrs.
Lopes's house. Only that the tooth had. Everything Grandfather
knew seemed to indicate that Ishmael flittered around, restless and
wandering. There had to be some gap between when he'd left it and
Rachel had found it, whether she had found it here or on the Cape.

Mama's perfect memory couldn't make up for the fact that she'd
resolutely avoided talking to Grandfather about Ishmael. Tia recalled
stories, but it was hard to tell what was true. Ishmael had not only
used a pen name for his stories in the *Spyglass*, but had also disguised
his identity in the letters he sent with them. Grandfather and Tia
guessed that most of the names and places in the old articles were
pseudonyms. Or made up entirely. I was looking for a man known for
his rampant fabrication and exaggeration. For his love of outlandish-
ness. We agreed he was real, but it was impossible to know whether
the details we thought we knew about him were true. He said he was
a sailor. The port-to-port route Grandfather had followed around
the world made that plausible enough. And his stories of hunting the
white whale made the Nantucket connection logical. But thousands of
men from around the globe had sailed from Nantucket.

I had a list of other places to search for information. Mrs. Aster
insisted the newspaper office should be my first stop, after wherever
the tooth led. Patience said I should wander around until I found high
school girls, who always knew everyone's business. But Mama, Tia,
Polly, and I agreed the library was the place to go. The Atheneum. An
esteemed institution, mentioned often in the writings I found about
Nantucket. A library was the type of place where I could walk in
with a wild story and walk out with something that would help me
tell it better.

It was easy to spot the Atheneum. Every other building I'd seen
in Nantucket so far was weathered shingles or red brick. But the
library was a lofty white box. Grecian columns propped up a pedi-

ment that displayed ATHENEUM in thin gold letters. A low wall surrounded a garden that spread from the broad front porch. I'd walked into some of the most glorious cathedrals and monuments in the world when I was a girl. But I was still a little nervous walking up the Atheneum steps.

The library was plain inside. Dark floors and simple rows of books. Paintings on the walls, busts perched on the ends of a few shelves. No one else browsing. A woman leaned on the librarian's desk, reading a copy of *The All-Story*. So wrapped up in it, she didn't look up at first.

"Excuse me," I said. She didn't respond. "I'm hoping you can help me."

She jerked up, blushing. "Of course! Yes, of course. How can I help you?"

"I'm trying to find the history of a house here in town. I believe a sailor I'm looking for information about might have stayed there once. My great-grandfather."

It felt exciting to call Ishmael that. Just being on Nantucket made him seem closer. Telling the librarian an address and description of the house gave me a fresh surge of hope. It wasn't such a dead end after all.

The puzzlement on her face threatened to dampen my spirits. But I could sense she'd lived on the island her whole life, even though she wasn't old enough to have overlapped with the time of Ishmael. She'd walked past the location in question many times.

"It's changed hands quite often these past few years," she said. She untangled her eyeglasses from her hair. Slid them down her nose. "To be honest, I can't seem to recall the names of any owners, at the moment. I suppose you've talked to the family living there now?"

"I'm renting a room from them," I said. "But Mrs. Lopes said the house was completely empty when they moved in."

"There will be records, of course. Some of the old boardinghouses and inns donated their guest lists to the archives. Though I can't seem to think of any name for the place. Do you know what ship he sailed on, by chance? We have excellent records of whaleships."

Tia said Grandfather had mentioned a ship called the *Perses* in the stories Ishmael sent to the *Spyglass*. But also that he knew that name wasn't real.

"Not exactly," I said.

"Pardon me, young lady, but this sounds like it's going to take a while."

An old woman in dark glasses and a straw hat with a bright blue ribbon was standing behind me, leaning on her cane. I hadn't heard her walk in.

The librarian stepped around the desk and put a hand on the woman's shoulder. "Good afternoon, Mrs. Prince. I'll get our visitor started on the records, then we'll go sit. You'll like the story I found for you today. It's rather riveting."

"I was talking to this girl here," Mrs. Prince said. "What sort of records are you looking for? I've got a good deal of records stored right here in my head. Might speed things up a bit."

I checked her path. Born on Nantucket, left as a girl, returned only recently. She'd been all over the island, but I couldn't see how she'd be much help. Maybe she could have crossed paths with Ishmael when she was a child. Unlikely she'd remember him if she did.

"Please don't fret over me," I said. "I can wait so you can hear your story. I'll come back tomorrow."

"I can assure you I am not fretting over you one bit. And I don't appreciate your pity," the woman said. "Now I insist you tell me what you are looking for."

I told her the address of the house, mumbled a bit about knowing someone who might have stayed there once. But she smiled, sharp and foxlike.

"Oh, I know that old place. My mother said the innkeeper made the nastiest chowder you'd ever tasted in your life when I was a girl. Yes, I remember that place well."

Even the librarian seemed surprised. I dug into my bag for my notebook, my palms sweating as I tried to find a pen.

"Do you mind if we sit and talk a minute? I have some questions you might be able to help with. Many questions, actually."

Her eyebrows shot above her glasses. "I would rather listen to my story, thank you. You can occupy yourself by following Water to Main, a slight right, a bit of a left, and left again at the house with too many windows. Bit more after that, then right at the mansion with the hideous garden. Take the narrow street off to the right. Walk like a lady or you'll break your ankle in the potholes. Look for a bedraggled little scrap of a house. I'm sure they'll love answering all your nosy questions."

I frantically sketched the route in my notebook. Hoped I could make sense of it. She didn't have to tell me twice. I shouted my thanks and was off and running.

~~~~~~~

THE WHALE WAS soft gray against ocean blue. Painted above the porch of a tiny shingled house squished into a row that seemed mostly abandoned, overgrown with climbing vines and flowers. I wasn't nervous to knock on the door. I couldn't wait to see what I would discover inside. A round, rosy-cheeked woman answered.

"Good afternoon," I said, still panting from my run. "Some folks at the library sent me your way because I'm told you can help me with . . . with a bit of a history question. It's a long story. May I come in?"

She stepped back, though she looked surprised. "Of course, dear. You make yourself at home, and I'll see what we can do."

The woman introduced herself as Ruth and showed me to an overstuffed armchair. She asked me to wait a moment and disappeared down the hall. I looked around a bit. The sitting room was sparse, with one other chair by the fireplace. But the walls were crammed full of pictures of whales. Prints from books and clips from magazines stuck up with pins. Framed pen and charcoal sketches. The largest were all paintings in the same style as the one on the porch. Whales twisting and leaping against the open sea, their figures formed by a few smooth brushstrokes. Most matched the species carved into the tooth I carried. Sperm whales, I'd learned from Mama. I settled into the chair, taking them all in. A cool, refreshing feeling seeped through my body. The way I imagined it would feel to walk into the ocean.

Ruth returned with two mugs. I'd never liked coffee, but I gave it a polite sip. It was sweet and milky.

"Hope you don't mind," Ruth said. "It's how we like it here."

She'd said *we* twice. Mrs. Prince had said *they* would talk to me at the house. Could Ishmael be just down the hall, ready to walk in at any moment? I told myself to wait. To be realistic. I'd find out more when it was time.

"Thank you kindly, Ruth," I said, turning up my manners as if Patience and Mama were watching. "I hope you don't mind me showing up unexpectedly, but I heard you could tell me more about an old inn here in town."

The pink flushed out of Ruth's cheeks as she gulped down the coffee she'd just sipped. She coughed, then laughed.

"Pardon me. It's been a while since anyone's asked about the Try Pots. Where'd a girl like you hear about the old place?"

I grinned at her. "It really is a long story."

"You're in good company in this house, then. We're familiar with long stories." She paused, studying my face. Staring as if she'd met me before and was trying to place me. "Where'd you say you came from again?"

"Out west," I said. "Idaho. But I was born in Massachusetts, as was my mother. I think I may have had some family here on Nantucket, at some point."

Ruth nodded. She appeared to be holding in a smile. "I bet that *is* a long story you have. But I think you've come to the right place. Give me another moment, will you?"

Soon she stuck her head back into the room and waved me over, speaking in a low voice as she led me down the hall.

"I must warn you, she looks well, but she is quite ill," she said. "She speaks very little, and it is a great struggle for her to do so. But she will understand everything you say. I'll give you a moment alone with her before I come in and assist."

She opened a door into a room with billowing curtains and open windows letting in a breeze that smelled of fresh fish. A thin, white-haired woman sat up in the bed. A yellow quilt wrapped her from toes to shoulders. The hem at her throat brushed against a necklace that appeared to be made of small, translucent bones.

Her path reached out to me before I could even intend to sense it. Like nothing I'd ever seen before. It was as if she were split in two. Severed. One part of her coming to Nantucket as a young woman and staying her entire life since. One part of her venturing to the farthest reaches of the ocean, icy seas and warm whirlpools and places too deep for light to reach. But as she extended a shaky hand out to me, I sensed the two begin to intertwine.

She smiled as the skin of her palm met mine. She took a long breath, as if coming up for air.

"I am so pleased to meet you, Antonia," she said. Her voice strong and clear. "I have been waiting."

The grandmother lags behind the others as they skim the sun-warmed waves. Ahead, the mother breathes out, the arc of air shattering the sunlight into sparkling colors. The daughter ascends beside her, breathing and bobbing, dipping beneath the surface and rising again. The granddaughter dashes beyond them all, racing, pushing, until at last she leaps. Her head twists as it rises, her gray body bowing until her belly is exposed to the sky. She does not appear to float or fly; she declares her immense weight. Spray erupts around her, a rush of white water that crashes into itself, sending up another crest that fractures into wavelets and ripples. Before the sea settles, she leaps again.

The grandmother trails. She drifts. Her great heart, so used to slowing when she descends to the deep, seizes, stops. It does not start again.

The daughter notices first, nosing the still floating figure. The grandmother's lids slide over her eyes, now lost among the scarred prairie of her head. A crashing cry gathers the others. They swarm her, shoving her sides, pressing their snouts to her head and fins. She does not respond.

They push her with them, their urging nudges flaking off papery skin nipped by fish as it diffuses into the sea. They push until hunger demands they leave.

She is alone, but not done. Sharks arrive, splitting the body. The rush of sinking leaves a cyclone of blood, drawing more. By the time she reaches the floor she is fragments, which settle into the sand. A long-limbed crab plucks blubber, a snail dissolves muscle, mussels nestle beneath fins, a meadow of worms grow on bone.

A squid slips past, its enormous eye blind to the body unraveled into splayed ribs and exposed spine, the skull still shrouded. With extended tentacles, it finds a fish huddling in the cove of the tail. Before it can eat, a call echoes through the expanse, the stunning announcement of a whale.

Part Five

EVANGELINE

Nantucket, 1905

Chapter 24

I HAVE BEEN waiting for you, Annie, Antonia, my saint of lost things. I am seventy-nine years old, as far as I know, so you may think I have had a lifetime of waiting. I suppose I have. Along the way I learned patience, which commuted waiting into something more. I have learned so much while waiting. I have seen, as I have always been so good at doing. And I have learned the limits of what I can see. Truth is, indeed, a slippery fish. Seeing does not always mean knowing; seeing does not always mean understanding. I have learned I must listen, and I must ask, to know. And sometimes I must wait.

You have come in search of a story, and I am happy to provide. I remember . . . most things. I remember Hosea's warm hands, the scent and sizzle of an onion in butter, the way to hold the knife to open a clam. I remember the smell of Rachel's hair, the roughness of Elijah's voice, the bounce in Freddy's walk, the ring of Tistig's laugh. And Ishmael—of course I remember him. But this is not a story about Ishmael. This whale's tooth you returned to me reveals as much. It was a gift from my friend Queequeg. It has always amused me to see you all believe it was Ishmael's, to hear you wrap it in legends, to watch you seek out its hidden stories. It is good to hold it again.

But I'm getting ahead of myself. I shall begin with what I remember.

It took me some time to appreciate the smell of dead fish.

~~~~~~

I BELIEVED MY determination would make Rachel's childhood easier. I'd had the will to live my life behind an illusion, even when it felt nearly impossible, so surely I could create a better life from the truth. She was my daughter, and I would not fear the consequences of her illegitimacy. No one said a word—at first.

I allowed my hired woman to make the chowder on the day Rachel was born, but I granted myself little rest beyond that. The demands of the inn would not relent merely because I'd given birth. When Rachel was two days old, I fashioned a sling from a sheet and carried her on my hip as I gutted fish and sliced salt pork and stirred my pots. My hips felt stretched, my legs loose in their sockets, my back wrenched and burning. My skin welled with sweat even more than usual in the sweltering, steam-filled kitchen, the flow of afterbirth filled the cloths I'd used to tamp it, and when Rachel fussed my breasts dripped milk. I rushed upstairs to change my sodden gown, laying Rachel on the bed, careful to keep her swaddled, praying she would stay asleep. Of course she did not. I fed her, half dressed, listening to the grumbles of the patrons below demanding their breakfast. I did not let myself weep, though I felt as if tears were pooling in my stomach, filling my throat. This was my daughter. This was my inn.

By the time she was a week old, I had learned to balance her in one arm and the chowder bowls in the other, and even coaxed her into the sling without tears once or twice. Hosea's cousin, Peter Coffin, arrived on Nantucket for business and stayed at the Try Pots, as he always did. He was waiting at the table closest to the kitchen when I emerged, and I placed the fullest bowl of clam before him. He knit his fingers together on the table and did not pick up his spoon. His face held the tense smile of a man who had been waiting to say something.

"Mrs. Hussey," Mr. Coffin said, speaking low so I had to stop and lean in to hear him. "I miss my cousin, as I am sure you do as well."

It was the first time he had ever acknowledged that Hosea was dead. I was unsurprised to hear it; word had quickly spread of Hosea's death once I stopped whispering my lies. Still, I did not expect what he said next.

"I regret very much Hosea isn't here to see his beautiful child."

I froze, my mouth agape, unsure I had heard him correctly. Did my old illusion have a greater hold on him than I realized? Could I have, in my exhaustion, said something to affect his mind? But no. I was bare to the world. Mr. Coffin was proposing an illusion of his own.

"It is unfortunate," he continued, "that a widow such as yourself should be working without a mother or sisters to assist you. I would propose my own wife come help, but she's quite busy with our own little brood, as I'm sure you can imagine. But if you were to sell the inn . . ." He trailed off, peering at me from beneath his hat with expectant eyes. "We would let you keep one room for yourself, of course."

"I appreciate the offer, Mr. Coffin, but I cannot accept," I said. "I will not be selling to you or to anyone."

Disbelief and annoyance flashed across his face. I noticed him clench his hands as he controlled his emotion, settling again into the soft voice.

"Surely Hosea would want his wife to be able to care for his child. Let me see the girl, won't you? My own dear little cousin."

He reached up and gently tugged the swaddling blanket away from Rachel's cheeks, ran a finger beneath the edge of her cap to reveal one dark curl. "Funny, she doesn't look a thing like him. Or you, for that matter."

I understood the threat, yet I was undeterred. Let Mr. Coffin say what he would like about me and my child. I neither asked nor expected him or anyone to pretend that Rachel was Hosea's. If I traded my inn for that lie, what would I have? A pocketful of money, less than the inn was worth no doubt, and nowhere to go. I preferred that my child be ashamed and fatherless than trapped in a single room in an inn owned by someone who would always despise her. She needed a home.

Mr. Coffin squeezed his eyes shut and ran his fingers down the sides of his nose. "Perhaps you do not understand me."

"I understand you perfectly well," I said, and turned my back on him as I went to serve my other customers.

I assumed the nasty stories would come knocking before long, but the desire of my neighbors to save face, even on behalf of someone who did not want them to, proved more powerful than my illusion ever had. Ministers and shopkeepers, young fishermen and old whalers, fine ladies and little girls, all of them referred to Rachel as "Hosea's daughter."

I declined to have her christened in a church, choosing instead to let my old friend Elijah, who after all was known as a prophet, say a prayer and wet her brow with seawater. He called her, as I did, Rachel Evangeline. I attempted to decline to have her registered with the town, but the clerk took it upon himself to show up at the inn one afternoon, record book in hand.

"She's a lovely little cherub," he said as he scratched *Hosea & Evangeline Hussey* into the book under *Names of Parents*. Beneath *Occupation of Father* he wrote *innkeeper, deceased*, cramping his immaculate handwriting so both words would fit in the line. He paused briefly at the final line, *Place of Birth of Mother*, before writing *elsewhere*.

"Very well, then, Mrs. Hussey, we've got that taken care of," he said. "Now, might I have a bowl of cod before I go?"

The townspeople's determination wore on me. I had once been tormented by the fear that I would be caught in a lie and left alone; now I discovered the exhaustion of having a lie imposed on me for the sake of community—and the shame of acknowledging how I longed for that lie to be true. I did wish she were Hosea's child. When I watched her before she awoke each morning, I imagined her opening her eyes to reveal the pale blue of Hosea's, instead of the amber of Ishmael's. It was so tempting to tell her stories and claim they were memories. Though life with a dead father was not easy, it was not uncommon on Nantucket. It might ease the pain I knew would continue to come for us. Finally I decided that, while I could not lie to her, I could allow her this one thing, this name. Ishmael offered no surname to me or anyone, and everyone already called her Miss Hussey. It made sense to let her have the name because it was mine, and she was mine.

~~~~~~~

I VOWED ON the day Rachel was born never to attempt to reshape someone's memory again. Even with power behind it, a lie was fragile, weak by nature, easily destroyed. To live in an illusion was to live in fear, and I would not raise my daughter in fear. But I allowed myself to continue seeing people's recent moments, as it required no manipulation of the truth. It was, I believed, convenient for a mother to have such a gift. When she was old enough that I could no longer carry her or tether her to me, I set her free to run about the inn, confident that I would know where she played while I worked. Much of the time she was a placid, imaginative child, content to entertain herself scampering around telling herself stories or playing with the wooden doll and ark of animals I'd saved up to buy for her. I stoked myself with pride when I paused from stirring my pots to watch such visions. But I could see her just as well when she snuck a hunk of warm bread in the kitchen or flung fish heads at Freddy, when she was neglecting the small chores I gave her or jumping on the bed in our room. I rushed to every unruly scene, plucking her off the tops of rickety chairs and dragging her from beneath shadowy tables, diving between her and whatever trouble she caused.

The nerves I thought had healed when she was no longer a helpless infant proved to be raw as ever. Even when she wasn't seeking mischief, danger could await her—the rusty nail in the muddy alley behind the inn, the vicious feral cat lurking beneath the stairs, the silent sailor whose gaze followed her every step through the public room. I ran myself ragged protecting her, pursuing her with a never-ending list of warnings, begging her to pay attention, to be good, to listen. Ellen, the latest of the widows I hired to help around the inn, suggested I hire someone to mind her until she was old enough to go to school, but I could afford no such help—and when I offered her the task, Ellen gave a snide laugh. I ignored it; I needed her in the kitchen, though I knew she would soon quit like all the others. The inn was busy as ever, in spite of everything. The sneers and talk about my situation writhed around Nantucket like a sea serpent, but the serpent did not strike.

I woke one night from a dream of depthless seas, plagued by the idea that, if only I had paid closer attention, if only I had watched him from the moment he left the inn, I could have saved Hosea. I reached out to find Rachel in the bed beside me, sleeping deeply as she always did, her head a sweaty mess of curls on the pillow. I wrapped my arms around her, listening to her breathe and feeling the rise and fall of her chest, until my own heartbeat slowed. She was with me, and even when she was not, I could watch her.

I set Rachel up scrubbing potatoes in the kitchen for the morning just to have her near me, but I relented when she pleaded to go play in the afternoon. I winced at the sound of her stockinged feet thumping and slipping on the floor above. If she was going to scamper around without shoes on, she should walk. I called her name through the still-swinging door of the kitchen, but she did not respond. I called again, walking through the public room, checking the porch. Finally, in impatience, I used my power to find her at the edge of the dark stairway of the second floor, tucking her dress beneath her so she could slide down, an activity I had warned her would hurt if she slipped too fast. She could hear me, and I knew it.

I stomped from the kitchen, wiping the starch from my hands onto my apron, my thoughts a jumble of fear and anger. It was dangerous to play on the stairs, I had told her so many times, and it irritated the guests, besides. It was such a simple thing to ask, and she was old enough to listen. She smiled down at me when I reached the base of the stairwell, her eyes enormous and brown, taking up most of her sharp little face. She looked so much like him. The reminder of it tipped my frustration into fury. Why should my child look like a man I barely knew? Why should he be able to sail away, knowing nothing?

"Rachel, come down this minute," I called up to her.

She shifted her weight and slid down a step, her teeth clacking together as her bottom hit the next landing. She laughed and stretched out her feet to slide again. How could my own child not listen to me? Did she care nothing for me, for all the things I did so she could live a life of peace and safety? I shut my eyes and tried to calm myself, but I heard her slip down the next stair, and the next. I peered into her mind and saw my own contorted face.

"Rachel!" I shouted. "You meant to stand and walk to me!"

The words left my lips laden with power, and I could do nothing to stop them. She stood as if in a fog, her small hand clutching the banister as she stepped down slowly, her feet level and steady on the stairs. And then she stopped. A furious light swept into her eyes. She broke my lie as if it were thinner than the most delicate vase, the shatter echoing in my brain as she scrambled back up the stairs, as if it was all a game.

I was distraught that I had broken my vow, and on my own child no less. I felt she had pressed me—everything had pressed me, forced me to a point of weakness—but I could not put the blame on her. I had once again fooled myself into believing I could shape the world to my will. I heard her call from the top of the stairs, but the sound was muffled by the ringing in my ears. I was tired, so tired. In fact, I'd been planning all day to go upstairs and take a nap. I did not recognize Rachel's power as I excused myself to my room. I'd had such a difficult night, and I deserved more rest. In sleep, my mind returned again to the sea, waves twisting wood until it splintered, cries smothered by water. This time I woke with the realization that even if I had watched Hosea that day so long before, even if I'd used my power to follow his every step, his every breath, all I would have done was watch him die.

~~~~~~~

I MUST APOLOGIZE, Annie. I have not spoken so much in many, many years, and I am tired. Call Ruth; she will make you supper. If she lets you choose between clam or cod, choose cod. Rest well, and I shall see you in the morning.

Chapter 25

DID RUTH MAKE you breakfast? I asked her to put the porridge on early, and to add raisins and cream. She is a better painter than a cook, though she is not so bad at breakfast, and she makes the most wonderful coffee. I hope you don't mind I had her wake you—we need the full day ahead of us. I have been saving these stories for you.

~~~~~

I REVISED MY vow after that day with Rachel on the stairs. When I first made it, I thought I was resisting fear by refusing to manipulate her memories—and when I failed to uphold that promise, I finally understood all the ways in which I had continued to let fear define my moments with my daughter. In my attempts to protect her, I had forgotten to trust her. Though she was still so small, so fragile, she was not helpless or without her own will. And so I vowed to give up using my gifts on my daughter entirely, to stop watching her with my mind, even if it meant leaving her vulnerable. I would even relinquish the habits any mother might have, following her and hounding her and demanding she share everything with me. I had to learn to let her have a life beyond my knowing, or soon enough she would drift beyond my reach.

Though I surrendered my illusions, the people of the island held on to theirs. By the time Rachel started school, the sea serpent of truth still wound its way out of the mouths of my neighbors, but it never quite broke the surface. In polite company, Rachel was Hosea Hussey's girl and the Try Pots Hosea Hussey's inn, run by his competent widow, yet behind closed doors she was a bastard child to a libertine woman. I was lucky, they said, to keep what I had—if only because none of them were brave enough to try to take it from me.

But children, who are so easily lied to, are also apt to reveal a lie's frailty. I had not considered that Rachel believed the stories about Hosea being her father until the day one of his cousins slunk through the front door of the inn. Martha Hussey Chase was a thin woman, thin-lipped and thin-nosed, her hair pulled back so tightly from her face it stretched her skin. She was nearly as young as me, but haggard from years of bearing and chasing children while her husband was out to sea. She had never entered the Try Pots, before or after Hosea died, and she rejected my offer of a bowl of chowder, though I'd made a new recipe that morning—bluefish lightly smoked over the stove, with rosemary and pepper and a rind of lemon I'd preserved the winter before, filling the inn with the scent of smoke and citrus.

She accepted a chair at an empty table, where she sat, glaring at me as I rubbed a dry rag across the pitcher I'd been holding when she'd interrupted me. She had obviously come with something to say, but I could bide my time until she said it.

Finally she flared her nose and said, "That girl of yours struck my Alice," elongating *girl* so it sounded like a filthy term.

"Did she now? I'll speak to her about it."

Light caught a smudge I'd missed on the pitcher, and I polished it with my cloth, ignoring Martha's continued glare.

"You'll *speak* to her about it?"

"What else would you like me to do? They're children. A schoolyard tussle is easily solved. They won't care in a few days' time."

She made a short, irritated sound. "I suppose you'll *speak* to her about being a liar as well, will you, my dear Mrs. Hussey?" Her voice slowed as she said my name.

I set the pitcher down and wiped my forehead. I had little patience for lies in my home, but equally little patience for priggishness.

"Well, Mrs. Chase, why don't you get on with it and tell me whatever you came here to tell me about my daughter? I have customers to tend to, and you've got no chowder in front of you."

She curled her lip but relented. "Alice came home yesterday, her hair all in shambles, saying Rachel hit her for insulting her father. I tell my daughter the truth, and I had informed her well before that your girl's father was a common penniless sailor who deserved harsh words—for what he did to you, of course, abandoning you here with a child." She wrestled her mouth into an attempt at a sweet smile. "But would you believe my daughter spoke back at me that I knew nothing, that Rachel's father was the good innkeeper Hosea Hussey and I was not to sully his name? She had the insolence to call me a liar, when she was repeating the lies of that . . . that little *girl* of yours."

I nearly laughed in her face. The impudence to insist that my child had woven some elaborate tale when all she'd done was repeat what all the adults pretended to believe!

I bent as if to pick up my pitcher from the table and paused inches from Martha's face, keeping my voice even and low. "I so appreciate you telling me, Mrs. Chase. I will be sure to speak with my daughter."

I went on with my chores, waiting for Rachel to come home. As I dusted my desk, I picked up the daguerreotype I kept of Hosea, taken when he was a young man, not long before I met him. My mind kept a perfect image of his face, but holding a material image of him reassured me that he was truly all I remembered him to be. I understood so well why Rachel embraced the idea that he was her father. I had wondered so many times what it would have been like to have him beside me as we navigated the miraculous and treacherous waters of raising a child. I tucked the picture into the bedside drawer in the room I no longer shared with Rachel, where she would not see me looking at it.

I had assumed my daughter was too young to wonder about her father's identity—she knew plenty of fatherless children on Nantucket, so her own father's absence could not seem too unusual. I had failed, however, to recognize how Rachel's keen mind would know the moment the truth was revealed, and I failed to recognize the looming peril brought on by letting the town carry on as they had. I should have known the lie would not hold; should have seen what pain would come with that collapse. But I had let it stand because, no matter how I hated to admit it, it helped me survive. I had sworn off my own power, but I had held on to theirs.

And she, I understood now, had her own, in more ways than I had recognized. I had no doubt Martha Chase had been whispering the truth about Ishmael to Alice her whole life; I knew as well that Alice was as incorrigibly conceited as her mother. Rachel could not have persuaded her to repeat the lie about Hosea without some strange power. My first feeling upon this realization was curiosity. If she had inherited her ability from me, in what ways was it like mine, and in what ways was it all her own? I realized how strong she must have been to change someone's memory with words in a schoolyard quarrel. She had not simply smudged, but entirely repainted what Alice believed. Panic threatened to wipe out my other thoughts as I remembered that day on the stairs when she was small, when she had defied my powers before my eyes but my only reaction had been to take a nap—as she had suggested.

I felt myself aching to corner her, to demand to know more, to beg her to let me teach her to control her power, use it well, use it wisely. But I had made a vow.

That evening I told her the truth about Ishmael and Hosea. I kept it bare and simple, an answer I thought was appropriate for a child. I longed to say how I wished Hosea had been her father, how he would have adored her, but it would not have been fair. Nor could I tell her how I sometimes wished Ishmael had stayed, when I always knew he would never return. She deserved more than illusions and impossible dreams.

Yet I couldn't bear to leave her with nothing but loss. I could see how she grieved for Hosea. I could only guess what desperation must have driven her to try to maintain the townspeople's lie, once she had seen it for what it was. It had been so long since anyone had comforted me, I struggled to find the words to assure her that her anger and pain merited no shame.

"A lie is a fragile thing, Rachel," I said, "but so is a heart."

I OPENED MYSELF to great risk by letting my daughter live her own life, and I opened myself to great risk by living my own. In the years after Rachel's encounter with Alice Chase, the sea serpent rose to the surface. It did not thrash, but merely bobbed and basked where all could see it. Hosea's relations and friends who had despised me since our wedding day quit forcing their smiles and greetings and returned to treating me with passive disdain. The islanders who feared my connection to the *Pequod* tended to avoid me entirely, as if I might conjure the ghost of the cursed ship merely by existing. They did the same to Rachel. I thought the myopia of childhood kept her from noticing; I know now how their whispers grated on her like sand.

The public room of the Try Pots grew quieter as wives began to shame their husbands for buying my chowder, and Mr. Coffin and others ceased recommending my inn to travelers. But the death throes of the whaling industry hurt even more, and the empty harbor meant empty rooms, empty hallways, empty days. At times I had no customers other than my friend Elijah. I worried for the man, for it did not take a prophet to see that he was growing old, his own powers waning. If he foretold anything in those times, he kept it to himself. I suspect he knew the number of his days. But he took great joy in conversing with Rachel, and still consented to hobble along the shore with me, taking in the sea air and warming himself with a bowl of chowder when we returned.

Nantucketers believed abolition was a just cause for war, yet we mourned as that war devoured even more from the island—men and ships and lives. The deaths of Freddy and Elijah should have been more than I could bear, but I no longer believed I could stave off loss. I paid for Elijah's final resting place from my own coffers, and from his graveside went to New Guinea and sat with Sarah's neighbors while she wept. I helped pack her trunk when she left for the mainland.

When I was young, in the days of Ishmael, I had so dreaded being alone. I thought if I fought hard enough, I would never feel abandoned. I did not understand.

I could have clung to Rachel, molded her to fill every hole in me. She was reaching the end of girlhood, one day a sprightly child racing through the halls of the inn and the next a solemn young woman dashing off on errands she would not share with me. I was no longer tempted to protect her from precarious heights and sharp objects, but other dangers lurked. Soon, no doubt, she would awaken to the troubles of life in a town that was crumpling in on itself, and I feared she would discover she had no place among what remained. From her birth she was haunted by the specter of the *Pequod* and the shadow of Ishmael, tainted by the scent of the chowder woman. Her power could only serve to set her apart even more.

I encouraged her love of school to feed her mind with other possibilities. I prayed for an unexpected path to open up to her, but I knew it was unlikely she could do anything other than leave Nantucket and build a life for herself elsewhere. Yet I knew the struggle of fleeing a place to start anew—and I had left no one I loved behind when I was a girl. If Rachel wished to go, she would have to leave me, along with the island. For all I'd lost, my life was still tied to Nantucket, to my inn, my chowders, the view of the sea from my window, the memories threaded through them all. I considered persuading her that her only hope lay in staying, in assisting me in keeping the Try Pots alive, in learning to cook the chowders she despised. We could rebuild our reputation, lure in the wealthy mainland tourists who didn't care about her name or parentage, who thought the *Pequod* was a charmingly terrible tale from a bygone era. If I convinced Rachel she needed no one else but me, perhaps I could save her the pain of learning that no one else might accept her. I would not need my powers. I could control her with guilt; I could control her with fear; I could control her with love. But each time I considered such a path, I remembered my vow.

That is not to say my vow meant I ignored my daughter. I heard plenty; I saw plenty. Though my closest companions were gone, I remained friendly with a few of the island's other misfits and troublemakers, and they spread stories like everyone else. Beyond that, I simply observed her. Even without knowing where she was going or what she was doing every day, I knew my daughter. I knew how her eyes narrowed and her fists quaked when she felt cornered or insulted, how her cheeks grew flushed and her words rushed when she was excited, even when she tried to disguise it. I knew how her steps slowed when her mind was elsewhere, and how often her mind was elsewhere. I knew she could not be contained.

And I knew when young Amos Starbuck drew her eye. The news that she had been frequenting the Starbuck store, despite Balaam's undoubted hostility toward her, found its way to me quickly. When she and Amos began making surreptitious visits to the book room at Shaw Mercantile, I told myself, as I had so many times since her childhood, that I did not need to know what they were up to. I had not raised my daughter to be a fool; I had promised to trust her. Still, I was certain that whatever relationship she had with the boy would end in disaster.

Miss Eliza Shaw had frequented the inn for years, preferring the early mornings or midafternoons when the public room was almost always empty, but we had spoken little due to her insistence upon reading while she ate. For this I liked the woman immensely. She was partial to cod unless I happened to have herring, as I did on the afternoon she arrived at the inn without a book in her hand. When I set the bowl before her, she beckoned me to sit.

I took the chair, though I hoped our conversation would be brief.

"I know what you've come to tell me, and I'll have none of it. I've heard enough already."

"I suspected you had, but wondered if you might like to hear it from a more sympathetic source." She stirred the chowder as she spoke, releasing the fragrance of thyme.

I leaned forward with a sigh, resting my face in my hands and breathing in the smell of fish until my mind settled. At times it took nearly as much effort to refuse to manipulate and interfere as it did to maintain my old illusion.

"Of course I want to know. But what could I do if I did? Trying to keep her away from the boy is bound to make things worse."

"I wasn't going to suggest you should," she said, tilting her chin, inviting me to inquire what she meant.

I wanted to end the discussion and free myself from temptation, but I could not bring my legs to stand. I dug my thumbs into the underside of the table, tapping the surface with my fingernails.

"I'll not spy on my daughter. She's practically a woman; she must be allowed to have business of her own."

"Just ask her, Evangeline," she said. "Ask her."

I had tried asking my daughter to tell me about her day plenty of times before. When she was younger, she answered with great detail and enthusiasm, but her willingness waned as she grew. It had not entirely bothered me, for I knew the things she hid could be no more than schoolgirl adventures, little dramas, and she deserved to treasure them for herself. But her interaction with Amos had consequences. Perhaps it was time again to ask.

I thanked Miss Shaw and returned to my kitchen, filling a small crock with the still-bubbling herring chowder. I had promised a delivery to a housebound old woman who lived in a single room of a grand old house now owned by distant relations, and who either did not know or did not care about my reputation enough to turn away my gifts. I had been unable to find another widow to work for me, so I left the inn and kitchen empty, confident that I would return to no new customers, confident that Rachel would arrive home in time to take on scouring duties, as she had since she was strong enough to haul the heavy pots, despite the vexing itch in the back of my mind suggesting this might finally be the evening she would not.

The only sound when I stepped back into the inn was the clang and clatter of her washing, the rich scent of soap overpowering the ever-present undertone of fish. My hand rose to my throat, to the string of cod bones I'd made so long ago in the same kitchen. My kitchen.

Hosea had been my home. Tistig, Elijah, Sarah, Freddy had been my home. I'd allowed Ishmael and Queequeg to enter, for a time. All had left me. The inn remained, and I loved each splintering floor-board, each threadbare counterpane, each crusted pot. In the days when Ishmael graced its halls, I had tormented myself with the fear that I would lose everything I had strived for, everything I'd clung to. Yet when that world shattered, Rachel was born.

When I saw Rachel's cracked and bleeding hands, the way she gnawed her lip to keep from crying, I knew Miss Shaw was right. I had to ask. She told me a story not far from what I'd expected, a dream of a new life, a man who thought new lives were easy. I wanted to ask her more. When she left my room that night, I told myself to wait. Leave her space to speak when she was ready.

Even after what happened next, I do not regret waiting. I do not regret my vow. I do not believe I could have changed the future if I had poured every drop of my power into keeping my daughter with me from the moment she was born. And all the things I wish I had said and done, I cannot go back and change.

I told her lies were fragile things, and this is true. But all things, all things are fragile.

Chapter 26

IN THE BEGINNING, there was darkness. I could neither hear nor see nor smell, my only sensations a faint impression of floating in an endless sea, the tang of salt on my tongue. In the beginning, I was nothing; I filled no space, had no will. I was utterly alone, but I was unaware of how much I feared being alone. I feared nothing in the darkness. I wanted nothing. I waited.

She was the first thing I heard, her call like the sound of rain pelting wood. I had no body, but I felt it. If I'd had fingers, they would have tingled. If I'd had ears, they would have rung for days. She was talking to her calf, who swam among the pod in their morning greeting, her soft white snout nudging the larger creatures, flitting down the length of their immense sides, taking in all the touch she could.

The call came again. *The mother*, I thought. *The mother*. The daughter swam to her, and I realized I had regained my sight. I remembered what it was to see, and I looked. A family of sperm whales swirled around me, tails waving. They broke for breath, dived again, their forms weightless and sun-dappled in the water. I watched them as they hunted and played, rested and fed. When the whales floated motionless in sleep, the darkness overtook me once more.

In all my waking hours I returned to the whales, drawn by the

tooth I had glimpsed in Rachel's hand, the scene of the graceful beast
at rest in the sea, a place for my mind to escape what had been done
to it. I learned the curves of the whales' backs and the contours of
their tails, the scars on their snouts and sides, the arcs of their fins.
Their language was like the popping hinges of an old door, the rock-
ers of a worn wooden chair against a worn wooden floor, the clink of
a spoon in a pot. It formed not words but pictures, patterns, readable
in light or dark, shallow or deep. The whales had names my mind
could not comprehend, but I learned to call them the mother, the
daughter, the aunt, the cousin, the grandmother, the friend, adding
as their family grew. I had no sense of time, but my days flowed with
theirs. I did not remember what my life had been like before them,
nor did I wonder.

After innumerable days and nights, unfathomable months and
years, a shadow appeared in the distance, a wavering blot on the surface of the water. I remembered a word: *ship*. The whales remembered,
too, the grandmother calling the others together. They rushed to the
surface to fill their lungs, plunging as the shape grew closer. Many
times I'd gone with them to the sunless world below, but this time I
stayed. When the ship passed, I followed it.

It did not move like a whale. It split the plane of the water, its
body heaving as the surface changed. It could not breathe, could not
leap, could not traverse the world without air pushing down on it and
water pushing up. It cracked and popped, but its sounds meant nothing. Still I followed.

One night the sky grew dark too early. The bands of light along
the ship's hull faded, then reappeared in jagged flashes. The sea
swelled and rose, doming above me, lifting the ship so it juddered
and reeled, churning the surface with a roar like thunder. A chunk of
wood jetted past, trailing a plume of foam. Something smoother fell,
something that stretched and contorted as it sank. I moved closer, circling it, wishing I could reach out and touch it. It had no fins, no tail,
but I remembered the words for hands and arms, legs and feet, billow-

ing dress and swirling hair, gaping mouth. I drew so near I could see its closed eyes. They opened, and saw me. *Remember.*

~~~~~~

WHEN I RETURNED to the world of my body, I had been asleep for nearly four years. On the morning Rachel left and my slumber began, Eliza Shaw had come for breakfast before opening the mercantile, running upstairs to my room when she realized the kitchen was empty and quiet, the chowder pots cold. She found me breathing softly, my eyes shut, my face relaxed as if in the sweetest dream. When she could not wake me, she ran for help. The doctor said I was good as dead, but Eliza refused to believe it. She cared for me, coming morning and evening to spoon broth and water into my mouth, to change my clothes and sheets, shift my body, read to me. She knocked on the door of every widow woman I'd ever hired who remained on the island and pleaded with them to return to the Try Pots, and all declined except the last and oldest—quiet, nervous Betty, who had served beside me so well until the days of Ishmael overwhelmed her. She brought along her hearty daughter Hannah, who had returned to Nantucket when her husband died, and her little granddaughter, Ruth. Their chowders were not so good as mine, but passable enough, and together the four women kept the kitchen open and the Try Pots—and me—alive.

When I awoke, the world seemed like the sea of my sleep: as if I were floating through it, an observer and passenger with no power to affect the space around me. Ruth was playing in my room, pretending to hide from pirates when she was supposed to be reading to me. Eliza had transported several shelves' worth of books to the inn, stacking them on every surface in my room. Ruth had abandoned a crisp copy of *Little Women* on the bedside table, and I could hear her whispering and snickering to herself beneath the bed. Of course I did not know her—for a moment, my clouded mind believed the small voice belonged to Rachel, a child again, all the years of strife and sorrow only dreams. As my senses awakened, I noticed the timbre of this voice was too low, the smell of the inn slightly too oniony, the light through the window too dim, blocked by curtains I did not recognize.

Ruth bounded out from beneath the bed, jousting with invisible enemies, gasping when she spun around and saw my eyes open. She backed away, then fled, calling for her mother. The rest of the day was a jumble of noise and color, my mind still too muted to make much sense of the chaos. My caretakers learned I could see them but not rise from my bed, hear them but not respond. I did not feel trapped, only formless as I had been for so long. It would take me some time to move in this world, as it had taken me time to learn to swim. When the effort of consciousness exhausted me, I drifted back into sleep, where the whales waited.

The routine the women had built translated well to my new, frozen, waking life. I still needed constant care, only now I could enjoy the stories and conversation they offered while they fed and cleaned me. Eliza read to me, ensuring that I was up to date on the literature from the time I was asleep, especially in regard to Jules Verne and Lewis Carroll. She read with expression, inventing subtle tones and cadences for each character. She had a voracious appetite for all sorts of other publications as well, and brought me newspapers and magazines, leaflets and essays, poems and children's books. She was never afraid to bring the goings-on of the outside world to me, and when she became involved in the movement for women's suffrage, she delivered many impassioned speeches to an audience of one. She always engaged me as if she knew my mind was sharp, asking questions and pausing to give me time to consider them, though I could not answer. I wished we had become friends long before.

Hannah spoke as if we had been friends for years. I had met her a few times when she was a girl, though she'd left at sixteen to marry a man from the mainland. Yet she remarked on her habits as if I'd known her well her whole life, referring to people and places in their Connecticut town as if I knew the streets as well as she. Little Ruth mostly stared at the floor and kicked her feet as she mumbled her way through a book when it was her turn to sit by my bedside, but on occasion she whispered schoolgirl secrets or made up her own stories, rife with surprises and villainy and wondrous creatures. When she took up painting, she often brought her easel to my bedside to practice, and I poured as much emotion into my eyes as I could to show her how I loved her sea creatures, especially the whales. She lamented that they were not good art, they looked nothing like the scientific illustrations they showed her at school, but she moved more of her canvases into my room.

Betty liked to reminisce about Nantucket's glory days, and I learned she treasured her first years at the Try Pots, though she'd left so shaken. She remembered stories I had forgotten: a day when Tistig's brothers had come to supper after returning from a voyage and drained an entire pot of clam chowder between them, a time Freddy tried to stow away on a whaleship at age eight. Once, when she thought I was asleep, she recalled Ishmael. "He was not such a bad boy, that anxious young sailor you took up with," she whispered. "Though I hope you do not miss him."

I missed Hosea. I still thought of him, returning to my memories of his smell and his tenderness, his smile on our wedding day, his large fingers so clumsy when they plucked leaves of thyme and rosemary, so steady when they guided a knife across the belly of a fish, so gentle when they touched mine. I had known for so long how to miss him, remembering felt more like sweetness than loss. At some point, though I could not ask for it, Hannah took the daguerreotype of him out of my bedside drawer and displayed it on top, always in my sight.

Ishmael I tried not to miss, though my mind rebelled against my will. I used to see him in my sleep, not visions, but dreams, for in them he was still a young man, his curls soft and brown, his eyes confessing every emotion. Excitement and fear and hunger and need. I had known him so briefly, yet in that time he had revealed so much of himself. When I awoke from those dreams, I would remember another dream, one I had tried to ignore, of a furious whale and a shattered ship. I knew the *Pequod* had never returned, its name become a curse, its sailors buried so deep in Nantucket's memory it was as if they had never sailed, never lived. But I remembered an image from that dream, a lone figure clinging to a slab, swirling away from the maelstrom. I had been so sure that the arrival of Ishmael portended the end of all I knew, but we were both of us set loose in an untamable sea, hoping the rafts we clutched were enough, drifting toward inevitable brokenness, unavoidable loss.

With all the time I had spent in my mind, and all I had seen in the days since Rachel left, I wondered sometimes if I could use my powers to find him, to see if he was alive and what that life was like. When the desire arose, I quieted it. I told myself to let him be, to forget him as he surely had forgotten me. And then one day he was there.

He sat by my bedside, unspeaking. I didn't wonder if he was real. I could smell the sea on him, thicker than air, as if he carried it. He was worn, his hair limp beneath his hat, his hands thick and scarred. A sailor's hands. They clutched a leather satchel, bulging with papers that stuck out through the gaps in the top.

"I have recently been in Greenland," he said, as if we talked every day, as if he had not stepped out of my life almost thirty years before. "I am continuing on to other countries, but have been briefly detained by my captain's wish to see an old friend. We sail again this evening."

His voice had a tremor I did not remember, something more than nerves. I could not respond, and he seemed to understand. I had not been out of my dream world for long and was slow to heal; I was still in a state of stupor, my voice absent, my face set. I could only attempt to show with my eyes that I'd heard him. I hoped he would sense my surprise at his return. The curiosity I had for so long avoided indulging. The sweetness I could not help but still taste upon seeing his face.

He wet his lips and wrapped his hands in the straps of the bag.

"I have written so much about the . . . the ship. I do not use its name. Do you remember when I signed my name to its roster? Do you remember my foolish joy? I remember you, Evangeline," he said, and for a moment I saw the boy in my kitchen, the young man in my bed. "There is no one left on this earth who ever loved me but you."

He opened the bag with trembling fingers and revealed sheaves of thin paper, pages ripped from ledgers, yellowed scraps, all covered in ink. "I have been writing what we did on that ship. Writing all I know. Some of it has been published."

He withdrew a copy of the *Spyglass*, familiar though I had never read it. "They say people find my stories amusing, or perplexing. I write even what no one could possibly want to read."

He read me one of his tales, beautiful, somber, and deep. *The Blacksmith*, he called it. Then he put the papers away, his face darting again to mine.

"It is all insufficient, though I try and try. I only am escaped alone to tell . . ." His eyes lost their focus, his voice dropped to a rough whisper. "If I cannot rest with them, perhaps they will rest upon my telling. They were none of them demons but what they made each other."

We sat in silence for a while. Comfortable together, as if so much time had not passed, as if so much pain had not shaped us both into far different people than we had been when we were young. I wished I could tell him about Rachel, return her to the world through my telling, give her story to him as she had given it to me at her death. I understand that wish, Annie, to repair what was broken, though your dear grandfather never knew the full depth of it. And yet he still sent you on the path that led to me, and to Ishmael, perhaps, when our time is through.

All I could do was let Ishmael go, as quickly as he had come. I have not sought him since. I hope he found what he was chasing, or escaped what chased him. Or rather, no. I hope he found what he was missing.

~~~~~

MORE THAN ANYTHING, in these days and hours and years, I have thought of my daughter. Sometimes my caretakers, my friends, talked among themselves while they dusted or gossiped or sang or shared a loaf of fresh bread in my room, briefly forgetting my presence. I did not mind those moments. They reminded me of being among the whales. As I observed these women who loved me, I learned that no one ever spoke of Rachel or alluded in any way to my having a child, and I knew that the visions Rachel gave me before I woke were real. She had once wrenched herself from my mind, nearly destroying it, leaving behind damage that could never be fully repaired. But in her final moments she returned what she had taken, and more.

I saw more readily how her struggles with the power she inherited from me were not unlike my own—we feared our power, fought with it, experimented with it, embraced it only to push it away again, stood in awe of it, used it. She saw her power as a curse, but in the end it was a gift. My own gift saved my mind from being broken, as my friends saved my body. I have replayed her life again and again in my mind, from my perspective and hers. It took me years to accept that her attempt to wipe herself from my memory was an act of mercy, as was sharing her story with me in her final moments.

And when she gave me back the memory of her, she gave me all of you.

Mara shone like a beacon on the dark ocean. I still watched the whales each time I rested, but I was drawn more and more to the child living in the distant forest. I longed to take away her pain, to slay the monsters threatening her happiness, to drive away every fear and give her a life of peace. But I had learned to watch, to listen. To marvel at how she and the people who loved her fought for that peace themselves. To be amazed as she discovered what she could hold on to, even as she was forced to leave so much behind. I know she tried to hold you too tightly at times, Annie, and too loosely at others. You can see the pattern in our paths. You never were afraid to see.

In waking life I learned to sit, to stand, to walk. Betty died. When Nantucket's population dwindled further and Hannah proposed the sale of the Try Pots, I approved, for all I loved in Nantucket was no longer contained in it. We bought this house, and we made it our home. Eliza died. I learned to feed myself, to dress myself, to express my will well enough, though I could neither speak nor write. Hannah died. My speech returned, though only in part, and I found some things impossible to say, until today. Someday I will die, and I will welcome death when it arrives. I have never been abandoned in this life, and I expect nothing less from that distant shore. *The strange untried*, Ishmael called it in his story. *The immense remote.*

But for now, I am here with you. This is still the beginning of a story.

Acknowledgments

MY THANKS, as deep and boundless as the sea, to:

Helen Thomaides, who saw the promise in Evangeline, Rachel, Mara, and Annie, and who helped me weave their stories together. Thanks also to the team at W. W. Norton who polished this book, brought it to life, and shepherded it into the world: Amy Robbins, Rebecca Munro, Julia Druskin, Elisabeth Kerr, Sarahmay Wilkinson, Sara Wood, and Lynne Cannon.

Chris Kepner for taking a chance on me when this story was barely formed, for your faith as I was writing it, and for your persistence when I decided to disappear into the woods for a week, while on submission, without telling my agent.

Everyone who read drafts of this book and helped make it better: Cara Hawkins-Jedlicka, Kendel Murrant, Kate Wutz, Esme Dutcher, Keene Short, and Jonathan Freeman-Coppadge; Stacy Boe Miller, who loved the Chowder Woman from her earliest existence; and Rhea Chipman and Miranda Hogue—you're the readers I always imagine I'm writing for.

The literary friends who have cheered me on through the mysteries of publishing: Amy Whitcomb, Sara Zaske, Alexandra Teague, and, especially, Sayantani Dasgupta (you were absolutely right that I would feel like a custard or jelly sometimes).

The women whose love and friendship get me through the day-to-day: Melissa Davlin (who loves me when I'm the absolute worst), Savannah Tranchell (sorry I didn't call this book *Love in the Time of Sperm Whales*), Hillary Talbott-Williams, Barb Kirchmeier, Caitlin Cieslik-Miskimen, Tracy Simmons, Leigh Cooper, Alexiss Turner, Melissa Hartley, Lindsay Brown, Willow London, Jodi McClory, Ashley Centers, Stacey Camp, the women of the Emmanuel Lutheran Book Club, and so many more.

My colleagues, mentors, teachers, students, and friends at the University of Idaho, especially Zack Turpin, whose great American novels class finally got me to read *Moby-Dick* and gave me space to write the first few scenes of this story; Walter Hesford, who taught me about American literature; and Daniel Orozco, who taught me about world-building.

The people who helped me with research and answered all my odd questions: Erin Green for Boston history, Corey Fabian-Barrett and Mary Bergman for Nantucket history and culture, A. Bowdoin Van Riper at the Martha's Vineyard Museum for Wampanoag history, Dale Graden for Brazilian history, Sonya Meyer and the Leila Old Historic Costume Collection at the University of Idaho for fashion advice, Rob Ely for sea shanties, and Rebecca Tallent for insights into Indigenous culture and history. (Any errors, omissions, exaggerations, or flights of fancy are entirely mine.)

The organizations, institutions, authors, artists, and scientists whose collections, research, and knowledge gave depth and detail to this book: the Nantucket Historical Association and Whaling Museum, the Nantucket Preservation Trust, the Nantucket Atheneum, the Museum of African American History in Boston and Nantucket, the Boston Public Library, the University of Idaho Library (especially interlibrary loan and Digital Initiatives), the Latah County Historical Society, *The Other Islanders* by Frances Ruley Karttunen, *Away Off*

Shore and *In the Heart of the Sea* by Nathaniel Philbrick, *Amazons, Wives, Nuns, and Witches: Women and the Catholic Church in Colonial Brazil* by Carole A. Myscofski, the photographers Cristina Mittermeier and Paul Nicklen, Sea Legacy, sperm whale experts David Gruber and Shane Gero, the Dominica Sperm Whale Project, and Project CETI. Additional thanks to the good folks at the Brass Lantern Inn on Nantucket, whose lovely inn served as a model for the Try Pots.

The Idaho Commission on the Arts and the National Endowment for the Arts for grant funding to support my research trip to Nantucket and Boston.

Maggie, my furry companion through almost every minute of writing this book.

The generations of grandmothers and aunts to whom this book is dedicated, especially Grandma Linda for your gift of determination, Grammy for your gift of patience, and Auntie Beth for your gift of books—and curse of writing them.

My grandfathers, Robert Karr and Daniel Moore, whose lives on Earth ended while I was writing this book, but whose love and pride I will carry with me for the rest of mine.

My parents, Paula and Patrick Karr, for reading books to me since before I was born, for guiding me as I've navigated the world, and for encouraging me to explore, question, understand, and write about the world for myself.

Tim, my best friend, my gentle partner, my patient listener, my mender of all things.

Henry and Danny, most of all. I'm honored to be the mother of such creative, intelligent, silly, compassionate, unpredictable people. You are my greatest adventure.